BLOOD AND SAND

A RUN AND HIDE THRILLER

JJ MARSH

PREWETT
BIELMANN

Blood and Sand
Copyright © 2024 by Prewett Bielmann Ltd.

Published by Prewett Bielmann Ltd.
All enquiries to admin@jjmarshauthor.com

First printing, 2024
eBook Edition:
ISBN 978-3-906256-27-6

Paperback:
ISBN 978-3-906256-28-3

This book is dedicated to The Sanctuary and its wise, creative and independent women

1

One song reverberated through her brain for the first two days: 'Who Let the Dogs Out?' She couldn't remember the name of the band or any of the verses, but that chorus wormed its way into Ursula's ear morning, noon and night. The only difference was her brain substituted the word 'cows' for 'dogs'.

Goa was overrun with bovines. Large horned beasts with a strange hump between the shoulder blades, they slept in the street, ambled along the beach, grazed on any patch of greenery they could find and trampled through hotel gardens. No one lifted a finger to stop them. Ask anybody which animal is sacred. Whether they've been to India or not, you'll get the right answer. She had run from a cowshed to find herself in a cow paradise.

It had taken over a month to travel to this odd little pocket of western India, mainly because she had spent three weeks in Mumbai, recovering from her injuries, doing her homework and shedding her previous skin to become Ursula Brown.

Her focus was laser-sharp and relentless. There was no time to look back and fret over the past. She had a job to do and realistically she was not up to the task. Her physical fitness was well below par due to months of sporadic activity and a meagre diet. Her combat training was about as fresh in her mind as her schoolgirl French. As for the talents required by an undercover agent, she had neither back-up nor intelligence, relying on nothing but memory.

The process of self-transformation starts with an image. *Who do I want to be?* In a similar kind of process to her A Casa da Prata application, Ursula began at the other end. What did they want? Who did they need? And how could she fulfil those requirements? The answer came as she soaked in the bath of her suite. They needed someone with connections, a fixer, a person who knew people. The only fly in the ointment was that Ursula knew no one. But that had never stopped her before.

If she wanted to convince people she was the real deal, she had to look the part and walk the talk. She gave her face and fingers time to recover from the injuries sustained on April Fools' Day but hit the gym hard. In her heart, she knew the damage went further than skin deep, but repairing her psyche would have to wait. She had a lot of work to do.

Most tourists with time to spend in a city like Mumbai would take a tour, visit the highlights, sample the food and marvel at such an extraordinary conglomeration. Ursula mostly stayed in her suite, scouring the web for information on the organisation she hoped to penetrate. It wasn't available through judicious use of the search engine, neither was it accessible from official records. The only way of establishing what aspects of racketeering these people currently controlled was by reading between the lines.

Thesis, antithesis, hypothesis. Ursula believed their headquarters was situated in Goa. However, that theory was built on nothing more than the word of a drunken old salt in a south

London pub. She had no proof the people she was looking for were even on this continent. Any evidence would be well concealed, practically impossible to find, unless you knew how to fish. Ursula selected her bait with care.

Step one was easy. Create an online persona, a rich young man with disposable income and a nose for a party.

Step two: fill invented persona's social media presence with generic images of jet skis, beach barbecues, skiing trips, scuba dives and indistinct suggestions as to his glamorous companions. It took her most of the morning to lay her traps, because she wanted it to look especially authentic. The decision that took longest was the name. He had to sound like old money. She browsed the society pages of British newspapers for a first name, surname then added a number, for maximum impact.

Harrington Locke III leapt into life at the touch of a button. Ursula felt like she knew him and already hated his guts.

Step three: inhabit the persona of Ursula Brown, concierge to the wealthy, key to the inaccessible, and personal aide at exorbitantly expensive rates. Although this woman should be impossible to find other than by word of mouth, she still required her own legend. Years of training as an undercover agent had taught her the necessity of memorising a fictitious background and career trajectory, how to drop thinly disguised names or 'accidentally' reveal her influence and most importantly, to hint that her identity was not all it seemed. When people went looking for Ursula Brown, they would find nothing more than a ghost. Exactly as it should be.

Step four: put out some discreet feelers as to where a young blood and his entourage could locate the right kind of venue, ensure every taste was catered for, arrange entertainment and source appropriate guests. All perfectly innocent and at the same time, for those in the know, it was 'Cristal' clear.

From there on, it was a question of cross-checking replies

and joining the dots. Ursula thanked all her respondents and assured them her client would make a decision soon. Meanwhile she swam in the hotel pool, ate fresh food, slept in a king-size bed and focused on the job in hand. Once her wounds healed, she hired professionals to help her shed a skin and invent a whole new identity. She'd changed her appearance before. This time was different. This time, there was no going back.

Ursula Brown stepped off the plane, collected her shiny new suitcases and emerged into Goa's Arrivals area. She wore jeans, trainers, a sports-branded T-shirt and sunglasses. Her glossy brunette ponytail swung as she walked, her skin glowed with health and her jewellery sparkled. As expected and paid for, a man was waiting with a sign bearing her name.

"Good morning! Directly to Da Gama Apartments, please. Could you take my bag?"

"Good morning, madam. This way, please." He wheeled her suitcases to a distinctly superior vehicle compared to the others idling in the pick-up bay of the Domestic Arrivals area. He opened the door and ushered her inside. It was dark, cool and sumptuous, with an array of soft drinks and snacks presented in a little box.

In comparison to Mumbai, Goa felt like a different country. The pace of life matched that of the ubiquitous, unhurried cows. People wandered rather than rushed, lingered over coffee or lunch, changed plans or direction at will and always had time to stop and smell the roses. Instantly, Ursula wanted to get out of the luxury sedan to stroll the roads with the other inhabitants. She'd been confined to an air-conditioned set of rooms for far too long. How she yearned to eat something with her fingers instead of silver cutlery, inhale something other than hothouse flowers or fabric conditioner. The scents and sights of a constantly changing view attracted her like a child to a sweet shop. She made no attempt to move, maintaining her image of the busy sophisticate here to judge the standards of service.

The Da Gama Apartments complex lived up to the photos on its website. A cool courtyard off the street behind protective electronic gates displayed understated five-star accommodation complete with pool, restaurant and a concierge. It reminded Ursula of a place she had once stayed in Manaus, but this place had fewer cats. She checked in, rattled off half a dozen questions to the receptionist and requested a local map. The journey from the airport to her lodgings should have taken half an hour, but the chaos on the roads doubled that. The best way to travel around this area was by moped. She made up her mind either to rent or buy one after the weekend. Her first meetings were not until Monday, so she had three days to scope out her surroundings.

The apartment was a step down from her Mumbai hotel in terms of space and luxuries, but a whole lot more comfortable than the cattle stall she had called home for the previous five months. This boasted a double bed, a balcony overlooking the courtyard, a clean ensuite bathroom with a shower, a desk, mini-bar and wonderful street view from the front window. Ursula Brown could be happy here.

There was one more thing she had to do before she let go of her previous existence. She set up her laptop, secured access to an anonymous browser and masked her identity. This was the last time she would permit herself a check of news from Pemba or Cabo Delgado. What happened in April was already an old story for Mozambique, unless there was an active investigation. No news, as they say, is good news.

Her heart leapt into her mouth when she finally found a month-old article on page seven. *CANTOPRETO MOURNS TWO DEAD AT PEMBA REFUGE!* The angle was all about the politician's sense of personal loss, so it took a minute's frantic reading before Ursula could clarify the names of the victims in an unprovoked attack. Apparently Mafalda Moutinho and Iris Simons had both been shot and lost their lives, one in hospital, one lost at sea. An adult male was also injured but had since been released from hospital. Arnaldo Cantopreto called for the community to come together in recognition of the women's work at a memorial service on Sunday.

Nowhere in the newspaper report did they mention bodies, funerals, an ongoing investigation or the future of A Casa da Prata. She was not surprised. Sad, but not surprised. She would grieve for Mafalda on her own terms.

To the world at large, her most recent identity was dead. That suited her fine. Because if Gil Maduro had received her letter, he knew different.

Wait for me, Gil. I'm coming back. I won't be the same woman you loved, but if I can, I will return.

2

O n Saturday morning, she went out to get milk, bread, coffee and to ask about renting a moped. By the time she returned, she'd bought a house. The only reason she entered the estate agent's office was to escape a sudden downpour and browse rental properties for her fictional clients. Then she saw a picture of a beachside property with its own vegetable garden, standing alone a good distance from the main road with a sea view. Her last few homes had varied dramatically, from beach shack to glorified cupboard, from sprawling farm to cattle shed. Now she was looking at the Goldilocks house – not too big, not too small, but just right.

She enquired about the price, and embarked on a lengthy and elaborate negotiation, invoking the estate agent's honour and her own vulnerability as a single woman. They compromised on a figure and shook hands on the deal. Then she paid a deposit, signed a contract and the agent shut up shop while he took her to her new home on his motorcycle.

"Okey dokey, this is it. Here are your keys. The big one is for the front door and the little one opens the back and the garage. You mind if I leave you here? It's just I want to get some lunch."

Ursula dismounted from the back of his bike, reminding herself to carry a helmet in future, and took the keyring with a grin. "Thanks, Vamsi. You drive a hard bargain. Go enjoy your lunch and your commission."

He grinned back. "You can bet on that. See you around, Ursula."

The bike kicked up sand all the way down to the road, where Vamsi hurled it into the unpredictable traffic. Ursula walked around the house, taking in the scenery and delaying the moment she examined the interior of her rash purchase. She sat on the rear deck, watching waves crash onto the empty beach below. Next she assessed the property through a cop's eyes. Built on top of a hill to get the best sea view, it had no fences or walls to keep out intruders, but that long sandy drive from the main drag gave a pretty good vantage point. The garden was neglected, but the morning's rain had washed some dust off the plants, showing some tendrils of green. In the centre was a tomato plant, bearing two tiny fruits. She bent to touch them and wondered how her little Brazilian pot was faring.

The thought of Brazil made her smile until reality struck. She wasn't going back. Why else would she buy a house, here on the coast of India? There was no blaming this on a momentary whim – Ursula was playing the long game. *I'm here to get the job done, however long it takes.* She got up, dusted the sand off her jeans and went to explore the house.

It really was just right. A decent-sized living room, a kitchen, bathroom, two bedrooms and garage, all on one floor. The second bedroom, evidently intended for a servant, was a narrow adjunct to the kitchen. Ursula decided to turn that into a utility room. Even though she could afford domestic help, she loathed the idea of some stranger inhabiting her space. Privacy was top priority, as always. The garage was destined to become her gym. Her mission depended on peak fitness. Running along the beach and swimming in the sea would form part of her regime, but no one needed to know how hard she worked out at home. That still left plenty of room for a Vespa.

Not a stick of furniture or single appliance remained from the previous inhabitants. The electricity didn't work, and turning the taps produced nothing more than a creaking sound. She locked the place, called a cab and walked down to the road, her eyes squinting in the harsh midday light. Time to go shopping for her new home. But first, food.

The cab was just turning into the drive when a motorcycle pulled up alongside. Since both rider and passenger were covered in dust, it took her a second to recognise Vamsi.

"Hey, Ursula, here's someone you gotta meet. This is Denzil Fernandes. He happens to have a job opening for someone exactly like you."

Ursula assessed him in a second. The man was lean and tanned, his collarless shirt buttoned to the neck and his posture stiff. Like Vamsi, he wore no helmet. His face creased into a charming smile while his eyes performed the exact same assessment as hers.

"A pleasure to meet you, Ms Brown. May I be the first to congratulate you on your new home? It is indeed a most astute purchase. My most fervent wish is that you will be very happy here. My name is Denzil Fernandes and anyone of any stature in this area will vouch for my credentials as a recruitment consultant. Please accept my card."

"Thank you, Mr Fernandes. How very friendly of you to offer your congratulations and your services so soon. As a matter of fact, I work freelance and have no need of a head-hunter."

The taxi driver flicked his cigarette butt past them. "Is anyone going to get in or should I look for another fare?"

Vamsi said something in a language Ursula didn't understand, then fired up his motorcycle and drove away. The driver shrugged and lit another cigarette.

"A head-hunter, as you deem me, often has need of a freelancer," said Fernandes, with an unruffled air. "Not only that, but a new homeowner usually has need of some furniture. I'm very well connected, Ms Brown, and I am firmly convinced our association will be mutually beneficial. Shall we share this taxi into the centre and talk business?"

Well connected was an understatement. Denzil, because by now they were on first-name terms, knew of a house clearance twenty kilometres away. While Ursula scarfed down two vegetable chapattis and drank a glass of lassi in a roadside restaurant, he made three phone calls. By Monday evening, she would have electricity, running water and all the basics on her list.

"I took the liberty of adding a few items," he said, sliding into the opposite side of the booth. "An electric fan, curtains, garden chairs and a mosquito net. The price remains the same, have no concerns on that score. A gentleman always keeps his word. Now to my side of the bargain."

Ursula was ready for him. She wiped her fingers on the flimsy serviette and took a roll of dollars from her handbag. "The bargain, as I understood it, was that I pay you for arranging to make my new home habitable. I appreciate your efficiency and I'm grateful for your help."

He palmed the money like a conjuror and it disappeared into his pocket. "I must stress in the strongest possible terms that it is extremely unwise to carry large amounts of currency on your person. The price you just paid covers the physical elements of your abode. My assistance in the matter is given freely. This is how we operate here – friends do favours for friends."

"Denzil, we've known each other for just over an hour. 'Friends' is stretching it."

"A stranger is a friend you haven't met yet." His sincere expression made it impossible to laugh. "We will become jolly good chums, I guarantee that. We operate in similar fields by keeping our promises. I understand you call yourself a fixer."

"Not exactly. I call myself a concierge."

"How interesting. Ursula, will you excuse my impertinence if I ask exactly what a concierge does? I would be intrigued to hear your business model."

"My business model is simple. I work miracles. My client wants New York bagels at 4am in a Cannes hotel room – I'll have them delivered. Tickets to that sold-out concert in Paris or baseball game in Philly – where would sir or madam like to sit? Haute couture tailors to alter your designer suit the night before the awards ceremony – consider it done. With a mobile office, I maintain an international network, but only accept clients by recommendation. 96% get the brush-off. The few I take on know damn well how lucky they are, which is why they stay loyal. I'm expensive and exclusive and *extremely* good at my job."

He rested his chin on his knuckles and examined her face. In full knowledge she looked the part, she let him stare while she took mental notes on his appearance. Greying temples, golden-brown eyes, manicured fingernails, clean-shaven and immaculately dressed in a linen suit, he had the air of a well-trained gentle Labrador. Yet Ursula suspected he had very sharp teeth.

"I would expect nothing less. My contacts tell me you are looking for five-star accommodation, with catering, entertainment and activities for a bachelor party of twenty men, is that correct?"

Ursula's story was out there, exactly as she'd intended. She feigned surprise. "Discretion is one thing I insist upon when choosing a venue for my clients. I'm sorry to say Goa has already fallen short in that respect."

"Yet you already bought a house here?"

She leaned forward, her tone confidential. "As I said, I can operate from anywhere in the world. It just so happens I feel the need to unwind, unplug, walk barefoot on the beach and gaze up at the stars from my hammock. To quote Garbo, I want to be alone."

"You're far too young to remember Greta Garbo. Let me assure you I understand completely and I hope you won't perceive me as patronising if I say you are not the first high-achiever searching for a deeper connection with the universe. Goa has always welcomed open minds."

Ursula shook her head. "No, no, no. You can forget all thoughts of *Eat, Pray, Love*. I'm not here to seek enlightenment. I'm here to source thrills and gratification for my client, whose daddy will pay me handsomely for tolerating his spoilt son's whims. That will serve me long enough. Then I can lounge on the beach for six months, drinking cocktails and eating fresh fish until I accept the next gig. Probably another nepo baby's birthday-of-a-lifetime or an attention-seeking A-lister's renewal of her vows. I guess I come across as cynical, right? There's a reason for that."

Denzil examined his fingernails. "I'm sure there is. When exactly is your client's event?"

"Late January, because the wedding is February 14. Valentine's Day." She rolled her eyes. "How's that for imaginative?" Part of her old self cringed. The happiest day of her life was when she married Salvatore Simon on Valentine's Day. She slammed the door on that sudden surge of emotion.

"I am in no position to judge others' choices or cultural preferences. But I admit to a degree of puzzlement. This is not

the wedding itself so such elaborate preparations seem dispro-
portionate. Who takes nine months to arrange a stag party?"

Ursula threw her arms wide, waggled jazz hands and
adopted a huge stagey grin.

"They must pay you a lot."

"Oh, they do. Because I'm worth every cent. You see why
I'm not interested in any part-time gigs, Denzil? I have my eyes
on the main prize."

He placed his elbows on the table, his hands in a meditative
pose, and ran the pad of his thumb across each of his fingers,
his gaze distant. Ursula fanned herself with the menu, biding
her time. If, and she was fairly confident in her assumption,
Denzil was hunting heads for one particular organisation, she
had to make him work for his commission. The greater her
reluctance, the lower their suspicions.

"What if we were to describe our potential collaboration as
a test run for your event? That would provide you with the
opportunity to trial all the relevant services and suggest
improvements, should you find them lacking. At the same time,
we are keeping my people happy and both of us earn a little
bonus on the side."

This was her cue. All it would take was an innocent question and she could be one step closer to locating her target.
Who exactly are your people? She said nothing, affecting serious
thought.

The waiter came to collect their plates and Ursula looked
up with a smile. "Thanks, that was great. Can I get the bill,
please?" she asked, pulling her purse from her bag.

"This is on the house, courtesy of Mr Fernandes," said the
waiter, darting a deferential glance at Denzil as he hurried off.

"Very kind, thanks. But the answer is still no. Please don't
take offence, but ever since I found myself in this role, more by
accident than design, I've always worked alone. You have my
sincere gratitude and my money for the house arrangements. I

have your card. If circumstances change, I'll be in touch. Thanks for lunch and see you around."

He didn't miss a beat. "Anything you need, Ursula, day or night, I'm just a phone call away. Welcome to Goa!"

By the time she got back to Da Gama Apartments, she was hot, sweaty and insecure. For a guy like Denzil to turn up immediately after she'd bought the house suggested he had special intelligence, or worse, surveillance. She checked her door for any signs of unexpected entry before venturing inside. Once she had swept the room for bugs, she retrieved her laptop from the safe and scrutinised that morning's footage from the tiny security camera she had installed above the doorway. Even though the recordings showed no intruders, she still checked the lockable suitcase containing items too large for the safe. Everything was in place: heavy-duty stun gun flashlight, miniature drone, night vision camera, stab- and bullet-proof vest, pepper spray, leather knife holster, belly-band gun holster and various wigs. Only when convinced everything was where it should be did she shower and face herself in the mirror.

It still came as a shock. She looked nothing like her old self. Or selves. Running and hiding always involved some kind of disguise, hair dye, costumes, a new identity, but now she had taken it to the next level. Not even Sal would recognise her as the woman he married.

Cosmetic surgery had never been on her wish list. She dismissed it as a vain desire to hold on to one's youth which fooled nobody. That was before prey turned hunter and breached enemy territory. The faintest chance her face might trigger a recollection in someone's memory was a risk not worth taking. She had to be unrecognisable. Hairstyle and colour were easy to change and tinted contacts weren't difficult to come by. Her face shape and age could be altered with a tuck, fill or lift, most of which would return to normal after a year or two. Hardest to achieve was a difference in posture or gait.

In her teenage years, Olivia Jones had been on the short side, wiry and athletic, with a compact physique, small bust and boyish frame. To infiltrate a criminal organisation's London headquarters, she added several pounds, wore push-up bras and make-up, and learned to walk in heels. Her identities since then included a dropout poet with long red hair, a glamorous gambler with movie-star disguises, a faded blonde farmer in dungarees and a scrawny volunteer at a women's refuge.

All those faces had appeared somewhere on security cameras or in the press. The transformation into Ursula Brown had to be something special.

Fuller cheeks and sharper jawline, Botox in forehead and lips, temporary breast implants, lifts in all her shoes, including sandals, hazel contacts and professional honeyed highlights in a brown bob. She was Everywoman, or at least every woman who had disposable income to splurge on looking like her peer group. She let out a snort, misting the mirror.

Oh well. If they got to her before she got to them, at least she'd look good in her coffin.

3

_____

The house clearance Denzil mentioned must have belonged to a Mughal princess. Either that or a Bollywood set. The four-poster bed was ridiculously sumptuous with swags of golden chiffon acting as curtains. The sofa was buttermilk leather, adorned by so many stuffed cushions there was no room for a person to sit. Mirrors, dining-table, chairs and desk all bore ormolu details, and the coffee table was a slab of onyx. Two golden vases, each capacious enough to conceal a toddler, were too large for any surface. Ursula placed one each side of the door. Thankfully, the fridge, washing machine, dishwasher and electric fan all operated as they should. The water ran clear, after a few rumbles and rusty expulsions. She fitted bulbs into every socket and arranged the garden bench and table on the veranda.

It took a large part of Monday evening to organise the place to her preferences, and there were still a few details outstanding when she poured some chilled tonic into a glass, added a slug of gin and sat on her terrace to admire the view. Unlike her Brazilian shack, the beach lay down a sandy track around a twenty-minute walk away. The distance didn't matter

– she could watch the ocean, admire sunrise and sunset, hear the roll of the waves and watch the palm trees sway. Warm winds brushed her skin, a perfumed caress.

From the other side of the house, she could hear traffic from the main road, but only as a distant grumble. This place was different to her previous seashore dwelling in other ways. Here she had solid concrete walls and decorative wrought-iron bars preventing entry via the windows. Should a gang of teenagers want to cause trouble, they'd have to work a lot harder than those surf dudes on Praia do Pesqueiro.

She toyed with idea of giving her dwelling a name, since the property was only known by a number on the road. Her most recent homes, A Quinta Douro and A Casa da Prata, were named after gold and silver respectively. A breeze lifted her hair and goose bumps rose on her skin. This might be the last place she ever lived. In which case, something cheesy like *Dunroamin* or *Little Bighorn*? Alternatively, she could look on the positive side. When the battle was done and the little guy, or in this case woman, came out victorious against the forces of evil, her home should reflect that struggle. *Tatooine*? *Silkwood*?

The sun sank below the horizon as if it was in a hurry to leave. Blackness surrounded the house, the only lights coming from other buildings along the coast and the first evening stars. The name floated into her mind as if waiting for its moment.

"OK," she said aloud. "*Nostromo* it is."

The first three nights spent at *Nostromo* were less than restful. The silence and security of an air-conditioned five-star Mumbai hotel suite was quite a different proposition to a house on the dunes, accessible from all directions. Ursula lay awake long into the night, alert for intruders, only sleeping when the sun glinted through the curtains onto her chiffon shroud.

When she arose around midday, she toured the building

again to increase security. A fence or alarm system would help matters, even if it was as basic as burying broken glass in the sand beneath the windows. The issue here was how to stay safe without looking paranoid.

Locks, chains, motion-triggered lights and self-defence weapons bought locally would attract attention, so she decided to venture into Panaji, the capital of the region. She planned the trip like an agent, prepared for every contingency. An empty suitcase, smart handbag, coordinated suit and shoes, with impenetrable sunglasses. Hard cash, two passports, and tucked into her jacket pocket, her favourite weapon – the knife.

Cab drivers like to talk, so tell them what they want to hear. *Why Panaji? Shopping, of course! A woman with a new house needs all kinds of little extras. No need to wait. I'll return when I'm ready. What can you recommend in terms of authentic restaurants in the Cansaulim region, by the way? My clients want to eat like locals. Yes, sort of a travel agent. Just a little more specialised.*

The driver was loquacious and bursting to share his knowledge. Thankfully, he kept his eyes on the road while he talked. She tipped him when he dropped her outside the Caculo mall and took his card, promising never to use another taxi driver. They both knew she was lying. Once he'd driven away, hooting cheerfully, she entered the building and walked out the other side. What she wanted was not available in a shopping centre.

She was examining some deadlocks in a hardware store when her new phone rang. Only two people had that number – Vamsi and Denzil. She could guess which one this was.

"Hi, Denzil."

"Good morning, Ursula. I trust you are well. My enquiry as to the condition of your new furniture is not intended as a nuisance, merely as a courtesy. Is everything to your liking? What else could I provide to make your abode ideal?"

"Hot tub, wine cellar, helipad? Relax, I'm joking. Your people delivered on time, and the amenities function. What more could I want?"

"All kinds of little extras, I imagine."

His echo of her words to the taxi driver was carefully chosen. He meant to make her feel scrutinised. Everything she did was public knowledge. She smiled. *Been there, done that. You're going to have to work a whole lot harder than that to intimidate Ursula Brown, Denzil, me ole mate.* She said nothing, leaving her silence open to interpretation.

"How about some *azulejo* for the kitchen? Believe me, I know the best artists in the area because I supply all the five-star hotels with authentic kiln-fired tiles. Or perhaps you are of a pragmatic bent and focused on security? One of my clients had a ten-foot fence erected around his villa by one of my companies. Anything you need, I can source it for you by tomorrow."

"That's reassuring. No offence, Denzil, but I'm used to looking after myself. Thanks for checking in. Gotta go now, I'm holding up the queue. See you."

"Ursula! Please don't hang up. I find myself in a predicament and wish to propose a mutually beneficial solution. Can you meet me for dinner this evening?"

She let the silence stretch out for few seconds. "No can do. I have plans tonight. An aperitif could work, maybe. Let's meet at the Postcard Bar at six o'clock. Bye." She ended the call before he was able to reply. Status games came easier than a hand of poker.

With suitcase full of security equipment, she hailed a different cabbie and instructed him to drive south. This time, she kept quiet. Her promise to the previous driver, whose card she'd flushed down a toilet, was long forgotten. She planned to drop the gear, ask the cabbie to wait and sally forth to meet Denzil. She wouldn't even change.

. . .

He was waiting on the deck, neat and upright, wearing pale yellow trousers and a mustard-coloured kurta. On the table in front on him were two similarly golden cocktails. She shook his hand, sat down and pushed the glass away.

"I prefer to order my own drink," she said, hailing a waiter. "Could I have a tonic water, please? You can bring it unopened and I don't need any ice."

Denzil did not seem at all offended. "It was only iced ginger and turmeric tea, but I admire a woman who takes no chances. Was your shopping expedition a success?"

"Partially. Household purchases complete but my next stop is to get myself some wheels. Taxi drivers are far too chatty," she said. "Particularly for a woman who takes no chances."

The waiter set down an empty glass, cracked off the lid of a bottle of tonic and stood, waiting for permission to pour.

She dismissed him with a nod. "Thanks, I can take it from here." High-handed behaviour towards waiting staff usually made her cringe but she maintained her role. "OK, Denzil, aka the best connected man in Goa, what's your predicament and how on earth do you expect the new girl to help?"

"Straight to the point. I like that."

Ursula was tempted to tell him how little his admiration and approval mattered to her, but she poured her tonic and tasted it, willing him to get to his own point.

"My organisation, much like yours, can provide a whole package for those wealthy enough to afford it. We insist on detailed preparatory notes on personal preferences from bed linen to food allergies. Nothing is ever left to chance."

She shrugged, as if he'd just told her the sun was shining, but let him continue.

"Surprises, unless specifically requested by the client, are not on the agenda. This is why a request I received this morning was most unwelcome. Friends of ours in Sri Lanka are in a similar line of business. Sadly, the weather is proving the weak link in their planning. A tropical storm is due to hit the south of the subcontinent, rendering Sri Lanka and the Maldives quite unsuitable for the party as planned. They pleaded with us to step in and rescue the clients, relocating the whole affair to one of our hotels. Logistically, it can be done. What I lack is a right-hand woman experienced in dealing with these types of rather demanding clients."

"Let me guess. The kind who expect private jets, limos and red carpet beneath their feet, for sunshine to appear on command, dolphins to leap and eagles to soar whenever they lift their cameras, and if there's a rain shower, it must be followed by a rainbow or someone's head will roll. Am I close?"

Denzil gave a conspiratorial smile but did not reply.

"Why me? You must have a team of people on call for such events who know the infrastructure and suppliers far better than I do."

"Two reasons. This is a week-long bachelor party, along very similar lines to the one you are preparing. As I mentioned, you could treat this like a trial run. Secondly, this sort of guest can be, how can I put this, somewhat bullish when it comes to dealing with Indian men. Whereas they are far more likely to take advice from a European woman, especially one used to handling herself. You would gain an insight into how the system operates by working hand in glove with me. The role is twofold: judicious procurement ahead of time, and trouble-shooting during their stay. It's not the easiest job in the world but it is very well paid."

The money was the least of Ursula's worries. However, an insight into how the system worked and some useful introductions were high on her list of priorities. "When?"

"They arrive next Friday. The seventeenth."

"The seventeenth? That's just over a week from now!"

"Indeed. The sooner we get started, the better. Are you on board?"

Ursula shook her head in faux exasperation. "Didn't I tell you I simply wanted to kick back and relax? Why would I spend two weeks buzzing around like a blue-arsed fly over some frat pack bullshit that doesn't concern me?"

"Frat pack bullshit," echoed Denzil. "I confess to sincere admiration of your eloquence. Entitled groups of young men can be insufferable, that is true. I will add that in my experience, women on a hen weekend can be equally dreadful. Between us, we can handle this and cover ourselves in glory. The powers that be will be most impressed."

"Well, bully for you. In my world, there are no powers that be." She emptied her glass of tonic and reached into her bag for a notepad. "We need a game plan. Let's start at the beginning. How many, how old and how much are they paying?"

4

From the outset, Ursula made three things clear. No drugs, no prostitutes and no hazing. Denzil agreed she need not be associated with any of those elements. They might still feature as part of the bachelor party, but Ursula could avoid working with drug dealers or pimps. As for hazing, if the group chose to pick on one member for an initiation ritual, they could not be stopped. Her role was to hand over to someone else in authority before things got out of hand.

Ground rules established, she and Denzil worked with great efficiency. By Friday morning, transportation to and from the airport was arranged, they'd booked three different excursions from zip-lining to quad bikes, and top-end restaurants knew when to expect a high-spending, boisterous and loud crowd of foreigners. The beach trip south to Palolem would occupy the rest of the week, with an associate of Denzil's overseeing scuba dives, jet-skiing and beach parties. Their last night would be a five-star dining and entertainment experience in Velha Goa before she packed them onto a plane and hoped never to see their faces again.

On Friday evening, Ursula took the files home to study over the weekend. It was vital she knew everything about each member of the party from medical conditions to political affiliations. Any information they had not volunteered, she was confident of finding on social media. In addition, she planned to double-check every third-party link in Denzil's supply chain for reliability and ensure she had an emergency number for every last one. If a bus broke down, a guide failed to show or one of the guests lost his phone/wallet/mind, she knew who to call. This was where she excelled, crossing the T's and dotting the I's. Attention to detail was supremely important when working undercover. Her legend had to be so plausible even she believed it.

In this situation, she employed two kinds of vision: intense focus and peripheral awareness. Some of Denzil's loose collection of associates must be working for the Osman-Vargas network. She feigned indifference and kept her eyes on the job. Her ears, however, were always open. In the last forty-eight hours, two things had piqued her interest.

First, Denzil took a call while Ursula was comparing boat excursions. When speaking Konkani or Hindi he usually continued his conversation in full confidence she did not understand. Only if his interlocutor was an English speaker would he move away to discuss business in private. On this occasion, his voice changed from authoritative to obsequious as he greeted the caller in Portuguese. Under the assumption Ursula's knowledge of Portuguese was non-existent, he did not leave his seat.

She ignored him completely, flicking back and forth between brochures, underlining random bullet points and circling prices. Within the first two exchanges, Ursula established that Denzil was speaking to a senior male connection.

He thanked the caller for taking the time to respond and apologised for the inconvenience. It was indeed correct that he had hired a temporary assistant to act as a representative on this occasion. Their clients tended to respond better to English-speaking types, especially professional women. No, her role was practical and their lines of responsibility were clearly delineated. Any special services were under Denzil's own command. He had to admit he didn't know, but he most certainly would find out. Normally such background checks were automatic but these were special circumstances. He was most grateful for the trust placed in him and wished the caller a very good afternoon.

He rang off and looked over at Ursula.

She folded up all the sailing brochures. "Right, these two are out, because they don't offer insurance. Between the others, I can't see a massive difference. Do you know any of these outfits? If so, why not pick one? I'll go with whatever you decide."

"You're very thorough. I should learn from your example. After all, I employed you on nothing more than your word. No references, no recommendations and your website is discreet to the point of obfuscation."

She rotated her shoulders and massaged her neck. "Don't mess me about, Denzil. You either trust me to do the job or you don't. To be honest, I've got better things to do with my time than cover your arse. I'm not your employee, we're free-lancers collaborating on a one-off project. Last thing I need is an associate who blows hot and cold. The first time we met I told you I prefer to work alone. Nothing's changed." She pushed all the paperwork across the table. "See you around."

"Please accept my most sincere apologies. Senior levels are asking questions but I can offer them genuine reassurances. You have already demonstrated your knowledge and ability."

She rolled her eyes. "Senior levels? I opted out of corporate crap a long time ago. Internal politics is your problem. You want to get the job done or not?"

On the second occasion, it was a face. Ursula took a cab to Velha Goa to negotiate a private dining area with a top-flight restaurant in Hotel Rosas Vermelhas. They kept her waiting in the bar for close to an hour. Outside in the dusty street with sun beating down, the delay might have been a problem. In an air-conditioned foyer with rotating fans, rattan chairs and filtered water, she didn't mind in the slightest. Even so, she kept her sunglasses on.

Young women wandered through in groups, businessmen maintained intense conversations and waiting staff checked regularly to ensure she was sufficiently hydrated. She flicked through a magazine showcasing glamorous events where the great and gorgeous displayed expensive frippery. Ursula noted the key players on Goa's formal party scene. Here was money and plenty of it. No wonder the remaining Osman-Vargas members fled to this pocket of privilege after the London bust. Money-making opportunities attracted them in the same way sharks scented blood.

A man came through the main doors and slouched up to the reception desk, his eyes scanning the waiting area. She glanced up for an instant then returned her attention to her glossy advertising, careful to show no sign of internal alarm bells. In her head, she was flicking through a Rolodex of faces, trying to place this carelessly arrogant individual. A cousin of the family, she was sure. One she'd only encountered a couple of times, but his demeanour was unforgettable. He exchanged a joke with the bartender, gave her a dismissive look and sauntered in the direction of the restaurant.

Ricardo? Ronaldo? Rodrigo? Before she had gone any further down her list, the barman called over.

"Hey, Berto, you left your cigarettes." He waved the packet in the air and tossed them across the foyer.

Roberto turned and caught the Marlboro Reds one-handed. Proud of his move, he glanced around, hoping for an impressed audience. Ursula kept her nose in her magazine. If Berto recognised her, the gloves were off. Their previous inter-actions had been often tense and sometimes antagonistic. Back then, she was under Milo's protection. Now she had no such shield. He swaggered through the dining-room doors like a cowboy entering a saloon.

Under the guise of a pensive expression, Ursula practised alternate nostril breathing, trying to marshal her emotions into some kind of coherence. Fear was her constant companion, whether a low-level anxiety at being found out as a fraud or immediate terror for her life. Both melded into one as she watched the restaurant entrance. Berto had never been the brightest light on the Christmas tree, but even he was capable of making two plus two equal four: a familiar face in a strange location spelt danger. There was every possibility he was making a phone call or loading his weapon while she sat gawping at perfume advertisements.

Conversely, a thrill pulsed through her nervous system, powered by a sense of vindication. If Roberto Vargas was in Goa, he was not alone. With all her sons jailed and her husband incapacitated, the old woman at the helm of the firm had resorted to scraping the barrel. Any one of the hundreds of guys flogging pineapples on the beach would be more competent than Berto, but Dolores only ever placed her trust in family. Big mistake, as Olivia knew to her cost.

"Miss Brown?" A soft voice at her shoulder snapped her back to her current reality. She was not Olivia but Ursula. She was not hunting an international criminal organisation, but simply making arrangements for a private dining room.

She stood up and pushed her sunglasses on top of her head. "That's me. Hello."

The woman wore her thick hair in a neat plait over one shoulder and a bindi between her brows. "Apologies for keeping you waiting. My name is Rakel and I am the Assistant Hospitality Manager, willing to assist with all your requirements. Would you like to follow me?"

The sky displayed all the colours of exotic fruits as it guided the sun below the horizon. On her deck at home, Ursula ate a bowl of rice with griddled shrimps and voiced her opinions aloud.

"Persimmon! No, apricot. That's tangerine, mandarin or clementine. Some kind of little orange, anyway. Mango with a dash of peach. Damson with a hint of blueberry. Blackcurrant. Alright, nothing on earth looks like that so stop showing off."

Ordinarily, Ursula stayed outside after the sun had set, gazing at the moon's reflection on the waves. It reminded her of Mozambique. Not tonight, because she had other plans. She washed up her dishes, made a pot of chai and sat at the dining table to dive into some in-depth research. The constant in-and-out motion of the ocean soothed her, like a living, breathing thing. Her recent security adaptations to the house added another level of reassurance so that she was able to devote her full concentration to the files.

You could learn a lot about a person by observing the gaps between their official persona and what they posted online. Kirkland C. Reece was 100% WASP, a high-achieving economics graduate of Yale, sporty, well connected and destined for a role in government. His social presence was probably handled by an agent, since it was wholesome in the extreme. But by burrowing into his 'Likes', 'Reposts', 'Shares' and personal messages, Ursula soon formed a more accurate image of the Ivy League jock.

The fact the kid had a sense of entitlement came as no surprise. Nor did his punching-down appreciation of unsubtle humour cause her any consternation. The only time she widened her eyes was on seeing his nickname. The group chat she'd hacked into was relatively innocuous – plans for a weekend cookout – but 'K-Klan Man'? Unless these guys were disconnected from reality, they had to see the reference. She made a note and moved on to the other males in the party.

Possibly more important than the groom was the best man. After all, the bachelor party was one of his key tasks, that and remembering the wedding rings on the big day. Ursula pulled up his picture and judged the two men almost interchangeable. Tanned, athletic, with chiselled jaws and white teeth, they could both be menswear models. She yawned. Noah Lloyd's CV made her feel very old and simultaneously very young. Three successful tech start-ups in Silicon Valley, two of which he started while still an undergraduate, had made him a multi-millionaire. King of the Unicorns, Zoomer-in-Chief, Starman and Limbic Dancer were just a few of the fawning monikers applied to this over-privileged pillock. Grudgingly, she noted a certain amount of philanthropy – a voice-activated assistant for people with physical disabilities; investment in sustainable conservation in Malawi; rehabilitation retreats for Rogue Rats. What the hell were Rogue Rats?

Placing judgement aside, she made a mind map for each member of the bachelor party, highlighting every single button to press. Flattery, nod to status, acknowledgement of influence and physical impressiveness were all tools in her kit. She wielded them less like a sword and more like a scalpel. When she went to work, they would never know what hit them.

Hello, boys, I'm ready for you.

. . .

In the early hours of the morning, she had one of her nightmares. She was running through tunnels, chasing something or someone just out of reach. Every time she turned a corner, a shadow disappeared around the next. She couldn't run fast enough because her legs kept getting tangled in a long skirt. She worked out the best plan was to stand still and wait for her quarry to come back. The place was an endless circuit with no visible way out. She pressed herself against the wall, taking long slow breaths and listening for footsteps. Moonlight glinted through the skylights above her head, throwing some illumination on the black puddles and grey walls surrounding her. Then something moved in front of the moon, blocking out the light.

Millimetre by millimetre, she lifted her head to look up. The roof was entirely made of glass and three gigantic heads were looking down at her, each grinning and pressing buttons on a console. She opened her mouth to scream but her mouth was zipped closed.

The only way to shake off such horrors was to drink a cup of coffee while welcoming the return of the sun. Her garden furniture faced west towards the sea, but she had placed a cane chair and side table at the opposite side of the house for just such an occasion as an early sunrise. She took her mug, a blanket and a cushion out into the darkness, her feet tucked into slippers. Still shaken from the bad dream, she placed her knife next to the coffee, before wrapping herself up against the morning chill.

Light gleamed on the horizon, pushing against the weight of the night. Ursula cradled her mug and inhaled the smell of Arabica. She was about to take her first taste when a deep comfortable sigh came from her right. She tensed, replaced the coffee on the table and took up her knife.

Ocean swells, sea birds and infrequent vehicles on the road below created an unobtrusive dawn chorus but the cumulative effect was still loud enough to obscure another person's breathing. Ursula inched to her feet and fumbled for the light switch. Just then, a long, loud fart ripped through the air and something heavy shifted on the sand.

The porch lamp illuminated four large white cows resting against the side of the house. One turned to face her, its droopy ears and liquid eyes conveying a mildly affronted expression. The other three were bent into sleeping postures, all bony angles and broad planes.

"Good morning," Ursula whispered. "I apologise for the disturbance and wish you a very nice day." She switched off the lamp and reflected on her good judgement in not purchasing motion-triggered security lighting. With visitors like hers, it would keep her awake all night.

She drank her coffee and watched the day dawn. Before the sun grew too intense, she spent an hour doing a yoga flow and focused meditation. When she opened her eyes, her overnight guests were swaying down the drive, tails flicking, presumably in search of breakfast.

5

The private jet arrived ninety minutes late, due to a late take-off in Mumbai and weather disruption en route. Neither Denzil nor Ursula was overly concerned. Cars, hotel and restaurants had been forewarned regarding flexibility. The only factor they could not control was the mood of their guests. Early signs were not good. Air traffic control alerted ground staff after the flight crew reported antisocial behaviour. Ursula sighed as deeply as any cow. *Here we go.*

Three security officers guided the arrivals through a private immigration channel, where Ursula waited to meet them. Through the doors, she could see Denzil taking charge of the luggage, directing an extraordinary number of bags into the people carriers. Ursula practised a bland smile and smoothed a stray hair from her brow. Her reflection in the mirrored observation window showed a smart, respectable woman carrying a clipboard and shoulder bag. The grey skirt and crisp white blouse projected a schoolmarm impression, one deliberately cultivated.

The doors opened and eight young men, all wearing sunglasses, emerged into the midday light. Some wheeled carry-on luggage, others wore rucksacks and all but one scowled.

"Good morning, gentlemen, and welcome to Goa. Please accept my apologies for the delay. As you already know, the weather is difficult to predict. My name is Ursula Brown and I'm your main point of contact."

"Hello, Ursula. I'm Noah. Good to know you." The best man shrugged off his rucksack and held out a hand. "Me and the guys are a little tired after a long journey. We'd appreciate checking into our rooms to freshen up." He flashed his teeth in a winning beam.

"Not a problem. Two vehicles are waiting outside to take you directly to the hotel. As requested, the place is exclusively yours for the duration of your stay. My colleague Denzil has already transferred your luggage. If you'd care to follow me?" She led them to the cars, allowed them to decide who went in which group, and hopped up to sit in the seat behind the driver.

"Let's go, Sanjay, and take it slowly, OK?"

"You got it, Miss Brown." He eased the bus out of the airport loop and onto the motorway. Ursula was so busy checking the traffic and wing mirrors to ensure they hadn't lost the other party that a voice in her ear made her start.

"Ursula? Whoa, didn't mean to startle you. Just wanted to say thanks for meeting us and sorry we took so long."

"That's OK, Mr Lloyd. All part of the service. Did you have a pleasant flight from San Francisco?"

"Call me Noah, yeah? The flight was OK, kinda long, but we slept most of it. Brodie got a little cranky when he couldn't vape on the connecting flight and he took some calming down. Just a heads-up, he might get on your case about that. You been in Goa long?"

"Long enough. It's one of those places that gets under your

skin and makes it hard to leave. This is your first visit to India, I'm guessing."

He waggled his head. "To India, no. I've been to Bangalore once but that was all work, no fun. Goa is completely different, I can see that already."

They watched as Sanjay steered around a cow urinating on the road. Ursula stole a glance at Noah as he took a photo with his phone. He was supremely confident in both body and persona, charming and convinced he could open any doors. He looked over his shoulder at his friends.

"You'll fit right in here, Thatcher!"

An Asian-American man at the rear flipped him the finger and returned to his phone.

"Noah, I'm sure you'd all prefer to rest after your journey. Perhaps at cocktail hour, I can run through the schedule with you so you get an idea what to expect. I sent a full itinerary by email, but it will make more sense when I fill in the detail."

"That works. Or you can come by my room and we can do that one-to-one." He pressed his phone against the window to catch a shot of three women in saris squashed onto a single moped.

"Company policy dictates we conduct meetings in public. It compromises no one and respects the local culture. I'm sure you understand. Shall we say six pm in the bar?"

He raised one eyebrow. "Whatever works for you, ma'am. Six is fine with me. Just be aware some of these guys push back against any kind of schedules, you get me? I get it, like herding cats, right? Just be patient with us, Little Bear." He bumped a fist to her shoulder.

"Little Bear?"

"Ursula Brown? Ursa means a female bear, at least in Latin-based languages. Ergo, Ursula means Little Bear. Kinda suits you, actually. Cute and fierce. Whoa, we here already? This looks great! Guys, check this out!"

She gathered their passports before the men got off the bus, enabling her and Denzil to complete check-in formalities while they explored the grounds. Hotel staff sent the bags to their respective huts so that by the time Ursula handed over the keys and passports, everything was ready to welcome the new arrivals. Most said thank you, some more sincerely than others, and only Brodie-the-Vaper still seemed bad-tempered and jet-lagged.

Denzil joined her in the reception area, waiting for the inevitable calls: the Wi-Fi's not working/need more ice/this pillowcase is not silk/where's the adaptor/can I get some Kombucha?

They satisfied all but Kyle's request for an urgent Ayurvedic massage because by the time a practitioner had been located, Kyle was already asleep. Denzil added one more charge to the bill, then left to participate in his niece's wedding party.

Ursula persuaded the masseuse to wait a while, just in case, bribing her with a pot of tea. She was a beautiful woman, with soft skin and green eyes, wearing her hair loose over her brilliant blue sari. Her hands as she poured the tea flowed with grace and delicacy. She offered the cup, holding the bowl like a religious offering.

Ursula accepted it with a respectful nod. "Thank you. I'm sorry about all the uncertainty. We only met these clients this morning and we're still testing the waters."

"Please, I require no explanations. My agency works with many hotels and tour operators. We know how it is. You're new to the scene, unless I am mistaken. My name is Perneet and I'm very happy to make your acquaintance."

"Ursula. Likewise. Yes, this is my first job. I hadn't planned to start work so soon, but Denzil was very persuasive."

"Denzil always is." Perneet blew across the surface of her tea, causing a wraith of steam to dance in front of her face. "My advice to you is to set boundaries. I tell my girls the same thing. Manage expectations and we all know where we stand. That goes for everyone, not just Denzil."

A moment passed as Ursula processed that information. "Last week, I established my boundaries. I stated that I don't want any part of sourcing drugs, extreme initiation rites or exploiting women. No offence to anyone who makes a living from such services. In fact, total admiration for those who do. I know how tough that work can be."

A breeze wafted through the reception area, swirling fallen petals in colourful eddies across the tiles. Sooner or later, the bell boy would emerge with a broom to sweep all the natural detritus back to where it originated. The water feature cascaded miniature showers from lily pads to pond, a soothing sound to calm jaded spirits.

Perneet lifted her lashes and fixed her pale green irises on Ursula. "Once we cross the Rubicon, we can only keep moving forward. Your stance makes sense. Escaping the whirlpool, a strong swimmer breaks for the shore and never looks over her shoulder. Unless to reach out a hand to someone drowning."

How this teatime chit-chat had morphed from polite introductions to philosophical musings escaped Ursula, but instinctively she knew they were on the same side. "Something tells me you're a stronger swimmer than me."

"All of us are just trying to keep our heads above the water. How do you like this tea? Nilgiri is most refined, in my opinion. It takes an educated palate to appreciate the scent and flavour but once a convert, true aficionados never drink anything else."

Ursula was about to sniff her bowl when the receptionist called over.

"The massage client is ready for you now. Hut number seven."

Perneet swept the skirts of her sari into her arm and bowed to the receptionist. "Thank you for the tea and the conversation, Ursula. I feel rejuvenated. I hope we meet again. Perhaps I can leave you my card?"

She tiptoed through the lounge and out across the lawns towards Hut No. 7, like a bird of paradise glittering in the sunshine. Ursula willed her good luck.

The ambience at the hotel complex was relaxing in the extreme, tempting Ursula to stretch out on a lounge chair over-looking the garden. Wind whispered through the palms, a uniformed waiter carried a tray of drinks along a sandy path to the pool where a solitary bather – probably one of the Castle twins – swam languorous laps. What better place to unwind? She would not allow herself to doze, no matter how conducive the environment. After all, she was still on duty. Instead, she went through her checklist for the evening for the twelfth time until she saw two figures crossing the lawn in her direction. The resemblance between groom and best man struck her afresh. The pair wore white linen shirts and jeans, Noah's deep blue denim contrasting with Kirkland's off-white, and both had opted for deck shoes.

Deep in conversation, their heads inclined towards each other as they climbed the steps to the veranda. They could be brothers or lovers, she thought, resuming her place at the table as they bounded up the step.

"Hi, guys! Did you get some rest?"

"Hey, Little Bear! We did, how about you?" Noah walked to the bar without waiting for a response.

Kirkland stood in front of her and held out a hand. "I was a little cranky after the flight and didn't introduce myself prop-erly. Sorry about that. Kirkland C. Reece, bridegroom-to-be and the main reason for all this fuss."

Ursula grasped his hand and shook it. "No need for apologies."

"Listen, I appreciate all you and Denzil have done at such short notice. Your itinerary ticks all the boxes. We just wanted to make a couple adjustments because we have an agenda." He swung into a chair and surveyed the restful surroundings. "This makes for a pretty good home base. Noah, you ordered those drinks, my man?"

Noah spun a chair around and sat with his arms folded on the backrest. "Three Cucumber Coolers coming up. I had to tell the dude the recipe, but believe me, this is the only way to kick jet-lag's butt. Did K-Man tell you the plan?"

"Not yet. I was waiting for you so we can explain our thinking." Kirkland leant forward and clasped his hands together, his expression sincere. "Ursula, we need you to understand us."

"We're not who you think we are," said Noah, gazing at her, his chin on his forearms.

Ursula looked from one to the other, her mind racing through options. Religious missionaries? FBI agents? A hit squad dressed as jocks? What kind of a set-up was this?

The waiter set a tray on the table with three tall glasses containing cucumber slices and cloudy liquid. "Would you like to taste, sir? I followed your instructions to the letter."

"I trust you, my friend. What a barman! You're my Go-to Guy in Goa! Cheers, you guys, and here's to an unforgettable week!"

Ursula chinked her glass to theirs and allowed the liquid to moisten her lips. She faked a swallow and widened her eyes. "What's in that?"

"Cucumber, basil, soda and ginger beer. Refreshment like no other. You like?"

"We like," said Kirkland, and took another swig. "Two of my five a day and I'm abuzzin'! Before the others rock up, let's level with Ursula. She's sitting here thinking we're a bunch of tech bros with no class and spring break expectations. For the record, we're not."

"We are so not," echoed Noah. "Truth is, Little Bear, we seek enlightenment. If all we wanted was to get wasted and chase chicks, Hawaii, Acapulco or Europe can do all that with extras. Why come all the way to India? We're here to seek a higher plane."

Kirkland pressed the first two fingers of each hand to the spot between his brows. "The Inner Teacher. The Third Eye. Wisdom, in the truest sense, lies within. Ursula, before I commit myself to marriage, I want to discover who I really am and that means stepping into the unknown. Because I have the greatest buddies on the planet, they're coming with me. This is way more than a bachelor party. This is The Reset."

She took a sip of her drink, playing for time. As far as she could tell, it was non-alcoholic and very pleasing. "The Reset? Help me out here."

"People come to India to find themselves, right?" Noah's expression was so eager and innocent, he could have been a puppy nudging a ball towards her feet. "Sure they do, ever since our grandparents' generation. Maybe before, who knows?"

"That's the path I want to follow. Spinning inwards and releasing all external perceptions of self. In a way, this is the ultimate ego trip – by letting go of the ego." Kirkland lifted his face to the sky. "I want to reset my mind."

"We want to reset our minds," Noah intoned in portentous tones. Ursula suppressed a laugh. "We are snakes, shedding our skin, reborn with clear eyes and fresh perspectives. That's why we want to insert twenty-four hours into our schedule. Scrap the zip-lines and jet skis. Been there, done that. We need one more day to acclimatise and then we're going in."

She stared at those two intense smooth-skinned, clean-shaven faces and absorbed the message. They didn't want sex, drugs or rock 'n' roll – they wanted salvation.

That wasn't in her contract.

Noah rested his hand on hers. "Denzil is sourcing the mushrooms. You're the nursery maid, holding our hands if we get scared. We won't, but just in case, you're our parachute. You get me, Little Bear?"

Ursula twisted out of his grasp. "No. My stipulations before accepting this job were clear. No drugs. I don't care if it's psilocybin or any other so-called natural hallucinogens, I want no part of it. Denzil can find someone else to hold your hands. Goodbye and have a nice ... holiday."

She stalked out of the hotel, furious with herself for wasting so much time. Goddamn Denzil and his 'contract'. No drugs, she'd said. Obviously that was insufficiently specific. She had no obligation to procure mind-altering substances, fair enough, but babysitting while they got off their faces? What the hell were they thinking? She hailed a cab and ignored the insistent ring of her mobile.

6

To her surprise, no one turned up to hammer on her door when she got home. Her mobile fell silent after she rejected the first half a dozen calls. She devoted the evening to working off her frustrations: a run along the beach, a strenuous swim and an hour's yoga on the deck as the sun went down. Dinner was a fridge-raid special – vegetable biryani and raita, with a glass of white wine. She was on her way back from the fridge with a refill when she heard movement outside the front door. In a second she had switched off the main light, snatched up her knife and pressed herself against the wall. Grunts, flapping ears and heavy bodies settling down for the night announced the return of the ladies. With a smile, she opened the door and walked to the edge of the building.

There they were, nestled against the wall, ghostly white boulders in the moonlight, fidgeting, shifting and releasing satisfied moans. Something about their presence reassured her and she watched them for a few minutes, taking comfort in the fact they had chosen her house as their home. At least for another night.

"Ursula?"

She whipped around into a defensive stance, her knife at the ready.

"Whoa, easy! I didn't mean to scare you." Noah stepped into the porch light, dressed in some kind of college blazer and tie. "Denzil gave me your address on condition I didn't disturb you until tomorrow. Don't blame him, Little Bear, he told me to leave you alone." His voice was thick with alcohol. "But no way could I leave things as they were. I had to speak to you and make you understand. So once I got the guys safely back to base, I took a cab out here. I can call the driver to collect me when I'm through talking."

"You are through talking. I suggest you call that cab and return to your hotel immediately. Why the hell would you think I am at your beck and call twenty-four-seven? This is my private time and space. I resent your intrusion. Please leave, Mr Lloyd. This minute."

He took a step away, blinking as if she'd pushed him, then stared over her shoulder. Such an obvious ruse was unlikely to distract a well-trained undercover cop. She stood her ground until she heard the breathing. The small crowd of bovines were on their feet, tails flicking, eyes focused on the intruder. The largest of the group stamped her foot, releasing a cloud of warm breath into the night sky.

"Call them off and I'll leave, OK? Call them off right now!"

Ursula opened her mouth to tell him they weren't guard dogs but wild animals. Then she changed her mind.

"Too late for that, Noah. They've already made up their mind. Just like me, they dislike intruders. The minute you turn your back, they're going to attack you with hard horns and hooves. Not for food. These girls are vegetarians. All they want is to eliminate the threat. My advice to you is to slip around the other side of the house. I'll open the back door and you can stay inside until they've calmed down. Then you call the cab and piss off. Don't run, just walk calmly around the building and wait by the door."

He reversed away, keeping his eyes on the disgruntled cows, and moved behind the wall. Ursula employed her dog handler training and used similar psychology on these large creatures. She sat down and breathed deeply, releasing all tension and blinking her eyes as if sleepy.

She spoke in calm, reassuring tones. "Thank you, my friends, I appreciate your help. Believe me, I can take it from here. My apologies for disturbing your rest twice today and I assure you it won't happen again. I wish you a restful night and a successful day tomorrow. Lights off now and sleep well."

The four animals continued to stare as Ursula took her knife and returned indoors, locking the door behind her. She waited a second and switched off the outside lights. Then she crossed the room and opened the rear door. Noah shot inside as if all the hounds of hell were on his tail.

"What the actual ...? Attack cows! Am I in a David Lynch movie?"

"Sit down and shut up. I'm turning off all electric lamps and lighting a candle. You're going to focus on reeling in those waves of agitation. This house will emanate nothing but harmony because we don't want to upset the cows again, do we? You wanted to find yourself. Start by meditating. Breathe in, breathe out. You are an observer of your own body. Focus on the breath. Feel your skin expand and contract."

Noah sat on the rug, looking around Ursula's house like a five-year-old on his first day at kindergarten. "Nice place. You lived here long? It's a little off the beaten track but I guess you prefer it that way."

Ursula killed the lights and lit the candle. "Breathe, Noah. Just fill your lungs and let it go."

"Sure, I'll try. Maybe a drink would help relax me. I see you have a glass of wine."

"In. Out. In. Out. Listen to the sound of the waves. In and out. In and out. Close your eyes and listen to your body. Allow yourself to relax. If it helps, lie on your back, feeling the contours of the rug. Notice everything, especially your breath."

He shuffled down to lie horizontally, his feet on the floor and knees in the air. "Five minutes, Little Bear, then I take the stage. Deal? You can play guru till the cows go home. But I came here to talk to you and I'm not leaving till I say my piece, you get me?"

"Whatever you want to say will benefit from clarity of thought. Breathe deeply, using your whole torso, and focus on what matters. Scan your body and identify areas of tension. Now breathe into those places. Direct your breath to ease taut muscles. Breathe again, noticing how your back spreads, your jaw releases and your forehead clears. Imagine you're lying on warm white sand, the sound of the ocean echoing your respiration. Every breath is healing. Every breath is nurturing. The only thing that counts is the air in your lungs. In. Out. In. Out."

In Ursula's limited knowledge of the man, Noah Lloyd abhorred silence. A gap in conversation must be filled, no matter how facile the utterance. Now he was quiet. She let the moment extend, noting the slowed inhalations and loosened limbs. For fifteen minutes, she observed the sleeping individual, then covered him with a throw, tucking a cushion next to his head. She poured a glass of water and left it within arm's reach. After performing her ablutions in the bathroom, she was on her way to bed when he mumbled something. She waited, listening.

"Thatcher, cat implants? Get a life," he murmured and began snoring.

Ursula blew out the candle and tiptoed into her bedroom,

taking care to lock the door and wedge a chair beneath the handle. Her knife, as always, was under her pillow. She gazed up at the swags of fabric over her bed, wondering if she had missed a major new trend. What the hell were 'cat implants'?

Despite the late-night disturbance, she slept well and woke shortly after sunrise. The first thing she did was open the window and check on the cows. They'd gone, leaving nothing more than a few splatters of muck along the track. She dressed in cargo pants and a short-sleeved shirt, pocketed her knife and opened the door to the living room. The floor was devoid of overnight guests and the throw was neatly folded on the arm of the sofa. Splashing sounds came from the bathroom.

Ursula filled the coffee pot, calculating how long it would be before she got rid of her unwanted visitor. She poured two cups of Arabica and wished she'd stuck to her original errand: buy bread, milk coffee and rent a moped. If she had her own two wheels, she could escort him off the premises herself. Priority for today – get her own transport.

The bathroom door opened and footsteps crossed the room. She looked up to see Noah wearing a clean white T-shirt and shorts, his pack dangling from his shoulder.

"Good morning. Coffee?" She pointed at the second cup.

"Wow. I turn up here drunk, interrupt your evening, upset your cows, crash on your floor and instead of kicking my butt off your land, you offer me coffee. I don't deserve that, Little Bear. You're class, pure class." He sat down, his expression as penitent as if he were wearing a hair shirt rather than a Mott & Bow crew neck.

"Listen, Noah, you can drink my coffee and have a normal conversation or you can walk down the drive and get yourself a cab. Just do me a favour and stop the bullshit, will you? I really don't care how many courses you've attended where they teach

45

you about eye contact, flattery and the use of first names. I did the same training and can spot fake charm a mile away. Do you want the coffee or not?"

He squeezed his eyes shut. "Not. That sounds ungrateful and I'm sorry. See, tomorrow is The Big Reset. Today, we prepare. All of us committed to taking no stimulants, eating only organic food and cleansing our minds. I could use a cup of herbal tea or some filtered water, if it's not too much trouble."

Ursula rolled her eyes. She fetched a jug of water from the fridge and poured a glass. When she returned to the deck, Noah was peering around the corner of the house.

"Moo!" she shouted, gratified to see him jump.

"Jeez, you scared me almost as much as they did. Where'd they go?"

Ursula shrugged and set his glass on the table. "I have no idea. They follow their own schedule. I just keep out of their way. Look, you came here last night with something urgent to tell me so now's your moment. Then I'd like you to leave so I can get on with my weekend."

He drank almost half his water in one go and fixed his gaze on hers. She spotted the attempt to read her mood and his intense sincerity right off the bat. With a theatrical sigh, she folded her arms and stared him down.

"You have sixty seconds, Noah. Cut the crap."

"OK, hear me out. It's not like we're taking acid or Class A drugs to get wasted and go crazy. We really want to explore what it means to alter the mind and test our boundaries. This is why we wanted the whole hotel complex to ourselves. We're going to be spaced out, all having our own inner experiences, not bothering anyone or each other. It's a leap into the unknown, and of course we've heard the stories about bad trips but honestly, no one ever got hurt taking psilocybin. It's a journey inwards, resetting brain patterns and discovering who we really are. All we want is a responsible adult around who will let us be. Someone like you, Little Bear. Someone non-judgemental and system-savvy in case anything goes haywire."

Her patience snapped. "Three things, Mr Lloyd. My name is Ursula Brown. You have my permission to call me Ursula or Ms Brown, nothing else. Referring to me as Little Bear is presumptuous and patronising. Secondly, I work to my personal moral code. No matter how much money is involved, I will have nothing to do with drugs. I don't care whether they're organic, herbal or made by masticating women in the Amazonian rainforest, I want no part of it. Lastly, this might be your holiday, but it's my weekend and I have things to do. Please leave now and return at your own risk." She tipped his undrunk coffee and remaining water onto the sand, went inside and locked the door. From the kitchen window, she watched him trudge down the drive, already on his mobile phone. She hoped he stepped in cow shit.

7

When she got home from her run later that morning, a bright blue Honda Activa moped was parked outside. She slowed and took an unnecessarily wide arc to approach the porch. Even from a distance she recognised the man sitting in her garden chair by his upright posture and two-tone outfit. Today, he wore midnight-blue trousers and a sapphire kurta, presumably to match his mode of transport.

Tired, irritable and in no mood for any more unexpected visitors, she leant against the porch and fixed him with an unsmiling glare. "You've got a bloody nerve turning up here. First you renege on our agreement and then you give one of those dickheads my address. Are you deliberately trying to piss me off?"

Denzil kept his composure, but each time she cursed, the muscles around his eyes contracted a millimetre. "Good morning, Ursula, and you are absolutely within your rights to be displeased with me. I had hoped to keep the young fellows' psychedelic adventures out of your sight since they will take place on Sunday. As we agreed, you do not work at the weekend." He gave a regretful sigh. "Unfortunately, Mr Lloyd is quite convinced you are the right person to supervise their 'trip'. What the client wants ..."

She wiped a forearm over her sweaty brow. "... the client gets? Including my address?"

"That was quite unforgivable on my part. I am deeply ashamed. Even though I insisted he leave you alone until the morning, I should never have run the risk. I pray it was not too troublesome having him spend the night with you."

Her jaw clenched and she ground her molars. "He passed out on my living-room floor, three sheets to the wind on what smelt like brandy. I'd have left him on the porch except he was afraid of the cows. First thing this morning, I kicked him out and from now on, I want nothing more to do with the lot of them. Or you, for that matter. Trust matters in a business partnership. You've let me down. No hard feelings, Denzil, but I'm out."

He bowed his head, touching two index fingers to the centre of his forehead. She recalled Kirkland doing the same. Her fuse burned shorter. All she wanted was a shower and her own space.

He lifted his face, his expression contrite. "When I heard Mr Lloyd had come here late last night, I was mortified. Denzil, I asked myself, how can you ever make amends? Through your indiscretion, you put a lovely young woman in danger. Shame on you! An apology will not suffice. Forget a bouquet of roses. If you have any sense of honour, you will beg her pardon and give her something useful. Ursula, I am profoundly sorry and whether you choose to forgive me or not, I would like to give you a present. According to my daughter, a modern woman should always have her 'own wheels'. Therefore, I bought you this moped." From his pocket, he pulled a fob with a key attached. "I hope the colour is acceptable."

She yanked the chair opposite from under the table, sat

down and folded her arms, ignoring the key completely. "How did you know Noah Lloyd spent the night here? What's your connection with the taxi drivers? Have you installed cameras in the house clearance furniture? I have to say, I'm starting to feel under the microscope. Maybe this isn't the right place for me or my clients. You can keep your bike, thanks, because I'm selling up and shipping out." She stood up, preparing to go inside. It was a good time to up stakes, when he was on the back foot.

"Please don't do that!" He jumped to his feet, an unusual move for such a calm personality. "My situation is awkward and I see you as my salvation. We can help one another, because two are stronger than one. I'm under pressure from my employer to prove myself or I will lose my status. Together, I believe we can deliver. This bachelor party is my last chance, Ursula, please. I'm asking you as a friend."

"I need a shower. Then we'll talk. But understand this: I'm not your friend and I owe you nothing. Whatever kind of working relationship we might have, honesty matters."

She used the time under cooling water to gather her thoughts. She emptied a bottle of water into a jug, threw in some ice cubes and took it onto the deck. When she emerged onto the porch, she was ready for a battle of wits. Denzil was waiting, his expression humble. She could tell it was practised.

Before she sat down, he began speaking. "If I were in your position, I would feel exactly the same. I present a good front but you have no proof I am an honourable man. The facts of the matter are that I work for a highly respected organisation. These people employ me and a network of other specialists to arrange their business. The suppliers don't know one another. Neither do the connectors, such as myself. We get a request, scramble to fulfil it and pocket a percentage. This time, I'm working with an outsider and the company is unhappy. All lucrative business goes through them. No exceptions. I hoped to fly you under the radar, but they know everything."

Ursula poured two glasses of water. "Not my circus, not my monkeys."

"Unfortunately, when you bring your circus here in January, you will require the services of very similar monkeys. That might prove rather difficult without approval from the top."

"Aha! Now we get to the point. You, and whoever you work for, want a cut of the action. This is no different to a protection racket."

"Thank you for the water. The wedding celebrations went on late into the night and I am feeling my age this morning." His tone, unlike hers, was modulated and calm. He held the glass with his left hand, holding his right under the base to collect any drops of condensation, and drank deeply. "Ah, that hits the spot. Much as I hate to contradict you, this is not a protection racket or as I think you meant, an extortion scheme. The people I work for do not want a cut of your profits. They have no need. Everyone you use, from driver to masseuse, is in some way linked to their businesses. Their only concern is that an independent outfit might challenge their dominance. This is why I ask you to meet a representative, with the sole purpose of proving your status as a one-off party planner."

Ursula shook her head, keeping her focus on the table. She had a pretty good poker face on most occasions, but the thrill of scenting her quarry at close quarters could give her away. "I don't need all this crap. All I want is a quiet life and space to do my job."

"Which will be guaranteed once this is done. It takes no more than half an hour and afterwards you can drive home with your own vehicle." He dangled the key from his forefinger. "Also, you can take the day off tomorrow. My niece's wedding celebrations have exhausted me to the extent that I will be quite content to doze on a poolside bed while eight young men stare at leaves or blades of grass in revelatory wonder." He rubbed at his eyes and Ursula saw his burnished glow had become grey and weary.

"OK, OK, I'll tag along with you this morning. Let me be absolutely clear, this is a courtesy call. I get one whiff of attitude and I'm out. Thanks for the bike. I just need a minute to fix my make-up. Shall I drive?"

A Land Rover, police patrol cars, her clapped-out Renault 5 and Dad's lumbering Volvo had never presented a problem. Even on Sal's powerful motorcycle, she'd never been afraid. Driving was just another challenge waiting to be conquered. The moped took some getting used to, especially its acceleration. As they left the house, she turned the throttle and promptly lost Denzil off the back. He dusted himself off and suggested a more gradual descent to the road.

By the time they drew up to Hotel Rosas Vermelhas, Ursula had learned how the moped worked, prepared herself to face her arch enemies and reminded herself that if she survived today's encounter, she must buy a helmet. *Not Berto*, she muttered as she parked the bike and located the kickstand. *Not Berto, please.* She excused herself to go to the bathroom, comb her hair and brush off the endless red dust which covered her clothes. Mostly, she needed a moment to think.

Denzil could be laying a trap. Maybe he knew who she was and planned to earn himself some Brownie points by handing over Enemy Number One. Her knife was unlikely to save her if the Vargas crew showed up in force. She faced away from the mirror and allowed her awareness to spread outwards in increasing circles, searching for threats, gaps or anything that disturbed her subconscious. She sensed nothing more than general grifting, everyone looking out for the next opportunity, but without malevolence. A pair of teenage girls came into the bathroom, laughing helplessly and clinging on to one another. Time to go. She gave the girls an indulgent smile, checked her lipstick and strolled out into the foyer, taking long, calming breaths to get into character.

Sitting in a faux Regency armchair opposite Denzil was Berto, his suit a touch too snug, and smoking exactly the same kind of cheroot he used to favour back in the day. Milo's sarcastic voice echoed in her ear. *He models himself on Clint Eastwood. Behind his back, we call him Tuco.*

"Ms Brown, may I introduce you to Roberto Vargas? I have had the great good fortune to be employed by the Vargas family in the recent past. Mr Vargas, this is Ursula Brown who is assisting me with a last-minute rescue mission. Since she is sourcing similar kinds of service for future clients, we chose to collaborate."

Instead of holding out a hand, she pressed her palms together and bowed her head. "It's a pleasure to meet you, Mr Vargas." She took care to pronounce his name as if it were unfamiliar.

Berto's head tilted to one side and he narrowed his eyes. Even if she'd never met the guy or his family before, she could have immediately deduced this bloke was all pretence and no substance. He blew out a stream of smoke. "Miss Ursula Brown, huh? How come I never heard of you?"

"Because you have no need of my services? Why would a well-connected man in your position require a networker? And it's Ms Brown. My marital status is no one else's business."

The little muscles around Denzil's eyes contracted as he indicated a chair. "Why don't we order a pot of tea and get to know each other?"

"I know all I need to know about you, Fernandes. You can talk a walk while me and *Mzzz* Brown get acquainted." He snapped his fingers in the air. "Two King's beers over here, Vik."

Denzil left with a reassuring smile at Ursula. She remained impassive as she took a seat.

"What do you want to know, Mr Vargas?"

He drew on his cheroot and ignored her, his eyes following the two teenagers emerging from the bathroom. His phone buzzed and he read the message, nodded and placed it face down on the table. Ursula folded her hands in her lap, maintaining a bland smile. Berto's status games were still laughable. The man was a bad joke: unfunny, cheap and in poor taste. If he had one ounce of the family's intelligence, he would be cross-examining her, rather than posturing to impress. She swallowed her disgust and thanked the barman when he brought the beers.

"Ursula Brown. Mind if I call you Ursi?"

"Please don't."

Berto's lip curled. "I gotta say, you're not making any friends here."

"Mr Vargas, I am here to do a job. Winning friends or schmoozing people is not part of my remit. As a rule, I work alone. Denzil needed a favour so I stepped up as a one-off and sort of wish I hadn't because the whole thing is a foul-up. Have no fear, I pose no competition to you or anyone else. All I want is peace, quiet and a decent glass of white wine." She raised a hand to attract the waiter's attention.

He stubbed out his disgusting cheroot. "You don't like beer?"

"No, I don't like beer, cigars, hard liquor or mind-altering drugs because my brain is my bullet. Hello, there. Your name is Vik, isn't it? Could you bring me a glass of chardonnay and a bottle of sparkling water? Thanks so much. Right, Mr Vargas, let's speed things along. What do you need to know?"

He poured his beer into his glass.

She looked at her watch.

The waiter brought her drinks.

He lit another cigarillo.

She took a tiny sip of wine.

He stared at her.

She gazed out at the garden.

"Who are you?"

This time she made him wait, pouring the water into her wine glass. "As you already know from Denzil, I'm a fixer, a concierge, a personal arranger. My USP is exclusivity. I work for one client at a time, devoting all my attention to their needs."

"That doesn't answer my question. Who are you?"

"You want my CV? Sure. Name, Ursula Brown. Born in Oakland, California to an American father and Australian mother. Studied politics and sociology in England, travelled the world. Introduced people to other people, learned how to meet needs, carved out a niche and set myself up as an entrepreneur. Single, flexible, imaginative and answerable to nobody. Anything else?" She reached for her glass.

He caught her wrist. "Why are you here? This time I want the truth, lady."

"Unless you take your hand off me in the next five seconds, I will publicly humiliate you in front of the entire pre-lunch crowd. No, don't waste time wondering if I mean it, Mr Vargas. Trust me, I will kick your flabby ass. Five, four, three ..."

He let her go and reached for his silver cigar case. "I don't like mouthy women."

"I don't like being hauled in front of a strange man to explain myself. Goa is open to anybody, last time I checked. My reason for being here is to relax, contact the right people, deliver a superlative experience for my client and leave no trace. Why does that cause you a problem?"

He lowered his brows and pointed a tobacco-stained finger at her nose. "If you cause me any problems at all, I promise I'll deal with you."

His *bandido* impression was so embarrassing she wanted to laugh in his face. "Let's agree to keep out of each other's way, shall we? Have a nice day, Mr Vargas." She left her barely touched drinks on the table and walked to the bar.

"Can I settle up? A glass of chardonnay and the water?"

Vik the barman shot a glance at Berto.

"Tuco can pay for himself."

The barman's eyebrows shot up. "Tuco?"

"My mistake. Berto." She threw a note onto the counter. "That should cover it. Keep the change."

She stalked away without a backward glance towards the exit. Denzil's shades of blue were visible under the shade of a palm tree and he straightened on seeing her.

"Everything fine, Ursula?"

"Apart from that asshole, sure. Let's get out of here." She swung herself onto the bike, already sweating in the midday heat. It was part impatience, part inexperience which caused her to gun the throttle the second his weight settled behind her. Once again, she accelerated too fast and lost her passenger. But this time, it was not a soft impact on sand.

Denzil hit the tarmac with a thud and a cry. A bellboy came running to offer assistance, followed by two of the gardeners. Ursula switched off the engine and abandoned the bike, racing to crouch by Denzil's side. His eyes were squeezed shut as if in pain. Blood trickled from his lip onto his brilliant blue shirt. He answered none of the urgent questions people asked him, simply cradling his upper arm. A woman in a sari appeared and knelt beside his head. She ran her hands across his shoulders and Denzil gasped, his eyes flying open.

"This man has a dislocated shoulder. Call a taxi. I'll take

him to the Das and Porvo Clinic and treat him personally. My name is Dr Das. Does anyone know this patient?"

"Me," said Ursula. "His name is Denzil Fernandes and he fell off the back of my bike. My fault because I'm not really used to it yet and we should have been wearing helmets ..."

"Yes, you should. Follow our taxi with your motorcycle and try not to injure anyone else."

Das and Porvo Clinic was a private hospital which specialised in gynaecology. The decor was grey and pink, the logo was a flamingo, and all the posters in the waiting room encouraged female health checks. Ursula sat there for an hour while other women came and went, each escorted by a nursing assistant in pink scrubs.

She had ample time to blame herself. Berto had rattled her, not with his Spaghetti Western shtick, but by bringing back ugly memories. Vargas men were master manipulators, alternating between threats and affection, unpredictable violence and love-bombing. Roberto had always been on the subs bench for the simple reason his ego got in the way. Nothing had changed. Still a loser who thought he was a player, and the financial backing helped him maintain the illusion. A cold shiver wafted over her neck. Berto hadn't recognised her because he was too busy admiring himself in the mirror. If she ever came face to face with Dolores ...

A young nurse stuck her head in the door. "Miss Brown? Mr Fernandes is asking for you. This way."

He looked like hell. A fat lip, a bandage around his head and one arm strapped to his chest. Only his eyes smiled.

"Shit, Denzil, I can't apologise enough! This is all my fault. Are you OK?"

He tilted his head in an approximation of a shrug and parted his lips. "It's not your fault. They say I will make a full recovery. Dr Das already reset my shoulder but this head wound must be under observation for the next twenty-four hours. I can't ..." His lip began to bleed and he pressed a tissue to his mouth.

"Stop talking. Stay here, rest and recuperate. You told me you needed a break after the wedding celebrations so a day in bed is exactly what you need. I'm truly sorry my bad driving landed you here. Obviously I need a lot more practice before carrying passengers. Listen, I know you're worried about the clients, but you can relax. My screw-up, my responsibility, so I'm going to fix this. I'll be there tomorrow to make sure those idiots don't do anything stupid." She was babbling so stopped to take a breath.

"Are you sure?"

"I said no talking! Yes, I'm sure. I'll leave you now and check in again tomorrow. Can I call anyone? Don't speak, just nod or shake your head."

He crinkled his eyes, moved his head a few centimetres left to right and focused on his stained and dusty kurta. "The ingredient is in my pocket."

"Get well soon." She scooped out the envelope and patted his leg. "I'll handle this, promise. And I'm really sorry."

For all the time she'd waited, she half expected it to be dark outside, so the mellow evening light came as a pleasant surprise. She fired up the bike, took off slowly and headed for home. Tonight, she had homework – the study of psychedelic drugs.

8

P silocybin is highly visual and opens an inner landscape involving all senses, a kind of synaesthesia. One is willing to surrender, to sacrifice the concept of self in order to explore an immense universe. It upturns all your understanding of meaning, leaving language insufficient to process what is happening. Emotions become overwhelming and fill every part of you, erasing any concept of being a human. You are a part of something infinitely greater. Consciousness is at its core. Losing your identity is part of that letting go of fear. Only the practised should attempt the 'Heroic Dose', e.g., 5g of dried mushrooms.

Ursula woke up with backache and a stiff neck, having fallen asleep over her laptop. She opened it immediately to ensure she'd shut it down, and noticed the time. Quarter to nine. She was due at the hotel complex in fifteen minutes. She stuffed her notes, some clean clothes and the laptop into her rucksack, splashed water on her face, rinsed her mouth with some unpleasant mouthwash and crammed on her brand-new helmet. Within three minutes, she joined the morning traffic, her stomach sour. Every instinct told her this whole thing was a Very Bad Idea.

The bachelor party was waiting in the breakfast room, mostly drinking herbal tea. The atmosphere was tense, with false joviality, and someone was missing.

"Ursula!" Kirkland got to his feet. "So cool you're here. We were expecting Denzil."

"Denzil had a minor accident so I stepped in. Where's Noah?" Her tone was sharper than intended.

The men exchanged awkward glances.

"Cold feet, I guess. We've not seen him since he got back from your place yesterday morning. I hope he didn't upset you."

"It takes more than an intoxicated Millennial to upset me, Kirkland. So does someone want to check on the best man just in case he choked on his own vomit?"

Their expressions were a mixture of horror, affront and confusion.

"I'll go." Thatcher ran off across the grass.

"Maybe Noah's not ready to let go of his ego, but everyone on The K Team is still going for it." Ethan stood up and made a sweeping gesture around the group. "Am I right, guys?"

"Sure!"

"Hell, yeah!"

"Let's do it!"

Their enthusiasm, Ursula sensed, was underwhelming.

"In that case ..."

"Wait up!" Noah, barefoot in pyjama bottoms and a T-shirt, ran across the lawn with Thatcher on his heels. "No way am I missing this. Sorry I overslept, monkey mind kept me awake half the night. Today is the day when Kirkland and his closest friends take a step into the unknown. Hey, it's Little Bear!"

She shot him daggers.

"Oh shit, I forgot, sorry! My bad. Ms Ursula Brown, I'm so happy you changed your mind. Me and the guys couldn't wish for a better guide. Gentlemen, let's take our medicine. See you on the other side!"

She stared at him for a moment, trying to ascertain if he was already off his head. His eyes were clear and his pupils seemed normal.

"Here's what's going to happen." She adopted a school-marm tone. "So listen carefully. Each of you gets an individual prepared dose. Take it and go lie down somewhere. I'll check in on you once an hour but if you need support, I'll be within calling distance. You're all hydrated and not under the influence of any other substances, correct? That includes last night's hangover."

Each head shook with complete sincerity.

She examined each face as she handed out eight little packets. The twins were already sweating. Kirkland and Noah high-fived one another. Ethan and Kyle wore beatific expressions as if about to meet their gods whereas Brodie looked like he was facing a proctologist. Only Thatcher took the drugs with as much interest as if it was a teabag.

"Take these back to your rooms, ingest the contents, close the curtains and rest, ideally in darkness. This evening, we'll deliver a light meal. Should you feel hungry earlier, just let me know. Stay within the compound, don't get into the pool and keep out of the sun. I think that's it. Have a nice trip. I'll be here all day and night if you need me. Anything at all, I'm at your service."

The weight of what they were preparing to do hit them like a wet towel. Kirkland was the first to react, pinching his packet between finger and thumb. "I have the best friends in the world." He wandered away to his hut, his dressing-gown leaving a trail across the dewy grass.

The other seven members of the party moved off without

any hurry, leaving Ursula hot, hungry and wondering how the hell she got here.

The morning started so pleasantly she should have known it wouldn't last.

First, Laxmi the housekeeper offered her breakfast. "The staff members are bored and the chef has nothing to do. Order something exotic and put him to the challenge. Use your wildest imagination. What can he make for you?"

"Oh, that would be very welcome, thanks. I overslept and had no time to eat. Coffee and some fruit would be wonderful."

Laxmi flared her nostrils. "You're having a free breakfast in a five-star residence, madam. Would you ask for fruit salad and coffee in the Waldorf hotel or the Ritz? I don't think so. Tell me exactly what your heart desires."

Ursula laughed, gave her order and asked if she could use the pool. Ten lengths later, she dried off, changed into a summery dress and enjoyed a fruit salad followed by Eggs Royale on waffles with pineapple juice and a pot of coffee. Her mood turned 180° and she could think of no better way of earning a crust than sitting in luxurious surroundings waiting for some rich gits to get off their heads.

With grateful thanks and compliments to the chef, she set off for her first tour of the huts. Most of the men had followed instructions and were lying on their beds with curtains closed. Ursula didn't disturb anyone, just made sure they were all breathing and left them to it. Cameron and Christopher Castle were together on the deck, one in a hammock and the other sprawled over a swing chair. Cameron's eyes were open and he made an attempt to wave but got distracted by the sound of wind rustling through the palm trees. The hammock, she judged, was a bad idea. Still, it was pretty low-slung so he only had about a metre to fall.

Back at the lodge, she tried to read a self-help book – *Mind, Body, Vision* – chosen carefully to reflect her assumed personality, and dozed off in the shade. After another tour of the huts to find everyone was still alive, she walked the boundary of the hotel grounds, delighting in the colourful abundance of flowers. She sat on a bench and sent Denzil a message, wishing him a speedy recovery. Then her thoughts turned to lunch. If the chef really was at a loose end, perhaps he'd knock up a Crab Xacuti?

A movement caught her eye. For a second she thought a dog was creeping through the gardens until she saw the dark hair flopping over its face. A naked man was crawling at some speed in the direction of the pool. She groaned. How did one handle someone tripping? Was it like sleepwalkers and you shouldn't wake them? The guy shrieked in pain and fell on his side. In a second, she was up and running. As she got closer, she recognised who it was.

"Noah?" She crouched a couple of metres away as if he was a feral hound. "You OK there?"

He got onto all fours, panting like a panther. "My skin's too tight. Too hot."

Even at this distance, she could see his knee was bleeding. "Uh-huh. How about a cool shower? That'll soothe you. Noah, what do you say?"

His head snapped up. "Who are you?"

"C'mon, I'm Ursula, or Little Bear, if you want. I'm here to take care of you, remember? Just in case those drugs give you a bad reaction."

He laughed and pointed at her, his eyes wild. "Drugs? You spiked my drink? Are you crazy? I'm calling the cops. Get away from me, you voodoo witch!" He reversed until his backside hit the trunk of a palm tree. The laughter turned to tears and he curled into a ball.

She let him cry for a few minutes, hoping this would fade into another mood swing, ideally something peaceful.

"I don't know how to get back," he sobbed. "I'm lost. I'm falling."

Even though she sensed a broader meaning in his words, she took him literally. "That's OK. I can guide you home. Take my hand, Noah, I promise to look after you."

His hand moved infinitesimally slowly, reaching in her direction. An instinct told her not to hurry the process and she waited, head bowed against the midday sun, until his fingers grazed her wrist. She clasped his palm and on impulse, kissed his knuckles.

"I'm your guardian angel, Noah. I've got you. You want to go home?"

He didn't react so she placed an arm around his shoulders and spoke simple, reassuring phrases, as if he was a kid who'd fallen off his bike. "Up you get. Lean on me if you like. There you go. Let's go home and chill. You're gonna be just fine. Just relax, I'm here. You got this. Just the steps now and you can lie on the bed. I'll bring you some water and take care of your knee."

He obeyed like an automaton, curling into the foetal pose on top of his sheet. "Hold me, Little Bear. Just hold me."

If the others were experiencing similar reactions, she had a major problem. Playing Nanny to eight adult males was a tough call. Unless she could get them to cuddle up in one big bundle, like a Teddy Bears' Picnic? She snatched a bundle of tissues to press against his knee. He didn't even wince. Then she spooned her body around his, leaning against his back and curling an arm around his chest. In seconds, he began to snore. She gave it a few minutes, dragged a pillow between them and replaced her arm with a rolled-up blanket. When his breathing continued uninterrupted, she slithered off the bed and jogged over to the lodge.

"Everything going to plan, Ursula?" asked Laxmi.

"One of the party needs close supervision. I don't think he's having a bad trip per se, but the effects are confusing him."

"That doesn't surprise me. These people have no idea what they're taking and I very much doubt they did meaningful preparation. Would you like me to check on the others while you stay with the troubled one?"

Ursula shook her head with a grateful smile. "You're very kind but I can handle this. The appearance of a stranger might make the others turn weird. I'll tour the other huts and return to number five. If he's resting, I'll come here for my lunch. If not, is there any chance you could send over a sandwich or something small?"

"The chef is testing new recipes today. Five-spice fish as a starter and Khatkhate with red rice for the main course. We can serve you here or at the hut. Good luck and take care. In an emergency, just call Reception and our doctor will attend to your people."

"Thank you. I appreciate it. I'm going to do my checks then let you know."

Six of the other seven remained in exactly the same position she had left them. Only Thatcher Carrington was sitting on the steps of his hut, looking up at the sky. He focused on her slowly, like an owl.

"Hey."

"Hey, Thatcher. All good?"

"I guess. What's going on with Noah? I saw him leave his place. Dude was butt naked."

It crossed Ursula's mind to ask him why he didn't help, but one glance at his pupils answered that. "He's experiencing some disorientation but I've got it under control. So long as you and the others are fine, I ought to keep an eye on him."

"Yeah, you oughta."

"OK then, catch you later." She strode off in the direction of Noah's hut.

"Ursula?"

She turned to see Thatcher wiping tears from his face. "Can I come too?"

At first it seemed like the perfect solution. The two men, alternately weepy or giggly, lay beside each other, reaching out occasionally for a comforting hug. Their co-dependence enabled her to administer first aid to Noah's knees and back-side, and encourage both to drink a few sips of water. After another round of supervisory visits to their friends, she found both Thatcher and Noah prone, eyes closed. That gave her enough time to eat her meal on the deck and check her phone. Denzil had replied to her message, saying he'd been discharged and was recovering at home. Everything was coming up roses. She stacked up her plates, planning to return them and shake the chef's hand, when Thatcher appeared at the door.

"Noah's in a bad way, man, like, really not good." His pupils were closer to normal and his diction clear. He waved a hand towards the interior. "Dude's pretty messed up and I think he needs some intervention."

Ursula assessed him with a clinical eye. "Thatcher, you didn't take the whole dose, did you? Be honest."

He dropped his eyes and shook his head. "One gram is all. Don't judge me, I have my reasons. But my bro's in trouble. I mean it, Ursula. You're supposed to be in charge here, right? We gotta take him to the Emergency Room. Do something, will ya! The guy's freaking out!"

She burst into the room to see Noah juddering, crying and dribbling from the mouth. Urine leaked from under the sheet. There was no way she could handle this alone.

"Go to the main lodge and tell them we need a doctor. Then come right back. Noah's going to need a friend, a voice he recognises as a touchstone, know what I mean? Hurry up, he's having a rough ride." She couldn't be sure Thatcher was entirely clear of mind, but an urgent task might help him focus.

Once he'd run off in the right direction, Ursula ran her hand under the cold tap and placed it on Noah's brow. It eased his struggles for a few moments, but once his eyes opened again, she could see nothing other than panic.

"No need to be afraid. I'm here, Noah, you're safe, it's OK. Don't be scared."

His mouth cracked open to release an unholy scream. Birds took off from the branches outside and the hairs on Ursula's arms stood up.

"Noah Lloyd, listen to me! You're not in danger, this is just a bad reaction to psychedelics, and to be honest, nothing special."

"I'm nothing special."

"That's not what I said. Your reaction is normal. You're going to be OK, you hear? You're going to be just fine."

"No, not fine. Nothing will ever be fine again." He burst into heart-breaking sobs.

"Miss Brown?" An elderly man wearing kitchen whites stood in the doorway, carrying a first aid kit with Thatcher at his shoulder. "My name is Dr Prabhu. This gentleman says you have a problem. How can I help?"

"You're the doctor?" Incredulity pitched her voice high.

"Yes, madam, I am the medical specialist for the resort and it is not the first time I have dealt with adverse reactions to hallucinogens. May I see the patient? You are most welcome to stay, as is Mr Thatcher."

"Mr Carrington, actually, Thatcher is my first name."

Ursula glared at the young idiot and he had the grace to

look chastened. Not that Dr Prabhu seemed to notice since his attention had turned to the whimpering man on the bed. He spent a few moments checking Noah's pulse and temperature, speaking soft soothing words in low tones. Ursula stepped outside for some fresh air, clenching her fists in frustration. This was exactly the scenario she wanted to avoid. Damn Denzil Fernandes and damn Kirkland C. Reece and damn these stupid frat boys and their foolhardy games to hell. She shouldn't even be here.

A gentle cough attracted her attention. Dr Prabhu was removing his gloves.

"I administered a sedative, very mild, but it will calm him until the effects wear off. He must be supervised for the next twelve hours, minimum. I recommend two people stay here, at least one of whom is capable of restraining him with physical force. It is unlikely to come to that but it would be remiss of me not to mention it. If urgent action is necessary, call Reception. They know where to find me. I will ask Housekeeping to clean up and change his bed. In the morning, I will return to determine if any further treatment is required. I wish you luck."

Ursula's profuse thanks met with no more than a curt nod before he marched off to the lodge. Shame suffused her. How the hell had she become entangled with an irresponsible bunch of playboys with no respect for their surroundings? Thatcher was the only one sober enough to catch the full force of her wrath.

"No housekeeper is going to clean up after your stupid friend. That is down to you and me. Go unhook the shower curtain and lay it on the sofa. Then we move him over there while we deal with the bed. The doc says he needs constant supervision, so you're going nowhere. When the rest of the space cadets come around, I'm going to punch every single one of them in the face."

. . .

It was not the longest night of her life but it came close. She and Thatcher agreed to take turns sitting beside Noah, who was sleeping soundly in the recovery position. The room still smelt of detergent after their efforts with the mattress, even though it was now outside on the balcony to dry. For the first two hours after she'd removed her rubber gloves, a wholly justified fury at herself dominated her thoughts. She should never have got herself into this position. Her aim was clear: find and destroy the remaining members of the Vargas clan. So how come she was babysitting a group of over-privileged drug-dabblers rather than infiltrating the organisation? Denzil was not to blame. Her target was no one else's responsibility but hers. By trying to take an easier route to her goal, she'd lost focus and got distracted. That had to change.

When she woke Thatcher for his supervision shift, she ordered her mind to switch off, curled up in the armchair and cat-napped. Complete rest and deep sleep was impossible, but she managed to doze for a couple of cycles.

"Ursula?"

She jerked upright to see Thatcher crouching in front of her. "What is it?"

"He's awake and sounds pretty lucid. He wants to talk to you."

She shook off sleep and the blanket. Noah was indeed sitting up, looking like death warmed up with the worst hang-over in the world.

She turned on the light. He recoiled, his hand over his face. "No lights!"

"OK, OK!" She hit the switch, her temper already flaring. "Are you feeling better?"

"I need to go home. Like immediately." His skin was waxy and his pupils dilated, he stank of sweat and urine and kept clutching himself as if to make sure he was still there.

"You're talking about getting a flight to the States? Don't you think you might want a shower, some food and a little time to get over what just happened? What about the bachelor party? You're the best man. Maybe I'll go find Kirkland and you can talk things over."

"I don't think you heard me correctly. I want to go home. Today. Please organise a private plane to get me out of here. I'm going to take a shower and then I want to leave."

"You know what?" Thatcher came to stand beside the sofa. "If he's shipping out, maybe I'll go with him. This is really not my scene. My guess is Brodie will wanna come too. You want me to speak to Kirkland?"

She bit her lip. *What I want is you people off my hands and I'll move heaven and earth to make it happen.* "Sure, go talk to Kirkland. I'm going to get some coffee and research our options."

The dawn was a beautiful sight, with dew evaporating into mist amidst the tropical plants and the rising sun tinting everything from hibiscus petal to gecko skin with glorious colour.

"They don't deserve somewhere this perfect," she muttered. "Good morning, Laxmi! Can I get some coffee? Because it looks like plans have changed."

By breakfast time, all eight men had assembled at the lodge. The atmosphere was awkward and unpredictable. Kirkland sat shaking his head for so long he began to resemble a slow-motion dog with a flea in its ear. The party fractured into unequal parts. Noah, Thatcher and nonstop whiner Brodie wanted to fly home that day. Loyal to Kirkland were Kyle, the Castle twins and Ethan. No surprise about the latter as this trip was all his idea. Everything about Ethan rubbed Ursula up the wrong way. His man-bun slicked to his head, his superior smiles and patronising shrugs, his revolting sandals and worst of all, the tiny goatee at the end of his chin which he scratched when adopting his 'pensive' pose. He had a habit of maintaining unblinking eye contact for longer than was comfortable, a technique he probably learned at some Burning Man festival in the desert. Few people in Ursula's experience had triggered such a strong urge to give them a damn good slap.

The men sat in silence, picking at their food while Ursula assembled quotes from private aviation companies and studied scheduled flight timetables. She took her laptop to Noah's table and pointed out their options.

"No way can I deal with a layover in Delhi. Book the private jet, Little Bear. Charge it to my company credit card and please arrange transport to the airport. Thanks, that'd be great."

"Never had you down as a quitter, Noah," said Kyle. "Gotta tell you, I'm disappointed."

Before Ursula could defuse the tension, Thatcher was on his feet. "Shut your mouth, Kyle! Did you sit there watching him suffer? Did you call the paramedics? Did you clean him up, wash his mattress and sit beside him on the sofa all night in case it happened again? No, you goddamn well did not, because that was on Ursula and me. Glad y'all had fun, but that was one of the scariest nights of my life. So take your 'disappointment' and shove it, OK?"

Ethan placed a hand on Thatcher's shoulder. "Take it easy, man."

"Don't touch me, Ethan. I'm not kidding."

"Hey, that's cool." He removed his hand and stepped into Thatcher's sightline. "All I want to say is ... c'mon, guys. This is Kirkland's bachelor party. We all need to chill and process our journeys. That's why we're here, right?"

Thatcher looked at Noah, whose mortified gaze was directed at Ursula. "Oh God, Little Bear, you told me the one thing you didn't want to do was babysit. And then you end up having to wipe my ass. I'm sorrier than I can say."

"I didn't ... it wasn't like ..."

"Please, just book the plane. I'm gonna pack my stuff. K-Man, I'm sorry."

"Sorry for being a chicken shit and ruining the whole week?"

"Not exactly. I'm sorry I agreed to Ethan's dumbest idea yet and boy, has there ever been some competition. Too bad my departure ruins your whole week, but right now I'm more concerned your bullshit drugs don't screw up the rest of my life. Catch you later."

The rest of the party watched him stride away, followed once again by Thatcher. Ursula picked up her phone, dimly aware of Brodie apologising to Kirkland, and Cameron complaining to Laxmi about his omelette. Just as soon as she had packed the first lot off to the airport and the second onto their minibus to Palolem, she was handing over to the tour guide in the south and going home.

Never ever again. No more frat boys, no more distractions, no more Denzil. She'd had enough.

9

The house was bathed in a fruit cocktail of colours when she finally rode up the drive, weary to her bones. It was the most welcoming sight she could imagine. Even the cows were sitting in a circle at the end, observing the sunset and chewing the cud as if discussing its merits. She parked the Honda inside the garage, grabbed a beer from the fridge and sat on the deck, letting go of the day just like the sky let go of the sun – quickly.

Five men had boarded a bus to Palolem right after lunch, all wearing sunglasses and each faking enthusiasm to varying degrees. Ursula waved them off, quashing her desire to flip them the finger. Next, she bundled three others into a taxi and escorted them to the airport. She managed to duck the farewells in favour of completing formalities so the last she saw of Noah, Brodie and Thatcher was their hunched shuffle up the steps of a Gulf Airstream. Once the plane took off, she called Denzil – no answer – and washed her hands of the whole business.

One beer on an empty stomach on top of a poor night's sleep was not the smartest idea. Stress faded like the light and triggered the urge to sleep. But first, a shower. She scrubbed at her skin, washing away forty-eight hours of pleasing other people, and emerged rejuvenated. Her phone buzzed as she was slipping into a clean T-shirt. The temptation to ignore it was powerful, but when she saw the name, guilt forced her to pick up.

"Hi, Denzil! You feeling any better? I have news."

For a second, she heard nothing but wheezing, then a female voice spoke. "Miss Brown, my name is Shripal Biswas, née Fernandes and I am Denzil's niece. He cannot speak to you because he is in hospital."

"Again? I thought he was recovering. I'm so sorry, this is all my fault."

"Last night two men turned up at his house, overpowered the watchman and climbed into his bedroom. On the instruction of his employers, we assume, they attacked him and regardless of his injuries, dispensed a brutal beating. My uncle is fighting for his life because he got involved with somebody outside the organisation. That would be you. Yes, Miss Brown, it *is* all your fault."

For a second, Ursula couldn't catch her breath. Images flashed through her mind like a slideshow of horrors – the drug runners' missing fingers, a whimpering man crouching under a barrage of vicious kicks, three terrified girls without a word of English pleading with their eyes, the blanched expression on Thanh's face when he saw how the Osman-Vargas crew administered punishment. Bile rose in her throat.

"Shripal, there's been a mistake. Denzil and I met a member of his organisation yesterday and cleared up any suspicion. Why would they hurt him when they know we're no competition?"

The woman exhaled a bitter laugh. "You have no clue how these people work, because you're stupid and naïve. Nothing more than a rich bitch playing in the sandpit. Take this as a

warning. Go back to where you came from. Or you'll be next."
The line went dead.

Total exhaustion transformed into mental overdrive. She
locked doors, checked windows, set alarms and turned off the
lights. In darkness, she ran over the conversation with Berto.
Confrontational, yes, but she hadn't been defiant and certainly
posed no threat to the Osman-Vargas monopoly. Why would
he send thugs to assault Denzil? He was small-minded and
petty, but surely if his nose was out of joint, he'd take it out on
the woman who offended his ego. None of this made sense and
she needed to speak to someone in the know. Denzil was out of
the question, for obvious reasons, and his niece sounded as if
she'd kill Ursula on sight. Vamsi was too far down the chain of
command to have any insight. There was another option. She
flicked through her wallet, found what she was looking for and
dialled.

"Come in, Ursula. I've made us a pot of Nilgiri." The entrance
hall of The Blue Moon was subtly designed to resemble the
evening sky. Deep blue walls draped with swags of shimmering
silk reflected the warm glow of lamps positioned on side tables.
Soothing classical Karnatik music floated from speakers and
the air was fragrant with the perfume of spices and fruits. A
dozen people, mostly in pairs, drank cocktails and relaxed on
sofas.

"Let's take our tea outside so we can talk in privacy."
Perneet led the way down steps at the rear of the building and
out into the garden. A few more couples were sitting on swing
chairs or rattan loungers, their murmured conversations
inaudible. A small summer house sat right at the end, with fairy
lights twinkling from its roof. Perneet placed the tea tray on a
low table and invited Ursula to sit on a divan.

"I hear things went less than smoothly for the bachelor party," said Perneet, pouring tea.

"No secrets around here, I guess." Ursula softened her words with a smile. "Thanks for meeting me. I really didn't know who else to ask."

"Ask what? Why Denzil got beaten up? Why people don't want you in Goa? Or perhaps you're more interested in the organisation itself and how it operates. Before I answer any of your questions, I want to ask one of my own." She offered a delicate glass in an ornate silver holder.

"Thank you." Ursula took a sniff, giving herself a moment to think. If Perneet double-crossed her, escape routes were limited. "Fire away."

"Are you police?"

"Police? God, no! Why on earth would you think that?"

Perneet surveyed the garden and her gaze eventually returned to Ursula. "Because I don't believe you are who you say you are. That in itself is not a problem – we all play our roles – but I would be foolhardy to share any information with an undercover officer of the law. You see my point?" She sipped her tea and smiled.

Ursula looked directly into her eyes. "I'm not a cop and no one sent me here. I came of my own accord."

They sat for a moment, studying one another by the light of the lamp, while the scent of tea and a citronella plant wreathed around them like a caress.

"If nothing more is forthcoming, I will take you at your word. You said you had some questions. Shall we start with Denzil?"

"Yeah. His niece told me he'd been beaten up by his employers. I can't understand why they would do that when we actually went to meet them. I mean, it wasn't the most cordial encounter, but I couldn't have been clearer about the lack of competition."

"Let me set a few things straight. Denzil wasn't beaten up by his employers. They rarely get their hands dirty. A couple of fists-for-hire were probably paid to rough him up a little and teach him a lesson. The problem with fists-for-hire is they tend to get carried away. I will stake my entire collection of vintage tea glasses that he was not supposed to end up in hospital. Neither did those thugs know he had just suffered a head injury after falling off your motorcycle."

Ursula rubbed her forehead. "I feel bloody awful about that. Even worse, I can't even call him to see if he's going to be OK."

"I know the family. I telephoned the hospital right after we spoke. His injuries are not life-threatening but he will be out of action for a few weeks."

A cat came trotting up the steps to wind itself between their legs. Ursula reached down to stroke it, feeling the purr reverberate in its ribcage. "The accident was my fault, no doubt. It seems the beating was also triggered by his collaboration with me. What I don't get is why they would summon us to reassure them, then go and give him a pasting after the event."

Perneet played with her earring, the ghost of a smile crossing her face. "We should clarify who 'they' are. The organisation has layers. It works like this. People like Vamsi, who sold you your house, are loosely affiliated lookouts. They spot an opportunity and contact the next level. This consists of people like Denzil, mostly networkers who have connections. When there's a demand, he and his ilk source the supply."

"He's certainly knows how to get things moving."

"Yes, the Fernandes girls married well. Business, government, utilities, they all have significant influence. Even the name commands respect. From there on upwards, we have three more strata of expertise. Next on the ladder is Berto. Everyone thinks he's an idiot but we are forced to humour the poor fool, because he has the ear of the boss. Berto manages corporate events, nothing more. He heard what you and Denzil were doing, and pretended to grant his permission. He should have known we'd already authorised it."

"We? You're part of this network?"

"Don't make assumptions, Ursula. Look beyond what you see. I could have sent one of a dozen girls to give your client a massage but I came in person. One reason was to give Denzil my permission for the bachelor party and the second was to learn more about you. Yes, I am part of the network. My role is one rung above Berto, but let me assure you, I am infinitely more skilled at what I do. Recruiting, managing and protecting sex workers while staying on the right side of the law is a delicate dance. I fought hard to gain my position. Harder still to retain it. Ethics come at a price."

It took a moment for Ursula's perspective to adjust. "You're right. I was making assumptions and I apologise."

Perneet waved a jewelled hand in dismissal. "You saw me as no threat. Being an optimist, I could take it as a compliment." She poured more tea and scooped the cat onto her lap. "I hold a relatively senior position due to my standing in the community. Denzil's mistake was to overlook the chain of command. Everyone knows what a bachelor party involves."

"Sex and drugs and stupidity?"

"Usually, yes. On this occasion, Denzil required no girls from me or foolhardy stunts from Berto. Drugs, however, go through Frankie."

Tiredness, confusion and the whole smoke-and-mirrors shtick were all getting on Ursula's nerves. "Who the hell is Frankie? What kind of bastard would beat up his own employees?"

"She. Francesca Vargas is second-in-command and the only daughter to the boss. Nobody supplies drugs to anyone in Goa without Frankie's say-so. From Class A to paracetamol, Frankie always takes a cut. Your clients paid a high price for their psilocybin experience, but Denzil paid a whole lot more."

Without warning, the cat took exception to Perneet's caresses. It swished its tail, hissed and struck out with an angry paw. Perneet gasped and the animal leapt from her lap to the grass, stalking away to demand affection elsewhere.

A deluge of memories and emotions threatened to overwhelm Ursula, so she clenched her fists and forced her mind back to the here and now. "Oh no! Did it scratch you?"

Blood beaded on Perneet's wrist in the lamplight. "Not for the first time. The beast is practically feral, but the girls love having her around." She took the tissue coaster from the tea tray and pressed it against her skin. "I should put something on this. And in any case, you look exhausted. Please take care on the way home. You look as if you're running on empty."

"I'm knackered, to be honest. Thanks for shedding some light on the situation. It's a lot more complex than I thought, and a little fish like me is better swimming in another ecosystem. When you have a free hour, I'd like to buy you lunch sometime, but now I'll leave you to tend your arm. Goodnight, Perneet, and I'm grateful for your kindness." She reached for the tea tray, so Perneet did not have to carry it inside.

Her hostess did not move. "Not a little fish. And clearly not a cat either. I see you more as a Bengal fox. Opportunistic yet cautious, with big ears."

What was it with everyone and zoomorphism? Bear, fish, cat, fox? "My turn to take an assumption as a compliment, I guess. Why am I clearly not a cat?" she asked, trying to maintain a lightness of tone.

"You lack curiosity. I just explained all how this organisation operates, all the way up to second-in-command. Most people would say that's a story without an ending. Don't you want to hear who's Number One? Unless, of course, you already know."

Ursula improvised, her brain sluggish. "I've no right to demand answers. All I wanted was to understand what happened to Denzil and why. Thanks to you, that's a whole lot clearer. If you want to be selective with your information, that's your prerogative."

Without offering a response, Perneet led the way across the lawn, leaving Ursula to carry the tray. They passed through the house where one girl relieved Ursula of her burden and another applied antiseptic cream and a plaster to Perneet's wrist. Then they walked outside to where the Honda was parked.

"I would be delighted to accept your offer of a ladies' lunch. I will call you next week to arrange a date. Please be very careful on your way home. To conclude our conversation, I really should join the dots. Berto and Frankie share a surname because they are cousins. The head of the organisation is Dolores Vargas, a truly cynical, exploitative, immoral human being. My advice to you is to keep well away from her. I don't know if you speak any Spanish, but Dolores means pain."

10

In her state of near paranoia, the journey home seemed to take four times as long. When she arrived home, Ursula's shoulders were stiff as concrete. The house was silent and unlit, with no vehicles in sight. That didn't reassure Ursula especially, but a lot of tension left her body when she saw the cows resting in their usual place. Even so, she checked all the doors and windows from the outside, inspected every inside space big enough to hide a human, and with knife in hand, ensured the garage was free of intruders. Only then could she allow herself to rest.

You look as if you're running on empty. That was an understatement. The stress and emotional seesaws of the last forty-eight hours had left her so exhausted she was practically delirious. She undressed, showered and considered packing up and leaving the very next morning. Logistically, it wouldn't take much of an effort, but she would have failed in her mission.

She replayed Perneet's words. *Francesca. Only daughter to the boss. Only.* Yes, she was their only daughter but more importantly, the only remaining Vargas child not dead or currently incarcerated. As Ursula brushed her teeth in front of the mirror, the girl's face floated into her mind so distinctly, it obscured her own. Francesca, or Chica as her family called her, was a genetically blessed vision of loveliness. Her father's side gave her honey-blonde hair, statuesque height and pale green eyes. Definitely some Viking in that side of the family. From the maternal line, her gifts were bone structure, thick arched brows and a flawless olive complexion. When Ursula first met her, Chica was just fifteen and already a jaw-dropping beauty. No wonder her brothers formed a protective ring around the girl. She was the family's most precious jewel.

She was also a hateful little bitch.

Manipulative and jealous, just like her mother. Cruel, spiteful and vindictive, like her father and brothers. But whereas they used their vicious natures to extend their power base, Francesca hurt people because she could. One time she took her three 'best' friends to Ladies' Day at Ascot in one of her father's cars. Gussied up and giggly on champagne, all four of them bet on the horses. Two of the girls picked winners, while Francesca lost over a grand. Instead of celebrating her besties' luck, Francesca and the third girl, Vivienne, went off to powder their noses. That was no euphemism. Even at the age of sixteen, Francesca used to snort her way through three grams of cocaine per week. She hoovered up two lines, summoned her driver and left her friends at the racecourse. When Vivienne expressed a twinge of concern for their welfare, Francesca instructed the driver to stop at a service station for a toilet break. She waited until her friend was in the stall, got back in the car and abandoned her at a Shell garage near Virginia Water.

Maybe the reason the girl lacked any sense of sorority was because she had five brothers. She was the youngest, junior to Milo by eight years, and fiercely possessive of her closest sibling. When introduced to his new girlfriend 'Zoë', Ursula's undercover pseudonym, Francesca faked great sisterly affection. At the same time, she actively sabotaged her and Milo's relationship. When she knew they were spending a night together, she always found a reason to call with some imaginary drama. Milo would either spend an hour on the phone trying to reassure her, or rush off to comfort his little sister in person.

If Milo bought Zoë jewellery or handbags, Francesca would express fawning admiration for a minute and then assume a Little Match Girl expression of wistfulness. Within a week, she'd be wearing or carrying something exactly the same, accessorised with a smug smile.

One Valentine's Day, Milo surprised Zoë with a ski break in Austria. After a full day on the pistes, they returned to their chalet, intending to unwind in the hot tub. No such luck. Forty-five voicemail messages from Francesca awaited him. She was standing on Tower Bridge, threatening to throw herself into the Thames. Instead of a romantic dinner *à deux*, Milo spent three hours on his mobile trying to talk her down. Zoë doubted she was anywhere near a bloody bridge, but adopted a worried expression and called every family member to come to the rescue of their beloved Chica. Duty done, she stood on the balcony, stared up at the stars and wished Sal a happy anniversary.

An undercover officer learns how to avoid people with excessive curiosity or wilful destructiveness. That was why she resisted Francesca's repeated invitations to a girls' night. Except on one occasion – 5th of November – otherwise known as Bonfire Night. A group of friends were having a party and she didn't want to go alone. "C'mon, Zoë, we never get to hang out together and bond because you're always busy. Won't you come with me for half an hour? Please, please, pretty please?" pleaded Francesca.

Zoë relented. "Half an hour max. I'm due at the casino for eight."

"Thank you so much! You're so sweet to me, sis!"

The party was at a house on Blackheath, an easy cab ride from the Docklands. It crossed Zoë's mind to ask why Francesca wasn't using one of the family's fleet but she couldn't get a word in edgeways.

"... anyway, I don't know if it's serious yet and that's why I wanted you to meet him first. He has a beautiful soul when you get to know his personality, but my brothers will take against him because of how he looks. They always hate every man I like. Why do you think I never had a boyfriend?"

Because you're a poisonous little viper. "No one wants to see you hurt. The boys are protective, naturally. What's this man's name?"

"Who?"

"The one you're dating? The one you want me to meet?"

"Oh, I thought you meant the cabbie! Ha ha! Hey, excuse me! It's right over there. That house with the flashing lights. You can park outside. Zoë, can you bring the wine? I'll go say hi and let everyone know I brought a guest."

Zoë paid the driver and lugged the case of wine up the garden path. She said hello to a bunch of strangers, poured a glass of water and walked through the entire house looking for Francesca. No one seemed to be the host or know a guest called Francesca, Chica or even Chi-chi, her social media user name. Someone lit the fire, others set off a few feeble fireworks, a couple of guys began grilling sausages on an insanitary barbecue and still Francesca was absent. Zoë dialled her number. Three times it went to voicemail. The fourth time, she picked up.

"Can I get a moment of privacy, please?"

"Francesca, are you OK?"

"Well, I was until you interrupted."

"I'm sorry. It's just you disappeared and I couldn't find you."

"And? You're not my big sister, Zoë. Piss off and leave me alone!"

The line went dead. Zoë thanked whoever was in the kitchen then went out and hailed a cab. She worked her shift from eight till two and walked into the staff room to change. All three Vargas brothers were standing in front of her locker. Dinis and Alex wore thunderous frowns; Milo's expression spoke of betrayal.

"What's going on?"

Milo held up a hand, a signal to his brothers. "Do you know where Francesca is right now?"

"No idea. She invited me to a party but as soon as I got inside, she vanished. When I called her, she told me to piss off. So I did."

Dinis stepped forward, pressing a finger into her breast-bone. "You took her to that party! You left her alone. She got drunk and took Ecstasy. God knows what would have happened if her friends hadn't brought her home. She's a mess and this is all your fault."

"But ..."

Milo rounded on her. "You left our sister alone with a crowd of strangers. What kind of woman are you? From now on, you and Francesca never go out alone together. You're either with one of us or a minder." Milo stormed out, with Dinis on his heels.

Alex came closer, his lip curled in a sneer. "Your time is running out, lady." He caught her jaw in a painful grip which would leave bruises. "Tick tock."

Zoë kept her mouth shut and her eyes downcast. In her mind, she snatched his wrist, twisted his arm and let gravity, aided by the weight of his flabby bulk, bring him to the floor. In reality, she waited until he grunted one last fetid breath into her face and left the room.

From now on ... those were Milo's words. So she was still part of the family.

Anger, impotence and a sense of injustice seeped through Ursula's system, guaranteed to trigger nightmares. She lay under the duvet, practising alternate nostril breathing, and brought herself back to the present. The rhythm of the waves, moonlight reflecting off her chiffon curtains, her clean skin slathered in cocoa butter and the knowledge that outside lay five large confrontational cows. Involuntarily she smiled, hearing Noah's voice, *Call them off!* She closed her eyes and refused Noah and his pals any head room. All her problems, past and future, could wait till the morning. Positive feelings are conducive to a restful night. Although her last waking thought was of Dinis and Alex in their current environments: inside a cell of a high-security prison, complete with slamming doors, grey walls and a tiny square of sky, surrounded by a bunch of psychotic bastards. She allowed herself another smile, this time of pure *Schadenfreude*.

Throughout her life, in all her guises, Ursula had been a light sleeper. As a police officer, she might need to leap into action in the wee small hours. As a fugitive, she never knew if that knock on the door was a hitman or a private detective. She couldn't remember the last time she had slept ten unbroken dreamless hours. And the first phrase to echo through her consciousness was Noah's plea.

Call them off!

She threw open the curtains, staring at the beach with clarity of thought and self-belief. *Call them off!* That's why she'd left the man she loved, travelled to India, reinvented herself and located her quarry. During her morning run, she pounded across the sand, watching morning light play on the ocean and seabirds dive for fish. All the confusion of the previous few days dissipated like dew. This was the endgame.

Nobody could call off the Osman-Vargas organisation so long as a single one of them still operated. In 2016, a fight between rival gangs erupted into a London-wide vendetta. The Osman-Vargas clan came out victorious, but the Osmans lost two out of five family members in the process. Gang warfare was not a good look for London, hence the undercover operation to dismantle the network. Ursula, Thanh and the team managed to jail patriarch Vitor Vargas and three of his sons. The three remaining Osman boys died in a turf war over the spoils. That left Dolores and Francesca Vargas, along with related dregs such as Berto. Their numbers had dwindled and power shrivelled, but the legend lived on. These networks were like an infestation of weeds. The only way to exterminate such a parasitic cabal was to pull out the roots.

She ran as far as the rock formation at the end of the beach, dropped to the wet sand and did thirty push-ups. Then she turned around and jogged towards home. No one knew more about those profiteers of people's misery than Ursula. She had to see this through, regardless of how scared she might feel. It was her responsibility to destroy the matriarch and her successor-in-waiting. Not just for her own safety, but to release everyone else under their control. Purpose was one thing, but she needed a foolproof plan.

Exhilarated and covered in sweat by the time her house hove into view, she tore off her T-shirt, trainers and shorts, and dived into the sea. The handy thing about a sports bra and knickers was that they doubled as a bikini. The waves buffeted her body, but she kept a careful watch on the beach. No tourists yet, just a few solitary beachcombers and some kids playing football.

In the kitchen, she poured a cup of coffee, fried an egg and took her breakfast outside to the deck, along with a piece of paper and pencil. Humming the tune to 'Chain of Fools', she drew a map of the organisation. The obvious way to break a chain was to target the weakest links. That meant throwing Perneet and Denzil under the bus. She'd already done the latter enough harm and Perneet had done her a favour by giving her an accurate perspective on her opponents.

One alternative was to remove the spider at the centre of the web. Realistically, she could never get close to the Black Widow. That paranoid old witch had too much protection. Her funnel web could trap an individual, tangling, dangling and torturing her victims until she was ready to finish the job. Ursula analysed the problem until the strength of the sun drove her inside. The coolness and shade of indoors helped her think. The Vargas net caught one person at a time, because it was fragile as a house of cards. Ursula smiled. She happened to be pretty good at cards.

"Good afternoon, Ursula. I hope you got home safely and enjoyed a good rest."

"Hello, Perneet. Yes, I'm fully recovered. Thanks for calling back. I hope I didn't disturb you this morning."

"Nothing disturbs me before I awake. My employees know I never rise before noon. Your message was delivered with all the others when I sat down to breakfast. You wanted news about Denzil, yes?"

"News, yes, plus your opinion of whether I can visit him or not. I feel responsible for what happened and would like to take flowers, a card, anything to show I care. Unless you advise me against that idea. I respect your opinion."

There was a brief pause. "My informant tells me Mr Fernandes is awake, communicative and ate a decent portion of *chana dhal* for lunch. Visitors are not yet permitted, although one of his daughters or nieces is constantly by his side. They have influence, you see."

Ursula read between the lines. "But I could send something to the hospital?"

This time the pause was a little longer. "We were talking about a ladies' lunch, if my memory serves. How about tomorrow? If you don't object, I will invite Shripal Fernandes, the one who called you, and Xenia, Denzil's youngest daughter. My hunch is you have a lot in common."

Now Ursula was lost for words.

"Ursula?"

"Surely they hate me!"

"People often hate things they don't understand. Come to Hotel Renascenca at three o'clock tomorrow afternoon, be as honest as you are able and I will do the rest. Have a good day."

11

Business, *government, utilities*. Perneet was right about the Fernandes family and their spheres of influence. Ursula spent hours at her laptop, digging deep into official documentation, governmental structure, corporate news and gossip sites. The most useful information came from the latter. No wonder Denzil had arranged for her home to be fully functional in one weekend. His family were everywhere. Other than eating and buying groceries, Ursula did nothing other than study key members of the Fernandes clan well into Monday night.

On Tuesday, the day of the lunch, she woke to the sound of rain battering the windows. Her morning run was out of the question. Instead, she decided to use the exercise equipment she had installed in the garage. The moment she unlocked the door, she knew something was wrong. The fluorescent lamp flickered into life, illuminating her Honda in the middle of the room, the punch bag, fitness rack, mat and weights. Nothing seemed to have changed, but the air was stale, with a faint hint of smoke. Still standing in the doorway, she pressed the button to open the electronic garage door.

A shout of pain made her look up and two men dropped from the metal struts above, one knocking the moped on its side. The other crouched in a combative stance. He was young and wiry, with short-cropped hair and scars, but carried no knife or gun that she could see. *Fists-for-hire.* She assessed them fast. The one who hit the bike was hurt, but trying not to show it. The fighter glared at her, showing the whites of his eyes. He was one ugly bastard.

She had a choice. In a hand-to-hand fight, she could probably kick both their arses. Unless they wore concealed arms. Or she could maintain her cover by screaming and shrieking for mercy. They were here to frighten her. So why not play scaredy-cat and let them think they'd won?

"Don't hurt me! Please! I have nothing of value in this house. Only the Honda, which might need repairing after you fell on it. Are you OK? You seem to be limping."

The injured guy swept his hair off his forehead. "Shut your mouth. I'm fine. You're the one who should be worried."

"That's right." The ugly one relaxed his fists and pointed at her face. "You and Denzil Fernandes think you can screw the system, right? Wrong. This is a warning, Miss Brown. Show some respect, or else." He moved closer and his sour breath reached her nostrils the exact moment his hand clasped her throat.

Before he could open his mouth to offer some clichéd threat, her temper snapped. She wrenched his wrist away, piled a fist into his groin and pushed him to the ground.

He howled in pain and threw a punch at her face. With her knee on his chest, she clasped one hand on the back of his skull and the other on his jaw.

"Try that again, sunshine. One sharp twist is all it takes to break your fucking neck."

Over his pained, fearful breaths, Ursula heard a sudden movement. His mate was trying to rush her, the imbecile. She sprang off the foul-smelling fool on the floor, not away from but towards her assailant. His momentum was such that he could not stop in time, tripped over her and landed on his associate. Ursula snatched up a dumbbell and hurled it at his face. It caught him in the ear, which was not optimal, but reasonably effective. He lurched sideways, clutching his head.

She cursed her own stupidity. Now both men were between her and the door to the house. One was curled over in the foetal position and blood seeped from the other's temple. The only advantage she had was to reverse roles and make *them* fear for their lives.

The gym-garage contained little in the way of weapons, so she would have to improvise. For some reason she thought of the Maori *haka*, an indigenous warlike challenge adopted by the New Zealand rugby team. Make plenty of noise, pull terrifying faces and intimidate your opponents. In the same way her ambush team impeded access to the house, she was blocking their escape route. There was a way to resolve this.

She ran around the rear of the fallen bike and grabbed her skipping rope. The handles were aluminium with a rubber grip and the cable itself was made of steel. Pretty painful when you hit yourself on the shins. With most of the rope behind her back, she gripped each end a little below the handles and started spinning them in the air, wielding them like nunchucks. Even she was surprised by the viciousness of the sound as they whipped through the air. She opened her eyes wide and her mouth wider, then released a banshee wail as she stomped around the front wheel of the Honda.

It was cultural appropriation at its most jumbled, but it worked. Already hurt and probably tired after waiting hours for her to emerge, these men were not going to put up a fight. Wounded Ear helped Sore Nuts to his feet and they scrambled away into the fresh morning air.

She watched from the window as they hobbled down the

drive, occasionally throwing looks over their shoulders. She wiped sweat from her lip and realised it was blood. Her nose was bleeding and her right eye was already swelling. That stinking bastard had made contact, but in the heat of the moment she'd not realised how hard. She let out another roar of outrage, partly to vent her feelings but mostly to put the wind up those cut-price heavies. She was only mildly gratified to see them break into a run.

She righted the moped and inspected the garage door. It had a human-sized rectangular insert with a simple metal bar keeping it secure. It wouldn't take much to jiggle that open and get inside. Those losers must have come around dawn, otherwise they would have disturbed the cows. She hammered a piece of wood into the door behind the end of the bar so no one could open it, and went inside. So much for maintaining her cover. Now Francesca's thugs would report that the mysterious foreigner was a lot more than a glorified travel agent. It wouldn't take much to raise suspicion and the Vargas family excelled in the field of mistrust. With one last look down the drive – where her unexpected guests were getting into a Jeep – she stood in front of the bathroom mirror. Great. She was about to meet three of Goa's high society ladies looking like a street-fighting hellcat.

The maître d'hôtel was not impressed by her swollen eye, grazed knuckles, bruised throat and scraped cheek, and insisted on confirming her invitation with the hostess. Once permitted into the building, she made her way to the first floor and the private dining room. There her injuries earned her immediate kudos with her three lunch companions. She chose to be economically creative with the truth.

"It could have been a lot worse. Two men hid in the garage and jumped me the second I opened the door. They told me to show some respect and then let fly with their fists." She allowed her voice to catch and took a deep breath before continuing. "Sorry. I'm just a little shaken. The thing is, I've worked all over the world. As a single woman in dangerous circumstances, I had to learn the hard way. Now I know how to protect myself. The second I drew my weapon, they ran out of there like a pair of rats."

Shripal was the first to speak. An unreadable woman, she wore a *chiudar kameez* suit in shades of white and gold. Her hands were still stained with intricate patterns of henna from her wedding day and her nails resembled pearlescent talons. Her jewellery added percussion to everything she said. "Those men are filthy cowards. To attack an injured man and a lone woman? They disgust me. Where is their sense of honour? I'm so sorry you got hurt, Miss Brown, and I apologise for blaming you for my uncle's injuries."

"No, no, you were right to do so. I waltzed in here with no idea of the status quo and trod on powerful toes. Typical over-confidence. Can I ask if Denzil is improving?"

Shripal deferred to Xenia. Whereas Perneet and Shripal wore traditional clothes, Xenia looked almost exactly like Ursula – minus the street-fighting hellcat part. Her navy suit was well cut and understated, her shirt a brilliant starched white and her hair cut into a shoulder-length bob. She had her father's gold-flecked eyes, somehow accentuated by small glinting crystals in her ears. Her hands, as she put down her water glass, were free of adornment other than clear nail polish. This was a woman who wanted to blend in.

"Dad's doing all right." Her accent, to Ursula's amazement, was broad Black Country. "The damage is mostly super-ficial, but he's under observation. The beating on top of a skull injury had the doctors worried, but they say he can come home at the weekend, most likely. I reckon the old sod's glad of the rest. Three days of celebrating wore him out. You should put some ice on that, Ms Brown, or you're gonna have a right shiner."

"Please call me Ursula. Thanks for your concern. I used an ice pack at home but it didn't seem like the right accessory for Hotel Renascenca. Great news Denzil's OK and I'm sorrier than I can say about dropping him off the bike. I wanted to send him something by way of an apology. Perneet suggested I ask your advice."

The women exchanged a glance. "Let's order a fish thali for four and discuss the situation," said Perneet. "I agree with Xenia about your eye and none of us cares if it matches your outfit. You need an ice pack. Waiter?"

The food, twelve little dishes on a huge silver salver, was exceptionally good. Ursula alternated between eating, pressing a tea towel full of ice to her face, and talking. First Shripal began by asking about Ursula's reason for being in Goa. All three women listened attentively to her story while spooning portions of saag aloo, okra bhaji, fruity bilimbi curry, fried kingfish, rice, clams in coconut sauce and hot red ambotik onto their plates. From then on, they eschewed cutlery and scooped up each mouthful with a torn-off bit of bread.

Once she'd finished relating her legend and detailing the incident at the stag party, she fell silent. A refreshing breeze blew through the balcony curtains, assisted by the overhead fan. For a few moments, all four women continued to eat. Ursula's face throbbed. She pressed the soggy ice pack to her eye. Cold water ran down her arm and dripped onto the tablecloth.

Perneet cleared her plate and wiped her fingers with a napkin. "We'd like to talk to you in confidence, Ursula. I already asked if you were a cop and you gave me your assurance that you are not. Still, I am afraid I doubt your party fixer identity and suspect you are here with a different motive. Your face when I mentioned Francesca Vargas gave a different impression. I asked you to be as honest as you can. Trust begets trust, you know."

Ursula took the ice from her face. "Trust is a luxury I cannot afford."

Everyone stopped eating and studied her. "In that case, we'll go first." Perneet dismissed the waiters. "Xenia?"

"Yeah, all right. The fact is, we could use you. I'm not trying to flatter your ego here, but even if you aren't actually a party planner, you've still got all the skills. Dad says you're the business."

"That's too kind, really. Denzil opened all the doors and made the introductions. All I did was use his network. Can I clarify, are you planning to set up a rival organisation?"

"No." Shripal took one of the little glasses from the tray. "You should try the *sol kaddi*. It's so refreshing after a spicy lunch. Not alcoholic, don't worry, just coconut with Kokum juice." She tipped the contents into her mouth.

Perneet and Xenia repeated the gesture, so Ursula joined in. It really was delicious.

"No, we have no plans for a rival organisation," Shripal continued. "What we intend to do is kick the cuckoos out of the nest. People in Goa have always catered for guests and earned a decent living from hospitality. Now long-established businesses like The Blue Moon are forced to hand over a percentage of their profits to the Vargas family for no other reason than plain extortion." Her voice was steady but her jaw tightened.

Ursula looked from one face to the other, trying to assess the situation.

"Let me guess," said Xenia. "You suspect us of being the soft soap alternative to the guys who jumped you this morning. Simple answer, we're not. Look, you gave us your life story. Dunno if Shripal or Perneet feel like doing the same, but here's mine. Dad paid for my sisters and me to go to university. Even though I'm the youngest, my education was the most expensive because I was determined to get my education in England, just like my dad. I studied biochemical science at the University of Warwick, graduated with first class honours and got a job with a pharmaceutical company in Birmingham. I would have stayed, 'cos I loved that job, but then I heard on the grapevine things had changed back home. So I came to see for meself. A smoothly functioning society had been infiltrated by a bunch of colonialist profiteers. Since then, I've been determined to get rid of those parasites."

"Parasite is the right word," agreed Shripal. "These people infest every level of society, seeking out the weak in terms of moral fibre, corrupting local government officials, police officers, members of the judiciary and financial fiddlers. They ask people for a one-off favour, like my uncle Denzil, and he suddenly discovers he is exclusively employed by them. If not, he's in trouble. They pay him well, but he is chained to their way of working and even worse, to their methods."

Ursula recognised the pattern. "Otherwise property inexplicably burns, contacts disappear and supplies dry up? Classic protection racket."

"Yes, it is, but those kind of rackets usually work where the government loses control. That's not the case here. There are no more half a dozen officials on their payroll. The rest want to clamp down on illegal activity. We plan to help them achieve that."

Ursula turned to Perneet. "What's your take? I had the impression you were part of the organisation. Is that not the case?"

"I am. This is why I am running an enormous risk by placing my faith in you." She said no more, her eyes fixed on Ursula's face.

"We don't know you," said Xenia. "Your reasons for being in Goa are suspicious. Your international concierge background is vague. We can't even be sure Ursula is your real name."

All three women stared at her, waiting for a response. The only sounds in the room were the rippling of the curtains and the tinkling of Shripal's bracelets as she flicked back her long hair.

Playing for time and using her instinct, Ursula placed her palms together, brought her thumbs to the space between her eyebrows, bowed her head and closed her eyes. She let her awareness expand and absorbed the atmosphere. At first she detected tension, but of the febrile kind, like in that vulnerable moment when you ask someone on a date. *Please say yes.* There was also warmth, willingness and strength. She gave it another minute and detected no danger from these women. Caution, yes, but they wished her no harm.

Meet them halfway.

She looked up, resting her chin on her fingertips and met each woman's gaze. "You're right. I'm not an international concierge and my reason for being in Goa is simple. I want revenge."

No one moved.

"Ursula *is* my real name and I'm here to punish the people who killed my sister. She was an undercover police officer who infiltrated the Osman-Vargas network. One day, she simply vanished without trace. Police inquiries found no explanation for her disappearance. The organisation had murdered her with impunity. If the law cannot act, someone else has to step up. I planted an olive tree in her name and swore an oath to avenge her death. Why an olive tree? Because her name was Olivia."

12

Invoking the loss of a sibling was a smart decision in a culture where family loyalty trumps all. The women's immediate sympathetic reactions did provoke a moment of guilt, but Ursula acknowledged that emotion as an old friend. She'd been living a lie for over a decade – it came as easily as changing clothes.

She accepted their condolences and tender pats, cynically aware that her visible injuries enhanced her pitiful status. The one thing she refused to do was cry.

Perneet came to crouch beside her and place a hand on Ursula's arm. "This is a long way to come for revenge."

Ursula met her eyes with a dry laugh. "You have no idea how far I've come."

Something in her tone seemed to convince the older woman, who rose to her full height. "Ladies, we should adjourn and continue our discussion somewhere a little more private. I believe the time has come to make a plan. Our reasons may differ but our aims align. I suggest breakfast at The Blue Moon tomorrow morning."

Shripal squeezed her shoulder. "I agree. Ursula is one of

us. Shall we say ten o'clock? Xenia, it's your turn to pick up the bill for lunch. Waiter!"

"Breakfast? I thought you never got out of bed before noon," said Ursula, looking up at Perneet's imposing figure.

"Never. Except on very special occasions. Go home, rest and put more ice on your face. Shripal, can you give me a ride?"

"Of course. Manoj!" The curtains to the balcony parted and a tall man in a white shirt and jeans entered. "Sorry, Ursula, but we couldn't be sure you were trustworthy. That's why I stationed my driver and bodyguard outside. We don't need to do that in future. Thank you for lunch, Xenia, and see you both tomorrow."

The driver opened the door to allow the ladies to depart. Ursula stayed behind while Xenia completed the credit card transaction.

"The food was lovely," she said with a smile. "Thank you for inviting me."

"Thanks for coming. Do you need a lift anywhere?"

"No, that's OK. Your father gave me a moped, although he probably regrets it now."

"He doesn't. He agrees with Perneet that we need you on our side. It really was a pleasure to meet you, Ursula. See you in the morning. Oh, yeah, Dad said that if I felt I could trust you, I was to give you this." She drew a beautifully wrapped gift box from her bag. "I do feel I can trust you and hope you feel the same about us. Open that at home, yeah?"

With a brief stop to buy groceries, Ursula rode up her drive just in time to catch the last of the light. She scoured both outside and inside the building for intruders, made herself a Chapman and sat on the deck to watch the sunset. She delayed unwrapping her gift until she could be sure she was unobserved. The sky put on another show to match her colourful mocktail of fruit and fizz. Her face throbbed and her left eye was almost closed, but she was celebrating a breakthrough. Savvy, influential, well-connected women were banging the same drum. The only problem was that Ursula had little faith in teams. Not since the Osman-Vargas bust in London. When your bosses throw you under the bus, how do you ever regain trust? *Simple answer: you don't.* She would play along and cooperate but always be alert for a trap.

When the sun sank below the sea, she went inside, lit a candle and tore the paper from Denzil's present. As she suspected, it was a gun. Her skin turned cold and she had the same reaction as always when facing a firearm. Some people had phobias about snakes, rats and spiders. Ursula, a highly skilled police officer who had aced her training, was afraid of guns. No matter how much practice, pride in her ability or gratitude for the times a gun had saved her life, she could never shake that feeling of malevolence. *A gun is only as safe as the person holding it*, Sal used to say. Maybe that's what scared her.

She screwed her courage to the sticking place and picked up the piece. A Beretta 92X, to be precise. Powerful, discreet and the ideal weapon to conceal under a jacket. Thoughtfully, Denzil had included five rounds of 9mm bullets. She loaded it, checked the action, tried carrying it in various garments and placed it in her bedside drawer. A useful gift, but only to be used in extreme circumstances. She would source an equally thoughtful but less lethal present in acknowledgment of his kindness.

Her face ached so she skipped the usual yoga flow on the deck with the mosquitoes, opting for a moving meditation in her bedroom. Focusing her thoughts was an impossibility, her mind leaping from suspicion to optimism to defeat at the scale of the task ahead.

You came here for one reason – to cut the head off the snake. You now have a potential team to help you reach that goal. A well-connected, smart and motivated group of people want to join forces. Together you can pull this off. After a while, the lone wolf act gets, well, a little lonely.

Knife in hand – old habits die hard – she performed her bedtime checks outside the house, noting the cows wandering up the drive. They were late tonight. She made a chai and waited till they settled, murmuring her greetings. They ignored her but for a couple of grunts, and curled into their sandy hollow. She finished brushing her teeth and completed her night-time ritual with extra care around her bruised skin. What a mess – again.

She slipped under the sheets and tried to forget about the gun lying inches from her head. It didn't work. She gave up, took it into the living room and laid it at the bottom of one of the ostentatious gold vases beside the front door. Only then was she able to sleep.

Her phone woke her at 05.25. She didn't recognise the number but picked up in case it concerned Denzil. "Hello? Who is this?"

"Here is Sandeep, Miss Brown. I am sorry to use your contact number but cannot reach Mr Fernandes. I have bad news. Your bachelor party guests are showing rotten behaviour and consequently are unwelcome at our resort. Nothing is to their satisfaction. They complain from dawn to dusk and expect the entire place to revolve around them. Last night they became most unruly and disrespectful in our beachside restaurant, upsetting many guests and staff members. We were forced to call the police and now two of your party are in custody. I want nothing more to do with these men and hand all responsibility over to you. Very sorry."

"Police custody? Sandeep, what happened?"

"Drunkenness and physical assault. I want them off my

property this morning. Please will you or Mr Fernandes arrange collection?"

"OK, OK. Mr Fernandes is in hospital but I'm his deputy. The drive south will take me around two hours, so I should be there by eight o'clock at the latest. Listen, Sandeep, I'm really sorry about all this."

"So am I." He rang off.

Ursula dropped her face into her hands, forgetting her bruises, and recoiled in pain. *What a way to start the day.* There was no way she could be at The Blue Moon by ten, so she sent a brief text message to Perneet with an embarrassed explanation. Of all people, Perneet would understand the urgency of dealing with troublesome guests.

Twenty minutes later, she reversed the Honda out of the garage, surprising the cows by rising earlier than them for a change. Once sure the garage door was closed, she buzzed down the drive, heading for Route 66. Two hours on uneven roads via moped, dodging cows, tourists and overcrowded buses would work her into a sufficient temper to handle those over-privileged asshats.

Sandy's Place was not the humble beach shack one might assume from the name. Rather, it was a glamping site, with twenty high-end luxury tents, a five-star restaurant, spa and private beach. Sandy was in fact Sandeep, a smart investor and businessman who capitalised on the shift from the beach-tar-on-my-feet vibe to vegan wellness with reflexology mind-set. Ursula pulled up at a café across the street to get some coffee and make herself look a little more convincing. Hair brushed, make-up applied, she changed out of her jeans and sweatshirt into a cheesecloth dress. Only then did she announce herself at Sandy's reception. Hopefully, the bruised eye and grazed cheek would stand out less with deep red lipstick and pretty floral patterns. While she waited for Sandeep to appear, she checked her phone. To her satisfaction, a minibus was available at a local rental firm, one of the chain hotels near the airport could accommodate a last-minute party, and tomorrow afternoon a private jet would take this bunch of big mouths far from her orbit. Now all she needed was to get two of them out of police custody.

A man strode across the foyer, immaculate in a cream suit and a neat goatee. "Miss Brown, thank you for getting here so promptly. I wish to apologise for being so short on the telephone this morning. In my defence, it had been a long and stressful night. Can I get you some tea?"

"If any apology is required, it's from your guests. You're Sandeep, right? Pleased to put a face to the name. A glass of water would suffice. I have a bus organised to get them out of your hair, just as soon as we spring the pair under arrest."

Sandeep led her to a mezzanine level, moving aside a sign saying CLOSED, and took two bottles of mineral water from a fridge behind the bar. They sat at a table by the window, overlooking the beach. It was extraordinarily beautiful, with palm trees stretching towards the ocean, clean white sands and irregularly placed sun umbrellas over cushioned loungers. A blue and white awning covered a little bar, from where staff in white shorts and shirts carried drinks and snacks to the reclining guests.

"Oh wow, I can see why this place gets all those rave reviews. It's paradise."

Sandeep poured sparkling water into her glass. "Paradise, at least by my definition, is beautiful, relaxing and peaceful. Most of our guests agree. A small minority behave as if they are on spring break, pursuing alcohol and sex like savages. The worst of them think they can pay away the problem. How does one repay the trauma of a sexual assault?"

The glass halted halfway to Ursula's lips. "They assaulted one of your employees?"

He closed his eyes. "Two. I have given both waitresses the week off on full pay and will support them financially if they wish to prosecute. Who on earth feels entitled to behave this way? I have worked in hospitality for fifteen years. Never in my life have I witnessed more disgraceful behaviour than the last few days. This is not your fault, I am aware, but someone has to teach these people they cannot take with impunity."

Ursula stood up. "Guess that's my job. Listen, Sandeep, I am sorrier than I can say. It's clear these men have upset you profoundly and your staff more so. I will get them out of here as soon as I can. This will never happen again, I promise. Poor Denzil will be mortified."

"How is he? You mentioned hospital. Obviously, you've been in the wars yourself." He gestured to her face.

"All my fault. Inexperienced with a moped, you see. I tipped Denzil off the back and fell on my face. Help me out here. Which of the guys are in jail and how do I get them out?"

"Kyle Arden and Ethan Rey. I don't know if the police plan to charge the men but I suspect not. You will need to assure the sergeant they will cause no more trouble and prove they are leaving the country at the earliest opportunity."

Another voice replied. "Oh they're most definitely leaving, Sandeep. That we can guarantee." Shripal walked up to their table, looking impressive in a green and gold sari. Her face was immaculately painted and both wrists glinted with jewellery. "My name is Shripal Fernandes and I am Denzil's niece. It's an honour to meet you."

While they exchanged greetings, Ursula marvelled at how fast Shripal had made the journey. More likely to have been a limo than a broomstick, but somehow it was magic.

"Ursula!" Shripal clasped her hand. "How are you feeling

today? A lot worse at having to rise before dawn to deal with ungrateful visitors, I imagine. Shall we take tea and form a battle plan? I expect an establishment as sophisticated as this can provide us with a pot of Nilgiri, am I right, Sandeep?"

The battle plan was unnecessary since Ursula had arranged transport and a hotel for the bachelors' last night, and confirmed their flight for the following day. Shripal used her influence at the police station to get Kyle and Ethan released, offering her personal assurance they would be leaving on Thursday. Ursula summoned Kirkland and the Castle twins to Sandeep's office, then read them the riot act. The presence of two security guards and Sandeep himself cowed them into silence, although Kirkland sat there shaking his head as if woefully misunderstood. Without actually mentioning the word 'deportation', Ursula hinted they were being asked to leave the country. She insisted they pack their friends' personal items and muster at reception by midday.

"Just so we're clear, I'm washing my hands of you. My colleagues and I have enough to do trying to persuade the police and hotel manager not to bring charges against your mates. At twelve o'clock, the minibus driver is leaving to take you to a hotel near the airport. If we can get Kyle and Ethan freed in time, they go with you. If not, they'll have to figure out getting to the airport themselves. When you get to the hotel, stay in your rooms, cause no one any hassle and behave like civilised human beings. I'd strongly advise against going out to explore, because if you get into any more trouble, you're on your own. Oh, and, Kirkland, any extra charges incurred by you and your friends will be added to the bill. We're done here. Get your shit together and piss off. Have a nice day." She motioned to the security guard, who opened the door and escorted them out.

The Castle twins looked like hell on earth and Kirkland's usual arrogance had deserted him. But that was nothing compared to Kyle and Ethan when the police vehicle ejected them at reception. A pair of bums in dirty, sweaty clothes, their faces drawn and hungover, they shuffled onto the bus without demur. A porter loaded their luggage and slammed the door, causing each passenger to wince. Ursula stood side by side with Sandeep and Shripal as the bus drove away. Not one of the bachelor party lifted a hand in farewell.

"No matter how successful a man or woman becomes, one should never lose respect," said Sandeep.

"No matter how successful a man or woman becomes, one can always learn a lesson," added Shripal. "Ursula, do you have to rush back to the north? Or should we have lunch here, overlooking the beach, and travel home at our leisure?"

"Lunch at Sandy's place would suit me perfectly. It's a lovely spot."

"Then that is settled. So long as we can find a private place to conduct our conversation?"

Sandeep bowed his head. "That will not be a problem, ladies. Please follow me."

He took them to an upper level containing only one beautifully laid table shaded by palms, and pulled out each person's chair as they sat.

"Miss Fernandes, Miss Brown, please may I make a recommendation? We have a catch of the day with caramelised onions, grilled vegetables and sweet potatoes. It is our house special."

"That sounds excellent. Would you be so kind to bring a platter for two and a bottle of Vinho Verde? As for an aperitif, I'd like a Dirty Martini. Ursula, you should try a Piña Colada. They say pineapple juice is the best for healing bruises."

Sandeep hurried off before Ursula could protest. "Sorry, but I can't drink alcohol because I'm on my bike. The roads were hairy enough before rush hour. After one cocktail, I'd fall into a ditch."

"You're not going home on the bike. I brought a people carrier in case we needed to transport those awful people out of here. Turns out you'd already organised a bus, like the Superwoman you are. We'll put your moped in the back and my driver will get us both home in comfort. Perneet and Xenia send their warmest regards and are sorry to postpone our brunch."

"Oh, you've spoken to them already. I left Perneet a message this morning, apologising. Is that what alerted you to travel south?"

"No, I only spoke to them on the way here. My father's phone is currently in my care, you see. When I awoke at six, I received Sandeep's messages and acted immediately. I have to say, I was very impressed to find you here, already in control of the situation."

"Denzil asked me to deputise, so that's what I did. Like it or not, we're still responsible for that bunch of ill-mannered idiots."

"Not anymore. My security team will be keeping a discreet watch over them to ensure they fly out tomorrow. You can relax. Talking of security, I told Dad about those guys attacking you. We agreed that in addition to the personal protection he provided, you should have a patrol visit your place, at least a couple of times a night. So if you see a couple of strangers on your property, don't be alarmed. Flick the lights on and off three times. The patrol will switch their torches on and off three times to reassure you."

"I don't know what to say. I am incredibly grateful for everything. Please tell Denzil his gift was absolutely the right choice."

A waitress appeared with two elaborate cocktails and a bottle of water. Conversation stopped for the ritual of tasting and approving. Shripal gave the girl a gracious nod and they were alone again, both staring out at the Arabian Ocean.

"Understand this, Ursula Brown, I want a pleasant meal in good company with luxurious surroundings and I'm paying for it. None of this is designed to ... sway you." She took her eyes off the sea and fixed her gaze on Ursula.

"Thanks, Shripal. You and your family are very kind. I'll be equally honest and say that I'm not easily swayed. I've worked alone for a long time and with good reason. Trust comes hard. Nothing personal, but when you've been burnt ..."

Her companion raised her glass. "No need to explain. You're an outsider without the network of company or family. I'm the opposite." She let out a little laugh. "You're not likely to believe this, but I envy you that freedom."

"I envy you that protection."

Shripal's eyes crinkled and her lips spread to reveal a warm smile. "To appreciating what we have and learning from each other."

"I'll drink to that." She removed a large chunk of pineapple which could have had her eye out and took a healthy slug of sweet, creamy, potent cocktail. "Goa is growing on me."

13

Appreciation for food was an attitude Ursula respected. She and Shripal helped themselves to crisp fillets of reef cod, freshly grilled vegetables and a spoonful of saffron rice, then devoted their attention to enjoying a moment of paradise. A light breeze blew in from the ocean, the wine sparkled lightly on the tongue, every item on her plate was delicately cooked, and the view of swaying palms against an ever-changing sea filled her with a rare joy.

"Bliss," she murmured, mostly to herself.

"Bliss," agreed Shripal, tearing into a flatbread. "I really should do this more often. Since this is your first time at Sandy's Place, all you need to do is eat, drink and listen. I'll do the talking. Here's the proposal. My uncle and I, along with Perneet and now my cousin Xenia, plan to rid Goa of the Vargas family forever. These people, as I'm sure you know, latch on to an imperfect but comfortably functioning society to exploit, capitalise and corrupt. We are going to stop them, ideally with your help and knowhow.

"The situation is this. The Vargas gang, and I don't use that word lightly, are a pack of criminals who turned up out of the blue. They made plenty of 'benevolent' donations – generosity to the police retirement pot, funding for a trio of hospitals, support for a political campaign, major boosts to tourism efforts, you name it. Like cuckoos, they kicked out any competition. The drug dealers who used to handle North Goa had their merchandise stolen, their runners recruited and clients poached. When they fought back, some ended up in hospital with mysterious injuries and at least two met an unfortunate end – one in a traffic accident and another drowned herself.

"Here in South Goa, they used a different technique. They simply flooded the place with better products. That lasted for a few months, by which time other suppliers had gone looking for new markets. Then standards dropped, but as the consumers are mostly tourists, who's going to pursue the point?

"They coerced my uncle Denzil and Perneet, amongst others, into working exclusively for them. They bullied hotels, taxi firms and other tourist services via a protection racket and fought any legal challenges or external providers with extreme aggression. Before we knew what was happening, they controlled most of North Goa."

Ursula trod carefully. "My sister never told me very much, probably for my own safety, but I think I can say for sure this is not their first time."

"That much is obvious. It's also not the first time they made mistakes." She placed her cutlery either side of her plate, reached into her handbag and flipped open a notebook. "A police undercover operation on London resulted in nineteen convictions, including father Vitor and three of his sons: Dinis, Alex and Milo Vargas." She closed the notebook and resumed eating. "Your sister did her job well. That's the standard we must match."

"Hang on, Shripal, the Osman-Vargas sting was a police job, run by London's Met. They're professional detectives and understand the law." She remembered her role. "As far as I'm aware. I don't know how the law works in India. Not even in England, to be truthful. The one thing I do understand is how violent and ruthless those people can be. The idea of trying to take them all down is terrifying."

"The alternative is worse. Perneet has fought hard to protect her employees, after two takeover attempts by that old dragon at the head of the family. Dolores wants to introduce a whole new ethic. Her plan is to use trafficked girls, turn them into drug addicts and therefore sex slaves. The next attempt at ousting Perneet, I'm pretty sure, will be dirty tricks, and I fear for the women's safety. Neither Francesca – I will never call her Frankie – nor Dolores has a moral code. We do. So do you." She nibbled one last piece of sweet potato and rested her knife and fork together on her plate. "Denzil trusts Sandeep with his life and I would swear an oath that my driver is discreet. Nonetheless, why don't we take a walk along the beach to ensure our privacy? What I have to say is for your ears only."

Sandeep refused to bring them a bill, hinting that the cost of their lunch would find its way onto the bachelor party's invoice. They expressed their thanks and appreciation of the food, left a large tip and walked down the drive to the beach. It was the warmest time of the day, so they stuck to the shade, beneath the palm trees.

Shripal's sari glinted and shone as they passed underneath the palm fronds. "We've been talking about removing this canker for some time. Now it seems everything has come to a head. Xenia's return, your arrival and that blatant assault on my uncle are all auguries. It is time to stop talking and act. What are our options? Well, we could start a bloody and potentially unwinnable war of attrition, which would claim far too many casualties. We could send a hitman after Dolores, except that the matriarch is completely inaccessible. We could work with the police to prevent their illegal activities, at least those who aren't on the Vargas payroll. Or, we can break the chain."

Her astute reasoning left Ursula speechless. That was exactly how the Met had infiltrated the London network. "And like a house of cards ..."

"That's it exactly. You see, each layer is dependent on the loyalty of those below. We destabilise one level which wobbles the next. Shake it hard enough and the whole thing comes tumbling down. This will require a concerted effort by every one of us, each penetrating a particular sphere of influence."

"Sounds like you have a plan."

"Oh, we've had a plan for a long time. Just one part was missing. Then along came Miss Ursula Brown."

The driver had to remove some seats in order to accommodate Ursula's moped, but he and a porter finally managed to heave the thing aboard the people carrier. Sitting the row behind the driver, Shripal and Ursula passed the journey in near silence; Shripal's thumbs flying over her phone and Ursula staring out of the window.

What the Fernandes family were planning was huge. If Ursula helped them pull it off, it would kill two birds with one stone, both parties achieving their aims: rendering the Vargas clan powerless and expelling what was left from Goa. But it was an almighty undertaking with far too many variables. To be honest, the fact they trusted a practised liar like Ursula was a red flag.

She could almost hear her senior officer's contemptuous tones as he picked holes in every element of a student's strategy during police training. "Yeah, right, of course he'll invite you to join his gang. You look *nothing* like a wet-behind-ears cop, do you? And then what? Offer him a beer, slip in some truth serum then call for back-up? I swear to God, you people get more naïve every year. This is NOT the bloody telly!"

The Fernandes' concept was fundamentally sound. No one working for the Vargas outfit saw themselves as personally to blame for the stranglehold. Each was simply doing his or her own bit. The key was convincing every link in the chain they bore equal responsibility. If one broke, the others would be weaker. The question was, why would anyone walk away from regular employment, unless there was an alternative?

That was where Shripal proved herself one step ahead. She and Perneet were building a shadow organisation, providing all the same services, but operating under fairer conditions. No threats or violence, no coercion or enforced loyalty, just a team of connected co-operators. Whether people would jump ship was a moot point. Maybe nothing more than wishful thinking. Even so, with the right kind of strategic support, coupled with resentment at the Vargas thuggish tactics, this plan was workable. A peaceful revolution.

As with all revolutions the problem was how to get rid of the previous administration. Once again, Shripal was prepared. Minor indiscretions by the Vargas network were usually 'overlooked' by the police, via pay-offs. Unless it was a serious infraction, they turned a blind eye. Something major had to happen, something so significant it would attract the attention of international law enforcement. Several family members caught red-handed in either drug or people trafficking could not be brushed under the carpet.

Ursula's pulse began to race, despite her exhaustion. She could do this. *They* could do this. With the right people in position, it was feasible for Goa's crime squad to intercept a drug shipment, covering themselves with glory. Next step, arrest Francesca. Obviously indicting such a close family member would weaken the mater familias to the extent she'd likely retire. She had no one left, other than Berto. Unless they could nobble them both at once? Impossible. The Vargas family stuck to their own lanes and rightly so because Berto was an utter schmuck.

Without warning, Shripal spoke to the driver in Konkani. The people carrier slowed and turned off the main road. After around ten kilometres, they pulled into another luxury resort. Shripal looked up from her screen and faced Ursula for the first time since Sandy's Place. She clasped her hands together and gave an apologetic smile.

"I managed to get an impromptu meeting with someone rather influential. Don't worry, Manoj is going to drive you and your motorcycle home. Tomorrow morning, the book club will be meeting at your place to discuss Amitav Ghosh, yes? Ten o'clock, I think we agreed. Please don't worry about providing brunch – I have that covered. See you in the morning. Get some rest!" She shimmied out of the vehicle and with a gracious wave, walked off under a palm tree arbour.

Book club? Amitav Ghosh? Ten o'clock? Evidently the text conversations Shripal had been conducting on her mobile had proved fruitful. Ursula switched her attention from bringing down a crime syndicate to worrying about whether she possessed enough crockery to cater for a ladies' brunch.

The driver looked into the mirror. "Are you ready to leave, madam?"

Ursula realised she was now the boss. "Yes, thank you, I'm ready." She sat back as the vehicle circled around the water feature and headed down the drive. The book club story was a cover, she was almost certain, but just in case ...

"Umm, it's Manoj, right? My name is Ursula. You don't happen to know anything about Amitav Ghosh, by any chance? Don't tell Shripal, but I'm feeling a little under-prepared."

He indicated, checked his wing mirror and joined the stream of traffic. "Although I have read every one of that man's novels, I would not presume to call myself an expert. Many say *The Glass Palace* is his finest work, but if you're new to his oeuvre, I would recommend starting with *The Hungry Tide*, an insight into the Sundarbans and the Bay of Bengal. As the title suggests, it covers man's constant compromise with nature, that delicate balance between futility and passion for life, or cycles of optimism and despair. I found it an education regarding a region of East India of which I knew little."

"Manoj, you are a fount of information. Tell me more."

Entertaining literary discussion and comfortable surroundings eased the journey so that it seemed to last no time at all. Manoj helped her unload her moped and she insisted on giving him a tip. They parted with a warm handshake. After a shower, Ursula changed into some white cotton pyjamas and drank a chai on the deck. She had no appetite since that enormous lunch. The sun offered its usual display, the cows ambled up the drive and all was well with the world. As she went to close the curtains, she caught sight of her reflection. Her pyjamas reminded her of a karate dogi and she snorted a laugh. Mistress of Martial Arts.

Whether that thought triggered a subconscious idea of using one's opponent's weight against them, she couldn't say. But when she awoke, the solution to bringing both the third-generation Vargas children to their knees was simple. Appeal to their egos, but separately. If Francesca knew Berto was involved, she'd veto the entire operation. The guy was all mouth and no trousers, more liability than asset. But if there was a way of convincing each of them the other required supervision, bingo. Two rats in a trap.

Perneet, Shripal and Xenia turned up at a quarter past ten in the same people carrier. Once again, the driver was Manoj. While the ladies settled themselves on the sofas,

Ursula helped him and a maid unload an extraordinary number of plastic containers filled with food. After everything was spread on the dining table, Manoj pressed his palms together and wished them a good day. Before he left, he pressed a book-shaped package into Ursula's hand. "My copy. Enjoy."

She thanked him and slipped it into a drawer after he'd left.

"Come sit down, Ursula," said Perneet. "Can I just check you have no staff in the house?"

"I have no staff, full stop. There's no one here but us."

"That's what I thought. And I have sent mine away, so we can talk freely. On behalf of everyone involved, and that includes my uncle, we are very glad you're joining our team. Xenia and I visited Denzil this morning and he gave us a list of points to discuss. Why don't we agree on an agenda, eat and share ideas?"

"How is he?" asked Ursula, sitting in the free armchair.

"Irritable, impatient and keen to get out of his bed," Xenia answered. "He sends his regards. Can we eat first and do official stuff when we've eaten? I make bad decisions when I'm hangry."

Everyone looked to Shripal for permission.

"Yes, go ahead. You eat and I will talk. Yesterday, while we were in Palolem, I told Ursula our plans."

Xenia grinned. "You were sorting out that stag party? I heard on the grapevine you kicked some arse."

"We assumed control of the situation, yes. Ursula listened, asked intelligent questions and agreed to join us. What I didn't tell her was who I went to meet on the way home."

Perneet, who was busy opening containers, paused for a moment. "Who?"

"My brand-new brother-in-law, Cruz Biswas, Superintendent of Police."

"We have a cop in the family?" gasped Xenia. "Nobody

told me his job when I was dancing with him at your wedding. Bugger! I quite fancied him as well."

"Firstly, his profession in law enforcement should be an attraction, not a deterrent. He's good-looking, intelligent, and very well paid with excellent prospects. You could do a lot worse. Secondly, he's not long been promoted and still idealistic about tackling corruption, etcetera. I asked if he'd like to chat and he happened to have an hour free. He's willing to offer us all the support we need. After all, which senior police officer would *not* want to nail the Vargas gang?"

"Those that profit it from it, I assume," said Perneet. "Otherwise they would have done it sooner." She settled on the sofa with a plateful of pakoras, bhajis and samosas. The colours on her plate reflected her sari, a blaze of oranges, ochres, yellows and browns. "He is aware he might make himself very unpopular, I hope?"

Shripal gestured for Ursula to help herself to the brunch buffet, but Ursula's mind was racing. "Excuse my ignorance and I'm sure you know your family best, but what if he's one of those taking kickbacks? Now he knows exactly what we're planning and can warn the Vargas clan."

Shripal shook her head with absolute conviction. "Cruz and Jay are cut from the same cloth. Honourable to their bones. In fact, it was Jay who suggested I speak to his brother. He knows how important this is to me. Please eat something, Ursula. My kitchen staff started cooking at six in the morning to create this selection. Perneet, I thought you could take whatever's left over back to the girls for lunch."

"Wait a bloody minute!" Xenia set down her plate and came to stand in front of Shripal, hands on her hips. "We have kept this concept strictly between us for a damn good reason. We scoped out Ursula and only when all three of us agreed we could trust her did we let her in. What right do you have to arrange a meeting with someone completely off the radar without our say-so? You're bang out of order, Shripal, and you know it."

Shripal rearranged her sari and swished her hair over her shoulder. "I apologise. I saw an opportunity and I snatched it. It was too good a chance to miss. Needs justify the means, I would say. Now we have a senior police officer in our corner."

Xenia continued to glare and Shripal gazed out of the window. Tension made the room brittle until Perneet spoke.

"Xenia is right. None of us talks to anyone else without express permission from all five of us. I appreciate why you did it, but I wonder, have you told your uncle?"

Shripal said nothing but turned her face away to survey the sea.

"It's quite normal for a newly married woman to feel a sense of power," said Perneet, her voice soothing. "You have influence, a new pool of relatives of whom to ask favours and a wealthy, magnanimous husband. Remember your roots, Shripal, and the risks that every one of us is running. Do not include anyone in our plans without asking all of us first. For the sake of clarity, all of us includes Denzil and Ursula. Now, let's move on. Ursula, if you aren't going to eat, bring me some more aloo gobi, a bit of dhal and a spoonful of saag paneer with a chapatti, please."

It was an effective ruse. With Ursula occupied by refilling Perneet's plate and Xenia returning to her own seat, Shripal's flush under the reprimand could fade without observation. Not only that, but the smell of all those spices triggered Ursula's hunger. Finally, all four women sat together and got practical.

Ursula's greatest fear, and one she could not dodge without blowing her cover, was that she would be tasked with Frankie. In the first thirty seconds of their discussion, her dread dissipated. Each person had a role: Denzil and Perneet stayed in place, Ursula was to inveigle her way into Berto's operations,

Xenia would tackle Frankie, and Shripal herself was to get as close as possible to Dolores.

"We share all our information, religiously," said Xenia, with a side-eye at Shripal. "When we know a large-scale drug delivery is scheduled, we all leap into action, including Uncle Superintendent."

It was all so naïve and underprepared, Ursula wanted to scream. Instead she played the wide-eyed ingénue. "How on earth are you going to do that? These people trust no one. I might have an outside chance with Berto because he's stupid and arrogant. Frankie is paranoid, violent and hates other women. At least that's what I've heard. And no one gets near Dolores. You told me that yourselves."

Shripal had recovered her composure. "We can't get close to Dolores because she lives on a yacht, patrolled by her security team. The only way of getting aboard is by invitation. Xenia knows some of the boat's suppliers and managed to befriend a stewardess."

Xenia preened but didn't say anything as she had a mouth full.

"The stewardess let slip that her boss is highly superstitious," said Shripal. "Horoscopes, the I Ching, Tarot cards, she consults them all. Xenia promised to source the best Tarot reader in Goa. That would be me. Yours truly is going to do a reading for Vovó."

Ursula's scalp contracted. How many years since she had heard that name? The tandoori fish in her mouth turned to ash and she only managed to swallow with the aid of a large slug of water.

"Vovó?"

"That what they call her. It means grandmother."

I know what it means. I heard it more times than I care to count. "You're going onto her yacht?" Ursula's voice had risen in pitch.

"Why not? The best way of getting close."

14

Last time she encountered Berto, the atmosphere was confrontational and she'd told him to keep out of her way. Now she needed to invite him for lunch. A *volte-face* was an embarrassment she had to accept in order to play the humble card. An invitation out of the blue would look suspicious. Ursula put herself in the shoes of a cocky, small-minded and petty gangster. He'd want something, a public admission of his superior status. She did her research, booked a table for two at Clube Nacional the following day and rode her moped over to Hotel Rosas Vermelhas. After a brief dust-down, change of clothes and reapplication of her lipstick, she sauntered into the bar. Her eye was still all shades of blue and violet, but the suit was Miu Miu and she had resurrected her Rolex.

She had every expectation of waiting another hour or two, but he rolled up before twelve in an ill-fitting suit. Obviously he'd gained weight since that was tailored for him by Jermyn Street's finest. He scanned the foyer and narrowed his eyes on recognising her. With an awkward scramble to her feet, she intercepted him as he stalked to the restaurant.

"Mr Fernandes?"

He stopped but did not turn to face her. "I thought I told you to keep out of my sight."

It was the other way around but she was not about to correct him. "You're absolutely correct, sir, and I'm sorry for the intrusion. It's just I've been dropped by my contact. You know Denzil, right? He wants nothing more to do with me after I caused a backlash. This means I have to start from scratch, sourcing accommodation, entertainment and ... extras for my clients. Everyone I speak to says to ask you. Look, we got off on the wrong foot because I made stupid assumptions. I've learned my lesson and I apologise. This is my first try at organising an event in Goa. Not my first for a bunch of millionaires, but here, I'm well out of my comfort zone. Say, could I invite you to lunch tomorrow at Clube Nacional? I need all the advice I can get."

"I'm a busy man. I have an appointment tomorrow."

Yeah, right, sitting on the verandah, smoking cigars and trying to look important. "Of course, you must get these requests constantly. I apologise for disturbing you. I'll look elsewhere." She bobbed her head and walked away.

"Hey! What do you mean by 'look elsewhere'?"

Ursula returned to stand in front of him, repelled by the reek of cigarette smoke. "Oh, don't worry, I won't seek out your competition. I could without any more black eyes." She gave a self-conscious laugh. "No, I think I might be better off relocating the event. Other possibilities on my list are Kerala and the Maldives."

"Clube Nacional, huh? Maybe I can move things around. I'll see you there at one." He pushed open the dining-room doors and went inside. Ursula clenched her hands together like a missionary, which looked like a gesture of gratitude but was mainly to stop herself from hurling her knife at his head.

She had secured an appointment. That was enough for

now. She returned to the ladies to change into her jeans and send a note to Shripal, only to find a message waiting.

Heading to the harbour in an hour. Vovó wants to see me this afternoon. But Xenia's drawn a blank with Frankie. Hope you're having more luck.

She inhaled sharply. A meeting with Vovó already? That was unusually quick. Trained to suspect everything and everyone, Ursula was always worried when things went according to plan. At least Frankie was behaving according to type.

Time to get away from the hotel and on with her plans. Firstly, rehearse how she was going to cosy up to Berto tomorrow. Second, coach Shripal on handling Vovó without letting on how much about the family she knew. Thirdly, come up with a strategy to assist Xenia. Before all of that, however, she owed Denzil a visit and an apology. She stopped outside an upscale jewellery store and, still sitting on her bike, brought the image of Denzil into her mind. Always beautifully dressed, charming, groomed and with an understanding of colour palette, the man had class. How to add to that? She rode towards the jewellery quarter and stopped outside one shop at random.

The second she parked the bike, the heat intensified, so she took off her helmet and got out of the sun's glare. Front and centre in the window was a display of Evil Eye adornments, supposed to ward off malevolence. She dismissed the pendants and rings as not his style, but focused on a leather and silver bangle with the blue eye at its centre. The price was over 100K, but that was Indian rupees. At the current exchange rate, it would cost her a tenth of that in sterling. He was worth a grand.

She attempted to haggle and got it 600 INR cheaper, plus gift wrapping, for a cash payment. Then she reversed the bike away from two determined cows intent on claiming her parking spot and rode to the hospital.

The staff refused her entry. She was not a relative and they were under instruction to admit no one but family. In one way, she was glad he had that level of security. She entrusted her gift and accompanying card to a nurse, crossing her fingers it would get to its intended recipient. Rumbles came from her stomach as she got back on the bike, her hair sweaty and throat dry. She could wait till she got back to her own kitchen or stop on the street somewhere. Close to the house, she remembered, there was a roadside shack selling *shawarma*. Cheap, filling and much easier than cooking for herself. She bought a vegetable-stuffed flatbread, a bottle of water and some slices of fresh mango, consuming them all while standing under the shade of an umbrella. Jeans were not practical in these temperatures. She promised herself a swim in the sea the minute she heard that Shripal was safely back on dry land.

Someone was staring, she could sense it. Two men standing three tables away were checking her out. Whether as a mark, a lone female or a familiar face, she couldn't be sure. She gave no indication of having seen them, wrapped up the remains of her *shawarma* and drained her water. As she threw the bottle into the recycling bin, one of the guys dropped his arm below the table, as if he was about to scratch his leg or whip out a knife from his boot. He did neither, simply curling his thumb over his index finger and splaying his hand to make the OK sign. He didn't look at her, just continued chatting to his friend.

Shripal's security team. With all the excitement of the past few days, Ursula had forgotten about her unofficial minders. She returned to the counter, bought two beers to stuff in her rucksack and rode home. The house appeared undisturbed, so she pulled on her swimming costume, covered up by a cotton wrap, ready for her swim. Three messages popped up when she unlocked her phone. The first was from Xenia.

F. told me to do one. Nasty little bitch. Not sure it's worth another go. What about B.? Another wanker? Xenia

The next was a photograph of Denzil, his face as crumpled and misshapen as discarded wrapping paper. His left hand clasped his right shoulder and on his wrist sat her bangle. The message contained no words but the warmth in his eyes sufficed.

The third was from Shripal, and Ursula did a double take.

We're in! Vovó wants me to use 'sozhi' or seashell cleromancy to divine auspicious dates for her family's future. My cowries cannot find truth, I said, without authenticity. My cowries?!? Xenia's going to source some before tomorrow.

Ursula laughed aloud, partly through relief and also through admiration. Shripal was a force to be reckoned with. She replied to each with an update, emoji or both. Much remained to be done, but now Ursula needed to swim. She locked the house, jogged down to the beach and after leaving her keys and wrap in a bundle on her flip-flops, ran into the sea.

From the beach, she swam out fifty metres and turned parallel to the shore, powering back and forth until her muscles screamed. Warm water with enough tidal pull and sandy salinity to act as an exfoliant scrubbed away all the stress and tension, leaving her with a clear head. The sun was low on the horizon when she finally padded up the beach track to the house. Cotton against her skin, sand between her toes, she watched nature's nightly spectacle and breathed.

The security detail would soon patrol the grounds, so Ursula slipped the two beers for them into a cool bag and left it on the porch. The cows, she hoped, would leave it alone. After a shower, she ate the remains of the veggie wrap and drank a tisane, while poring over a mind map of connections: Dolores, Francesca, Perneet, Berto, Denzil, Shripal, Xenia and herself. Shripal had been successful so far, but she was overly confident and under-informed. Xenia had missed her chance with Francesca and another attempt to get close would raise red flags. If Ursula could curry favour with Berto at lunch tomorrow – and she remained pretty confident she would – they had two sources of information. Was that enough to take to Cruz and the police?

Her inner professional gave a scornful laugh. *What do you think?* Much as she hated doing it, she returned to her police training. *Get as close as you can to the strategists.* Berto was low on the ladder and unlikely to have quality intelligence. She could pump him for the little he knew, but it wouldn't advance their cause. Dolores was still in charge, at least nominally, but the head honcho was clearly Francesca. Someone had to infiltrate the inner circle. Trying to become an ally or a friend would set off klaxons. Somehow, she had to lure them to her.

Familiar sounds came from outside; heavy bodies settling into the sand, huge lungs expelling breath and the flapping of large ears as they shook their heads free of flies. Their presence relaxed her and she sat cross-legged on her yoga mat and closed her eyes to open her mind.

She put herself in Francesca's shoes. No, *Frankie's* shoes. If that was the persona the woman had adopted, Ursula had to think the same way. Frankie was an old-school gangster just like her big brothers. In order to control her turf, she needed to attract money. Traditional tourism was chicken feed. That's why she controlled a network which offered the whole package – sex and drugs and rock 'n' roll – for those who could afford it.

But times were changing and the Vargas model was old school. Her thoughts floated to Kirkland and his 'bros'.

Why come all the way to India? We're here to seek a higher plane. The Inner Teacher. The Third Eye. Wisdom, in the truest sense, lies within. Before I commit myself to marriage, I want to discover who I really am and that means stepping into the unknown. This is way more than a bachelor party. This is The Reset. Spinning inwards and releasing all external perceptions of self. In a way, this is the ultimate ego trip – by letting go of the ego. We are snakes, shedding our skin, reborn with clear eyes and fresh perspectives.

Her eyes snapped open. 'Old school' was exactly the right description. In the 70s, hippies came to Goa to get stoned and find themselves. That was over forty years ago. Those free spirits with flowers in their hair were probably grandparents now. Today's youth searching for different ways to alter their brains had the same ambition: to glean a deeper meaning in life. As always, they knew best. Far more importantly, they could afford to pay for it.

The marketing line formed itself: Goa: The Reset – How to Change your Mind.

A grin spread over her face as she imagined her evangelical pitch to Berto, with an emphasis on simplicity. Source psilocybin and provide a safe space for trippers, throw in a chef, a couple of minders, maybe a medic, and hell, why not, a guru, then stand back and reap the rewards. No need for prostitutes, jet skis, cocaine or techno parties. This was taking candy from very rich babies.

Once she had dangled the shiny stuff in front of his eyes, all she needed to do was change her mind. *Sorry, I'm not sure Goa has everything I need. Kerala looks much more promising.* Berto would tie himself in knots trying to convince her to stay, even to the point of enlisting Frankie.

Her grin vanished. The chances of Frankie seeing through her disguise were way too high. Yes, the surgery, yes, the tinted contacts, and yes, the physique, but all it took to give herself away was a mannerism or a distinctive gesture she didn't even know she used. She had to become someone else. One of the best ways to engender trust was to mirror the target.

Oh, shit. She had to become Frankie.

She was applying moisturiser when sounds of a scuffle on the porch brought her back to the moment. The cows? The security guys fighting over the beer?

"Ursula! Get these guys off of me!"

She couldn't place the voice but it was male with an American accent. She dropped her face cream and ran to the spyhole. The same security team she'd seen at the bar flanked a terrified-looking man she'd seen before.

She opened the door. "Noah? What the hell are you doing here? I put you on a plane to California!"

An aggressive exhale drew her attention. The cows were on their feet and evidently pissed off at the intrusion. The security guys appeared worried about both the intruder and the animals.

"OK, look, I know this person. You can let him go. Please don't go anywhere because I might need your help. That bag on the table contains two beers for you. If you sit down and drink them quietly, the cows will go back to sleep. Thank you for doing a great job."

The shorter of the two spoke. "You're welcome, madam. We will be waiting here for a while. Thank you for the beers."

She stood aside to let Noah in, only then noting the suitcase. He was a wreck, red-eyed, crumpled, sweaty and none too fragrant. He stumbled inside as if about to collapse.

"I say again, Noah, what the hell are you doing here?"

He looked at her through bloodshot eyes. "I came back for you, Little Bear. The drugs messed me up, sure, but one good thing came out of it. I realised something profound. Since I flew out of here, I couldn't stop thinking about ... oh, um, sorry, can I use your bathroom?"

He rushed away and closed the door. She took her chai onto the rear deck to give him some privacy and gazed up at the stars. *This? Now? Why?*

15

I t took a while. So long, in fact, that Ursula knocked on
the door.

"Noah, you OK in there?"

"Uh, um, can you give me a minute?"

"Sure. But the security guys are still waiting and I need my
sleep. Why don't I call you a taxi and we'll talk tomorrow?
Where are you staying?"

Silence.

"You thought you could sleep here? You're kidding me!
Clean yourself up and get out. Unbelievable arrogance," she
muttered, and picked up the phone. She soon found him an
apartment available in the Da Gama complex, where she had
first stayed. Pricey, sure, but he could afford it. "Two nights to a
week, I think. The client has just arrived and is unsure of his
plans. He'll be with you in under an hour and the name is
Noah Lloyd. Thank you so much." She immediately dialled a
cab and sat with her arms folded until the bathroom door
opened.

Noah looked as bad as if not worse than Denzil. "Hey, I

am more sorry than I can say about tonight. Guess I ate something bad. Not how I wanted this evening to go, believe me."

"Not how I wanted my evening to go either. Take your bag and go to your hotel. I have a busy week but I'll check in with you tomorrow, if I get time." A horn honked outside. "Right on time. Goodbye, Noah, hope you feel better in the morning."

"Ursula, I have something really important to tell you. Can I invite you for dinner in the next couple days?"

"I doubt it. As I said, I'm busy and really do not appreciate unscheduled interruptions. Your taxi is waiting. Bye-bye and get well soon." She opened the door and ushered him out.

As promised, the bodyguards were standing to attention. Noah took his case to the cab and turned as if to say a final goodbye. He was intercepted by a bovine grunt. He got into the car and left with a pathetic wave.

Ursula didn't wave back, instead turning to her minders. "Thank you so much for waiting. You're really good at your job and I intend to say so to your boss. Goodnight."

"Goodnight, madam, and thank you once again for the beers."

She shut the door with a smile, locked all the doors and windows, switched off the lights and flopped into bed. She released a sigh deep enough to compete with the cattle and closed her eyes. Why was life always so complicated?

Waves tumbled over her head, spinning her like a seashell, until she wasn't sure which way was up. Something caught her around the chest, dragging her with powerful force to the surface. Her head burst out of the water and she took huge, gasping breaths. Trembling legs found firm ground and she staggered onto dry land. Sal. Salvador, her beloved husband whose name meant saviour. Except when she looked back at her rescuer, it was a leaner, darker man with a burn scar on the right side of his torso.

She opened her eyes and concentrated on steady breathing to expel the night frights. Drowning, out of her depth, losing orientation: so far, so clichéd. But it was Gil Maduro who drew her to safety, put her right and waited in the wings. Her mission was clearer than ever. Burn the Vargas organisation to the ground and return to the man she loved. Presuming she could find him. She got out of bed, and made a pot of tea and some concrete plans. Golden rays of dawn began to brighten the sky as she set the alarm, switched her phone to silent, kicked the cushions off the sofa and curled up under a throw. Nightmares rarely happened in daylight.

Almost immediately she sank into sleep until a loud knocking came at the door. Her eyes flew open with a gasp. How was it possible she'd heard no vehicles approach in the last five minutes? A glance at the clock showed she'd been out of it for at least an hour.

"Ursula? Are you there?" Xenia's voice was cheerful. "I tried calling but you didn't pick up. I've got tea for you."

Ursula opened the door. "Hi, Xenia. It's nice of you to come over, but I was just catching some rest and I've got plenty of tea and coffee, thanks."

"Ooh, you look knackered. Bad night? Better freshen up before you meet Berto. No, not tea as in a cuppa. I mean gossip. Look, you sit down and I'll make us some strong coffee. Here, I brought us some *pasteis de nata* from the deli. They're enough to put a smile on anyone's face." She shoved a box in Ursula's direction and went into the kitchen. "Where's the coffee machine? Oh, a Moka pot. You're so European. Right, so, here's what I learned this morning."

"Wait, Xenia, let me have some caffeine before you begin your update. What happened with Francesca yesterday?"

Xenia scowled. "She's a piece of work, isn't she? I went to

the same salon to get my nails done. Slipped the staff some dosh to get us seated together. I made every attempt at conversation and finally got her going on the subject of ecotourism. She's not a fan, I can tell you that much. When we were done, I suggested we go for a coffee to discuss how businesses can greenwash activities like jet-skiing and so on. She gave me a snooty look and said she had plenty of ideas of her own. Horrible cow. I can only say that to you, obvs."

"Say what to me?" Ursula's brain was running on three simultaneous tracks.

"Calling her a cow as an insult. Everyone else here thinks cows are beyond reproach. Do you want milk?"

"Yes, no, yes, please." She bit into a custard tart and concentrated on her concerns. But Xenia was not to be stopped.

"Anyway, I took some cowrie shells round to Shripal to do her fortune-telling shit. At least she got one foot in the door, even if I fell flat on my face. She's going to the yacht again this afternoon. The old bat wants her out of there before four, because that's when the family arrive and they would not approve." Xenia gave her a significant look. "Whatever you say to Berto will be repeated fewer than two hours later."

The pot began to boil and the smell of freshly brewed coffee lifted Ursula's spirits. "That's good to know. I'll make sure to use that information."

Xenia warmed some milk and poured two cups. "Yeah, I thought you'd wanna know. What do you think about switching places? You tackle Frankie and I'll flirt with Berto?"

Ursula didn't answer, blowing on the surface of her coffee.

"Pass that box over, I'm starving. I missed breakfast because I had to collect those ridiculous shells from Perneet's place. Do you want another one of these?"

"Sure. Natas are my favourites. Let's play it by ear with Berto and Frankie. My plan is to reel them in by walking away.

I want them to chase us, not the other way around. Plus we shouldn't underestimate her. She's seen your face and if you two cross paths again, she'll smell a rat."

Mouth full of Portuguese pastry, Xenia could only waggle her head from side to side. She seemed upset at being side-lined, but the risks were too high to keep her involved for the sake of her ego.

They ate and drank in pensive silence for a few moments. Concern for Shripal preoccupied Ursula. Several elements of Xenia's account were troubling – tipping the nail bar staff to seat her next to Frankie, a clumsy attempt at becoming an ally and a lack of openness in presenting herself. Every persona required a grain of truth. Xenia should have used her father's trusted connection, offering to represent him in his stead. Frankie would only have needed to ask a couple of questions to find out the real identity of her attempted New Best Friend. If she had, Xenia was a marked woman. Worse, wary of infiltration, Frankie would suspect any newcomer close to the family, leaving Shripal vulnerable.

"Tell me about the seashell divination thing."

"Dunno much about it. They throw shells in patterns and read meaning into it. As far as I know, Shripal has never done it in her life. But she'll put on a damn good show. Hey, guess what else I heard? Those stag party guys you and Dad were hosting? One of them is back. I know the manager at the Da Gama Apartments. A guy called Lloyd checked in last night. The receptionist asked if his visit was work or pleasure and he said, get this, he's here on 'unfinished business'. You think he's got a beef with you and Dad?"

Taking her own advice, Ursula was partially honest. "No, I don't. Noah Lloyd is on a different kind of mission. He turned up here late last night in a bit of a state, jet-lagged and not particularly coherent. I refused to engage and sent him away. If you want my opinion, his drugged-up mind accentuated certain factors of his Goan experience. The guy's deluded. He perceives my babysitting him through a bad trip as symbolic and thinks we're soul mates. Let me assure you, we're not."

Xenia's eyes widened. "A single millionaire came all the way back from San Francisco just for you? Poor bugger." She licked some pastry flakes from her fingers. "Don't dismiss him too fast. You never know, he might end up being useful. I gotta go. Dad's coming out of hospital today. You want to come over for dinner later? Shripal will be there so we can talk tactics."

"I'd love that, if Denzil doesn't mind."

"Mind? It was his idea. Come over around seven-ish because we're having champagne. Do you want this last nata? Mind if I take it?" She scooped up the cake and tapped her watch. "Good luck with Berto. Where are you meeting?"

"Clube Nacional. I booked a table for one o'clock."

Xenia put down the pastry. "Clube Nacional? How the hell did you manage that? What are you going to wear? This is a seriously upmarket place and you still look like something out of Fight Club. Have you got any designer gear, jewellery or handbags? Don't even think about riding there on your moped – you can use my car and driver. Get in the shower, quick, and I'll do your make-up. In fact, let me organise everything. Lunching is my superpower."

Ursula stepped into the bathroom, already getting into character.

Money. Everyone at Clube Nacional had it and flaunted it. Clients arrived in chauffeur-driven luxury cars, sporting flaw-less blow dries, wearing eye-wateringly expensive clothes with statement accessories. And that was just the men. Women, whether wearing Western or traditional dress, fluttered, glit-tered and drew attention like exotic butterflies. Ursula marvelled at the way they used their hands like dancers.

Thanks to Xenia, Ursula fitted right in. Her make-up, heavier than she might normally use, covered all the bruises (even if Xenia's enthusiastic blending technique had probably added a few more). She chose a modest yet striking Alexander McQueen rose-printed dress with a collar. For accessories, she used her statement watch, an eye-catching Esse necklace, matching diamond earrings and a stack of Dior bracelets. Her handbag was Stella McCartney and her nails were as false as her smile.

She kept her gaze above all the other clients as the waiter led her to the table in a discreet booth on the mezzanine. Berto was waiting. As she approached, he lifted his phone and took her picture. The old-fashioned shutter sound removed any doubt.

"Good afternoon, Mr Vargas, and thank you for meeting me." She gave a bow rather than offer her hand. Who knew how secure that nail glue was?

He didn't stand up, merely looking her over as if he was interviewing her for the role of lunch companion. "Siddown, Miss Brown." He smirked at his facile rhyme. "I got here a little early to try what's new on the cocktail menu. They change things up every coupla weeks. I chose The Godfather."

From Tuco to Fredo. The involuntary laugh which escaped her went unnoticed as the waiter pulled out her chair and flapped open a napkin to place on her lap.

"What can I get you to drink, madam?"

"Oh, I think I'll follow Mr Vargas and have a Banana Daiquiri."

Both men gave her a look of puzzlement, but at least the waiter was a pro. "Coming right up. Catch of the Day is king-fish and our specials are kedgeree and Vindalho da Galinha." He backed away and left her to face her dining companion with a sinking heart.

"As I said, Mr Vargas, I'm grateful you could spare me an

hour. Since I arrived in Goa, nothing has gone to plan and I find myself with very little time to establish the infrastructure of my operation before next year. Denzil said he could pull all the strings I needed, but it appears that was not the whole truth."

"That guy's a loser. Over the hill and on his way out. He's worked for us, what, two years now, and I have to watch his every move. He's looking for a way to funnel clients into his own organisation. Exactly why he pounced on you. You'd make a good recruiter." His eyes searched her face.

God, he was repulsive. No particular feature stood out but everything about his sneering lips, supercilious expression, arrogant posture and powerful wafts of smoke masked with aftershave repulsed her. She would order a vindalho. Hopefully the pungent smell and ferocious heat would overpower this nauseating stench.

The waiter set her cocktail on her little leather coaster. "Are you ready to order?"

Berto answered before she could speak, waggling his empty glass. "First, I want another one of these. Then we'll have the starter plate of pakoras, bhajis and samosas to start. After that, we'll have one Catch of the Day and a kedgeree, with bread. Also, a bottle of Bordeaux, a 2009 if you have one."

"And for *my* main course, I'd like the chicken vindalho, please. Could we also have some still water with ice?" Ursula's tone was calm and pleasant as she handed the menu to the waiter.

"One sharing starter and three main courses?" The waiter's head flipped between them.

"Yes," Berto snapped. "She's paying."

The waiter gave a gracious smile and as he gathered their menus, caught Ursula's eye and pinched his lips together in sympathy. She didn't react but took comfort from the fact that not only she saw Berto as a boor.

"To be completely truthful," she lied, "I was very naive when I chose Goa as a potential base. Maybe the old hippie vibes of the 70s swayed me until I saw what kind of operation people like you and Denzil are running. I don't want a cut of your cake, Mr Vargas, not even the crumbs. My start-up is a very different beast. I mean no disrespect, but what you do is rather traditional, cumbersome and top-heavy. What I seek, and I choose that word precisely, is something more forward looking, leaner, better targeted and a whole lot more profitable. Put it this way, 'the experience of a lifetime' these days means something more than beach volleyball, getting stoned and feeling up the local girls." She took the opportunity of the waiter's arrival with Berto's second cocktail to take a sip of her daiquiri.

"You invite me to lunch only to insult me?" said Berto, immediately taking a slug from the new drink. "Why should I sit here and listen to this? You're wasting my time." He showed no signs of moving.

"In a way, I suppose I am. You see, I'm taking my business elsewhere. After I spoke to you yesterday, I found a connection in the Maldives who can source everything I need. That's why I'm relocating south. On the other hand, since we're here, we could forget the idea of a collaboration, have a nice lunch and part on friendly terms. Who knows, maybe you might find my blueprint useful? I don't have any kind of copyright and I'm very happy to share my concept with an entrepreneurial mind. By the way, you can call me Ursula."

It was clear from the warring emotions on his face that Berto was used to directing the conversation. He had no idea how to listen. "What concept?"

Ursula did a subtle-not-subtle glance over each shoulder for eavesdroppers. "What if I told you the average event I run draws down a 400% profit? You think I'm kidding? This is exactly why I honed my business plan. All I need is the right venue, suppliers and staff. Clients? No problem. These guys are hammering on my door, demanding I provide them with something special."

Berto's focus sharpened. "Keep talking, Ursula, and yes, we can drop the formalities. My name is Berto."

She gave him a conspiratorial smile and raised her glass. "Good to meet you, Berto." She took care to pronounce it Burr-toe, with a mid-Atlantic drawl, rather than Bear-to like a Portuguese speaker. "You were right about these cocktails. They're pretty good."

"The bartender here is the best. OK, I'm listening."

"People like us, service providers, need to keep up with changing tastes. For decades, people flocked here for enlightenment, freedom, beautiful beaches, plus the usual sex and drugs and rock 'n' roll. Times are changing. Let me ask you something. How much is your average client worth? Don't answer that, but keep a ballpark figure in mind. Got it? OK. The guy who hired me to arrange his bachelor party is worth 700 million dollars. No need to take my word for it. His name is Harrington Locke III and one look at his online profile will tell you all you need to know. His friend, who is pestering me to be next in line, is a billionaire."

She let that sink in.

"We're talking people with money to burn, but not on hookers and hashish. A whole new generation who don't want to get blind drunk or snort coke because they care about their bodies, who dismiss shooting safaris and big-game fishing because they respect the environment, and regard racing cars or private yachts as classic use-it-up-wear-it-out Boomerism. Experiences, in their view, should be internal, not external."

He looked suspicious. "They sound boring as hell."

"I won't debate their ethics with you but I can divulge what they really want."

The starters came on a silver platter and Berto made a pretentious show of tasting the wine.

Only when the waiter departed did she continue.

"Here I'm going to level with you, Berto. The stag party Denzil persuaded me into was a mercy mission due to a weather event spoiling their plans. He had no intention of stealing your business but saw an opportunity. Eight men with an agenda was a great way to do a trial run. Denzil's a smart networker and we agreed to work together. It wasn't perfect, but that was the point. This is how one learns to hone one's craft. I only want one of these or I won't finish my vindalho. What do you recommend?"

"A pakora. The bhajis are good but too spicy. Try a pakora with the mango chutney. You still haven't told me your big concept."

She picked up the little golden bundle, dipped it in the sauce and popped it into her mouth. Hot, sweet flavours exploded on her tongue. So very moreish. No wonder Berto had eaten most of the plate. "You were right. Light and delicious but packed with taste. To the concept. It's the opposite of big. We're talking small, manageable, people-pleasing and incredibly profitable. The most important element of all is the base principle. Goa: The Reset – How to Change your Mind."

She spoke with quiet intensity throughout the meal, convincing him of the minimum outlay, maximum profit and ease of delivery. The one element she purposely omitted was the client base.

His attention was so intense that she speeded up, hoping to make him panic. "That's it in a nutshell. Top quality psilocybin, a handful of professionals in case of problems, maybe an expert in guided meditation and a five-star residence where your high-paying guests can wander around safely under the influence." Inspiration struck. "You know what? I can introduce you to one of the previous party. He's back again already, eager for more. I just can't handle another event when I'm about to ship out. He'll explain far more articulately what these extraordinarily wealthy people are willing to pay for. More wine?"

Berto had eaten most of his fish and over half the kedgeree, washed down with almost the entire bottle of Bordeaux. He looked sweaty and uncomfortable.

"No, you finish that. I have to leave for another meeting. Bring your contact to Hotel Rosa Vermelhas for a drink tomorrow evening at six. I want you to meet my cousin. We handle strategic changes in our lines of business together. Lunch was good, thanks. Bye." His normal saunter replaced by an urgent scurry, he crossed the restaurant in the direction of the bathrooms.

Schadenfreude at his discomfort was dampened by the prospect of drinks with Francesca, Berto and Noah making chit-chat over a Gin Fizz. She poured the last of the wine into her glass, avoiding the sediment, drank it in one and beckoned the waiter for the bill.

She had a whole lot of work to do.

16

Xenia's driver dropped her at home. She changed into jeans and a T-shirt, grabbed her helmet and flicked open her knife before unlocking the garage door. It was devoid of human presence, housing nothing more than her exercise equipment and her moped. She rode down the driveway and along the main drag into town, heading for the Da Gama Apartments.

As she passed Vamsi's office, she glanced inside, ready to offer a wave. What she saw was Noah Lloyd standing on the threshold, shaking Vamsi's hand. She veered into the path of a bus and only just managed to keep herself from falling under the wheels. Holding her hands up in apology, she restarted the bike and made a speedy U-turn amid a cacophony of angry horns. She caught up with Noah as he was browsing a street stall selling hats.

"What the hell do you think you're doing?"

The way he swivelled to face her was telling. This man had no fear, dreaded no enemies and turned with a pleasant smile. When he recognised her, he broke into a broad beam.

"Little Bear! Sorry, I mean Ursula. I called at your place

earlier. Guess you were still at lunch. But hey, you tracked me down. Wanna get a cold drink?"

She heaved off her helmet and parked the bike on what passed for a pavement. "What were you doing at Vamsi's office?"

He looked blank. "Sorry?"

"The real estate agent? I saw you two shaking hands just a minute ago."

"Oh right, yeah. I asked him to let me know if a place just like yours comes on the market. The apartments are a great base, but I'm looking for something a little more permanent, you know? Sorry to sound ungrateful."

Ursula shook her head in exasperation and stalked off towards a café with colourful tiles and palm umbrellas. She ordered two beers and sat in the shade. As she expected, Noah followed, but only after he'd bought himself a hat.

"What do you think? I figured straw, you know, unstructured, light and airy but protective enough to keep the sun off. Oh, would you listen to me? I'm babbling. Nerves, I guess. Let me say right off the bat, I apologise for last night. Turning up at your place with an upset stomach was not part of the plan. I'm really sorry. Are you still mad at me?"

"Well, if I said I'm pleased to see you, I'd be lying. Why did you come back?"

The waiter brought over two bottles of King's.

"Oh, no alcohol for me, sorry. Do you have kefir?"

"No. Sprite, Fanta or Ice Tea."

"An iced tea sounds great. Sorry, Little ... Ursula, it's just I gotta keep a clear head. I have a couple things I want to get off my chest."

"Noah, please shut up. You do realise that every time you open your mouth you say 'sorry' but display no signs of contrition? Yes, I deserve an enormous apology for your repeated transgressive behaviour. The problem is, I see no signs of it stopping. I am going to ask you for the third time, what the hell are you doing here?"

He clasped his hands together and rested his forehead on his knuckles. Ursula poured the first of the beers into her glass. She had a feeling she might need the second. The waiter set a can of Ice Tea next to Noah's elbow, along with the bill. Ursula beckoned for him to give it to her and counted out the necessary rupees. The waiter checked the amount, thanked her for the tip and jerked his head at her companion, a question in his eyes. She could do nothing other than shrug.

Half a glass of beer later, Ursula was planning what to wear for drinks with the Vargases tomorrow night when Noah lifted his head.

His sad eyes and earnest expression were exaggerated to Disney levels. "I don't have the words to express my journey inwards. Even if I had, the narrative would sound phoney. All I can say is this: now I understand."

Growing impatience threatened to shatter Ursula's calm. "Let's get one thing straight, Noah Lloyd. I don't give a shit about your journey inwards. Nor do I intend to tease out your 'narrative' with perceptive open questions, because I am not your bloody therapist. Keep your revelations to yourself. Hang out in Goa or piss off back to America, it's up to you. Just leave me in peace to get on with my life. The last thing I need right now is another pain in the arse."

To her astonishment, Noah laughed, clapping his hands together like a seal. "This! Exactly this. Never afraid to tell it like it is. Shoot from the hip and screw the consequences. From the first moment we met I knew you were the real deal. Then you stepped up to guide me through the nightmares, always capable, kind, strong, gentle and present, no matter what. Since I left Goa, I couldn't stop thinking about you, morning, noon and night. My journey inwards delivered twice. I found myself, but I also found my soul mate. For the first time in my life, my heart and soul have overruled my head. Deep in the core of my being, I understood something profound. That revelation terrified me at first, but when I learned acceptance, it all made sense. I love you, Ursula, and I always will. The reason I came back was to convince you of the truth. We are meant to be together. You are the most authentic person I've ever met."

She didn't know whether to laugh or cry.

All's fair in love and war, said her cynical side. *Don't slam the door in his face. By the same token don't give him the key either. He could be useful.*

Her decent half disagreed. *It is immoral to string someone along simply because he's an asset. Tell him you cannot return his affections. Be your better self.*

She played for time. In a stumbling speech, she explained she wasn't looking to get involved romantically, that business took priority and she was accustomed to operating alone. That said, perhaps if they spent some time together, getting to know each other from scratch, there might be some common ground.

Her cynical side rolled her eyes. Her decent half gave a disappointed shake of her head. She was letting both her selves down, neither hard-nosed grifter nor moral beacon.

"That would mean a lot to me, thank you." Noah reached for her hand, and she withdrew it with a jerk and knocked over her beer. Napkins and apologies flapped around the table, until Ursula stood up, her jeans wet down one leg.

"It's fine, Noah, it was my fault. Let's ease off the throttle and take it one step at a time, OK? Lunch tomorrow?"

"Or dinner tonight?"

She raised her eyebrows. "Didn't I just say one step at a time? Anyway, I already have plans this evening. I'll pick you up at half past eleven in the morning for a general tour and some quality food. Enjoy the rest of your day." She put on her sunglasses and scooped up her handbag.

He gave her the abandoned puppy look all the way back to her bike. She ignored him but sensed another stare. A car with tinted windows was parked outside the mobile phone store on the opposite side of the street. That had certainly not been there when Ursula arrived. The driver's window was open and he seemed to be pressing buttons on his phone, with no curiosity about her. Maybe he had no interest but his passengers might.

She ignored the vehicle, got onto the bike and buzzed away into the traffic, glad of the sunglasses. As expected, the car pulled out behind her, purring along in her wake. Who on earth was following her now? Berto, recovered from the squitters and playing status games? Maybe. Or Frankie's people, watching where she went and who she met? Highly likely. The tail could even be something Shripal had organised, in addition to the security patrol. Her gut told her not to stop and find out. Instead, she ducked down an alleyway between two blocks, secure in the knowledge the sedan could not follow. It wasn't the smoothest run as she had to dodge children, chickens, effluent and a pair of playful goats. The end of the alley grew closer, sunlight indicating a gate to freedom. Just as she swerved to avoid a stray dog, the light changed. A large black sedan blocked the exit. She reversed, beeping her horn, and made a U-turn. Halfway back up the route she had come, she spotted a smaller passageway between two buildings, clearly not meant for anything bigger than a bicycle. She swung the Honda right and wove a cautious path between litter, wandering cats and discarded shellfish. Once out of the lane, she inhaled fresh air and twisted the accelerator to cross the road into another back street. Whoever was following her couldn't bring a wide sedan down these rat runs. At the same time, nothing stopped them getting out of the car and pursuing her on foot. They must know these tangled paths far better than her.

She jerked into another rutted route, criss-crossed by channels of waste, and paused to consider her next move. The black sedan crawled past the end of the alley, close enough now for her to see shapes behind the tinted windows. If she could see them, they could see her. She snapped her head from left to right in search of escape. Two mechanics' yards, a smallholding crowded with chickens, a tannery and wholesale florist. Only one of those had a bearable stench, but at least two were plausible for a motorcyclist. *If in doubt, do the unexpected.*

She parked the bike amongst the wrecks in one junkyard, walked through the shop where no one looked up from their phones, turned right on the street and entered the flower store. The florist initially refused to sell to a private customer but caved after blatant bribery and Ursula walked out with a beautiful display bouquet for Denzil. After a few moments of casual chit-chat until the black sedan turned the corner for another circuit, Ursula thanked the woman and ran outside to grab a taxi. Home was not an option. She needed a safe space.

"Where to, lady?"

"The Blue Moon, please."

"But who would want to tail you?" asked Perneet. "I don't understand."

They were taking tea in the summer house and Ursula's pulse had finally returned to normal. Few places felt as safe as Perneet's garden.

"It's the kind of thing Shripal would do, out of protectiveness."

Perneet wobbled her head, clearly unconvinced. "Shripal hires professionals, not thugs. Whoever was following you wanted to be seen and wanted to scare you. This worries me. If

Berto is the one who ordered that car, and it would be typical of his heavy-handedness, I'm concerned about your meeting tomorrow. We know where and when the rendezvous is scheduled so nothing prevents us from planting a few of our own as observers. Just to keep you safe. You cannot walk into the lion's den, innocent as a lamb."

For once, Ursula overlooked the animal comparisons, more concerned about her motorbike currently stashed in a junkyard. "Yeah, good point. Let's discuss that with Denzil tonight." She realised her assumption a moment too late. "You are coming to dinner, no?"

"No. My presence is required here this evening as we are hosting a party of VIPs. The appointment with the Fernandes family is at seven, yes?" She checked her watch. "To retrieve your motorcycle, drive home, freshen up and change will be tight in terms of time and very likely dangerous. I will send one of my bouncers and a driver to collect your vehicle and take it to your place. They can also look around for any strangers near your house. It's between hours for my business so they'll be glad of something to do. The post-work rush will be gone by six and the party crowd rarely arrive before nine. Meanwhile you can use the upstairs changing room. Pick an outfit, have a shower and I'll arrange a driver for you. I have to say, your make-up is very impressive."

"That was Xenia's doing. I'm amazed it's lasted this long."

"I wondered." Perneet gave her a knowing smile. "Persuade one of my girls to help you reapply. They love to experiment. One or two might even loan you some jewellery."

Ursula bowed her head. "You are so generous. I am more grateful than I can say."

"Be careful, my dear. I'm going to make some arrangements. Top floor and the dressing room is on the right. Take your time. This pot is half full."

. . .

When Ursula stood in front of the mirror, she let out an incredulous gasp. Dressed in a deep red sari decorated with golden leaves, her hair pinned up and her eyes rimmed with kohl, she barely recognised herself. Perneet assessed the transformation. She dabbed the tip of her little finger into a pot and pressed it between Ursula's brows. "That is a bindi, signifying your marital status. Who knows, it might offer a little extra protection. Good luck and don't forget those flowers."

A side door led into a little garage which was in constant use. Perneet's employees left and returned at regular intervals, each in an upmarket vehicle with driver. She waited in an anteroom, clutching the flowers, until a familiar face looked in with a smile.

"Manoj! You're my driver?"

"Indeed, madam. I am to take you to the Fernandes residence and home again. Would you like me to carry those?"

"Thank you. I'm so glad to see a friendly face."

Manoj opened the rear door of a Jaguar. "I am likewise pleased to see you safe and well, madam. I understand there was some unpleasantness today."

"Yeah, but I wriggled my way out of it. That book you recommended is the best thing I've read this year. Thank you so much."

"I had a feeling you might appreciate it. Ghosh is not the only writer to offer insights into the subcontinent, although he does shine a light on regions other than Mumbai. May I say how well you suit a sari? Not everyone can wear such a garment with confidence."

"I was worried, to be honest. The whole cultural appropriation thing can get you in hot water. But Perneet herself gave me this bindi."

Manoj concentrated on the traffic, navigating his way

through the early evening chaos of cows, buses, motorcycles and tourists. "Wearing a sari, kurta, bindi or dhoti is a matter of choice unless proscribed by one's religion. Our clothing also has a practical function. To see a foreigner adopt our style is a compliment. Ms Brown, please don't be alarmed, because I am going to take an unnecessarily complex route to our destination."

He wasn't lying. They drove up to three different hotels, went in and out of a supermarket car park and stopped outside a chic-looking bar for five full minutes. Manoj said nothing and Ursula followed his lead. At quarter past seven, he pulled into a broad driveway, saluted the watchman and drove into the property. The Fernandes villa was expansive and beautiful, with low-level lights showing it at its finest. Well connected was an understatement. Manoj jumped out to open her door and hand over her flowers. A maid waited under the portico, so Ursula scooped up her sari to ascend the steps. Under the pretence of waving goodbye to Manoj, she sent out a radar, searching for threats.

"Madam? The family are waiting for you."

Ursula gave a polite bow and followed the girl inside. A large room towards the rear was divided into two sections: a long dining table with elegant settings and a U-shaped sofa around a tiled surface the size of a ping pong table.

Shripal, Xenia and Denzil stood up to welcome her, effusive with compliments at her attire and floral tribute.

"These are extraordinary, thank you so much," said Denzil, squeezing her hand. He looked very poorly, bruised, tired and stiff, but his eyes shone as brightly as ever.

"How are you? I am so sorry about everything."

"No need to apologise. You are part of our family now and fighting alongside my girls. We have much to discuss. What would you like to drink?"

Ursula dithered, uncertain of protocol.

"Give her a glass of fizz. We're celebrating," said Xenia. "Right, tell us what went on this afternoon? Perneet says you got hassled by some tossers in a blacked-out car."

The story didn't take long to relate and Ursula suspected the two women already knew the basics from Perneet.

Shripal tapped her fingernails together. "Makes no sense. Who wants to scare you, when you have a meeting with Berto and Frankie tomorrow? What do you make of this, uncle?"

The three women gazed at him as he thought. This evening, he was wearing tones of purple and violet, as if to match his bruises. "I don't intend to be in any way patronising, Ursula, and I hope you understand why I say this. The people following you could have snatched you off the street in a second. My belief is that it was a test. They want to know if you are as clean as you appear. To evade capture and disguise yourself so well that they lose you suggests a professional. In other words, they think you're a cop. You demonstrated skills, strategies and training which reinforce their beliefs. We'll have to work much harder to convince them you're nothing more than a fixer."

"How?"

"Right now, they think you're dangerous and have you in their crosshairs. Make a mistake. Lower the bar. Delude these people into thinking you are no threat. Then, when they look away, you shoot them in the back."

Ursula swallowed.

Xenia pushed herself to her feet. "What he's trying to say is you have to fuck it up. Not on an epic scale, because that brings us all down. But you've got to fall flat on your face in order to save it. Right, I'm hungry. Mumtaz, please serve the food and then you can leave for the evening."

Shripal indicated Ursula should sit between herself and Xenia.

Denzil sat opposite and Ursula saw there was an empty place on that side of the table.

Denzil caught her expression. "Shripal's brother-in-law Cruz will join us in a little while. He's currently having a family dinner in a restaurant downtown. We wanted you to be here beforehand in order to come to an agreement. How much are we prepared to share with the Superintendent of Police?"

"I see." Her pulse sped up again, in near dread of meeting Cruz Biswas. True, she looked very different, especially tonight, but a senior police figure had access to information denied to the general public. He would check out her story and investigate Ursula's dead sister Olivia Jones. When he did, he would learn that she was very much alive and on the run from the London Met. He would also discover that fugitive Olivia did have a sister. Her name was not Ursula and she was not out to wreak vengeance on a criminal gang in Goa. She was most likely in Dewsbury, tackling nothing more dangerous than a parrot with psittacosis.

"I think we stick to the facts," said Xenia. "No need to mention our grand plan to replace the entire network with our own people. I don't think we should even mention that Dad was beaten up."

"Shall I tell him I walked into a door?" asked Denzil, with raised eyebrows.

Ursula jumped in. "No. We stick as close to the truth as we can without incriminating ourselves. It's true that you had an accident falling off my moped, due to my bad driving. It's true that I feel terrible about it and brought you flowers by way of an apology. It's actually true that I am a fixer, although an international concierge is an exaggeration, and I prepare special events for clients. That's why I am meeting with two members of the Vargas family tomorrow, to ensure smooth cooperation. What we want to do is gather intelligence on the family's illegal activities and deliver a tip-off to the police.

What we expect in return is for law enforcement to act on it and arrest the ringleaders."

"Exactly!" said Xenia, grabbing the bottle from the ice bucket to top up their glasses. "Keep it simple and we all sing the same tune."

"He'll want to know why. At the risk of sounding Bollywood, what's our motivation?" Shripal asked. "Uncle?"

He placed a hand over his glass, refusing more champagne. "No, thank you, I will have a sparkling water, if I may. Xenia and Ursula are right to say that simplicity is best. Our motivation, as Shripal puts it, is independence. We resent being under the yoke of these interlopers, unable to operate our own activities unless we give them a cut. They are putting locals out of business and flooding the place with serious narcotics. Before they muscled their way in, we had a fairer, more egalitarian way to give visitors a memorable experience, while sharing the profits among a wide group of providers. Now, money funnels in one direction and everyone is squeezed. That is why we want rid of them and look to the authorities to make that happen."

"Good speech, Dad. Let's eat. Just help yourselves. Ursula, how do you feel about telling Cruz your real reason for wanting to take these guys down?" She lifted the cloche off a silver platter.

Despite Ursula's pressing need to hide her story, the sight of the golden pile of fried food stopped her in her tracks. "Don't tell me that's fish and chips?" she asked, inhaling the smell of battered cod, vinegar and mushy peas.

"Yeah. I missed it. The family indulge me on special occasions. Tuck in, everyone!"

"Thank you. I love fish and chips! As for my history with the Vargas family, I'd rather we kept that to ourselves. If my reasons for pursuing them became clear, I could be a scapegoat for anything that might happen. I say once again, stick close to the truth. Just enough information so we can work together on this one operation." She took a portion of fish and a scoop of chips, and breathed in the scent of home.

They ate with enthusiasm but Denzil was the first to admit defeat. "I'm not saying I dislike this kind of food. It's satisfying in the first instance but as with so many European dishes, it lacks depth, not to mention colour. Ursula, do you have a strategy for tomorrow's meeting? Perneet suggests planting a few people in the hotel restaurant in case things get ugly. I agree to that as an insurance policy. Forgive my impertinent enquiry, but how do you plan to persuade Francesca Vargas to take you on trust? In three years, I have never got close."

"I have a secret weapon. His name is Noah Lloyd."

Denzil folded his napkin and his face creased into a smile. "How intriguing! Tell me more."

The atmosphere changed and all attention rested on Ursula. "It's the other way around, isn't it, Denzil? You are an opportunist who saw what's going on in Kodaikanal and decided, with admirable foresight, to get ahead of the game. Am I mistaken?"

Shripal and Xenia's heads switched from one to another as if watching a tennis match.

"Correct. I have been keeping an eye on Tamil Nadu for some time. The potential for psilocybin in Goa is phenomenal, under very similar circumstances as the bachelor party. What I did not want to do is hand over this business model to the Vargas clan."

Xenia, the only one still eating, put down her cutlery. "Hold up a minute! I'm gonna need subtitles for this conversation. What have Kodaikanal, Tamil Nadu and psilocybin got to do us?"

With a nod of respect towards Ursula, Denzil checked his watch and began speaking. "Our new friend and ally is smart, capable and surprisingly well informed. The region of Tamil

Nadu grows large amounts of hallucinogenic mushrooms and Kodaikanal is its hottest spot. Harvesting and selling such products is illegal, but somehow, when you know the right people, things work out. I keep an eye on trends. That might be fashion, sports, holiday destinations and recreational drugs. Young kids and immature adults still chase short-lived hits such as weed, cocaine and alcohol. Wealthier types want mind-altering experiences on a more profound level. Ursula and I provided exactly that for Kirkland C. Reece and friends. I understand the best man, Noah Lloyd, has returned to mine this rich seam."

The doorbell rang and everyone froze.

Shripal stood. "I'll get it. Let me do the talking. Just agree with everything I say."

17

Superintendent Cruz Biswas was a force of nature. Over six feet tall, he wore a sandy-coloured uniform and black leather belt and a broad smile, and carried his hat in his hand. Energy and intelligence radiated from the man causing a frisson of fear to ripple through Ursula. For a second, she wished the custom here was to shake hands. One could pick up a great deal by touching someone's skin.

As it was, she followed the lead set by their hosts, pressing her hands together in a bow. Shripal made the introductions and offered him a drink while Xenia cleared away the fish and chips.

He focused his attention on Denzil. "I am very sorry to see you have been injured but pleased you are out of hospital. Did you report the incident? I will personally see to it that the perpetrators receive justice."

Denzil gave a gentle smile of reassurance. "The perpetrators are sitting beside and opposite you. Ursula was unfamiliar with the acceleration speed of a moped and I should have been wearing a helmet. The first mishap occurred on sand. The second was on tarmac. I suffered some bruising and slight concussion but no broken bones. These beautiful flowers are an apology from Ursula, not that one was necessary. An accident is an accident, as I well remember from when my daughters were learning to drive. Back then, I was younger and fitter, bouncing like a rubber ball. Now, old age is catching up with me. Welcome to my home, Cruz, and can I say what a pleasure it is to see you since we barely had a chance to chat at the wedding."

Xenia re-entered with a tray of glasses. "Gin and tonics for us, water for Dad and Shripal. Him because of his medication and her because she wants to impress her brother-in-law." She placed their drinks on the table with a grin at Cruz. "There's a very good reason we call her Bubbles."

With effortless diplomacy, Cruz managed the situation like a pro. "I feel honoured to be here, even more so to be entrusted with the results of your enquiries. May I propose a toast to the health of Mr Fernandes, the success of my brother's betrothal to his beloved, and great health and happiness to Xenia and Ursula!"

He met everyone's eyes as they drank. Ursula lifted her gaze for a second and the electricity emanating from that man set off alarm bells. All her instincts acknowledged danger, but she could not ascertain what kind. She adopted a passive role, eyes lowered, ears open and her radar febrile. Shripal spoke at length, sticking to the script, supported by Denzil. For once, Xenia kept her mouth shut and head down.

After Shripal finished her pitch there was a moment of silence, and Cruz took three swallows of his drink. Ursula looked at him, trying to gauge his mood. He was statuesque, filling the space with his large personality. Without a trace of a beard or moustache, thick black hair neatly trimmed and clear hazel-green eyes, he presented an imposing figure. His expression remained impassive.

"Your proposal is not without merit. What you must guarantee is solid intelligence. I cannot and will not commit police units unless I am sure there is concrete evidence we are pursuing genuine criminals. Ursula, if I understand correctly you are meeting with two senior gang members at six tomorrow evening. Would you be willing to wear a wire? We can coach you in protocol."

A wire? While trying to lure the Vargas family into an illicit operation fleecing billionaires with prohibited substances?

"I would be prepared to gather intelligence on condition my colleague and I are guaranteed impunity. We're dangling a carrot, Superintendent, confident they will bite. When they do, and they most certainly will, they're all yours. But should you feel it necessary to scrutinise our methods, we might well prove to be unreliable witnesses."

Cruz fixed his gaze on her, his lips twitching in amusement and curiosity. "I can assure you, neither you nor your colleague will suffer any consequences. The only reason I suggest an electronic recording is for avoidance of doubt. Tell me, how did a person like you end up embroiled in such a situation?"

"Right time, right place? I am just glad I can assist Denzil and his family by removing the threat to his livelihood." She dropped her eyes, feigning modesty but actually escaping the intensity of his stare.

"Very well. I will assign a surveillance team to assist you and listen in on your conversation. Come to the police station for four o'clock and we can make the necessary preparations. Shripal, Denzil, thank you for the drink and for entrusting me with your confidence. Depending on how tomorrow goes, I will be in touch. Goodnight, Xenia, goodnight, Ursula."

Shripal saw him to the door. Once they were safely out of earshot, Xenia let out a sigh. "Such a shame he's a copper. What a total fox."

"He has a certain presence," Ursula agreed. "Is his profession that much of a deal-breaker?"

"Yup, 'fraid so. Plus the fact he's Shripal's brother-in-law. Too close to home. Anyway, I plan to marry a scientist or surgeon or businessman. The kind of bloke who will come in handy one of these days."

"You could do a lot worse than the Superintendent of Police," said Denzil. "In my opinion, that's the very definition of handy."

"Don't you start with the matchmaking, Dad, I told you I want to choose for myself."

"And I agreed you should. I'm just saying he's respectable, solvent and with excellent manners. If you did change your mind, you would most certainly have my approval."

Shripal returned, looking like the cat who got the cream. "Ladies and gentleman, I think we have a plan. My next meeting with Dolores is on Friday afternoon, so let's hope whatever she says tallies with your information. We could have this all sewn up by the end of the month."

Ursula suspected the end of the year was overly optimistic, but kept her mouth shut. Shripal seemed to think a few cosy chats were sufficient to tease enough rope from the Vargas clan with which to hang them. But she didn't know them as well as Ursula. If Frankie had the faintest suspicion the family was under threat, she would strike like a scorpion. The person right in the line of fire would be Ursula.

The following morning, her pessimism had evaporated and she set out on her run with a clear-eyed determination. It was up to her to pull this off. First, to talk Noah into assisting with her sales pitch. She made up her mind not to mention the wire or the police team in support. The fewer people who knew about that, the better. Then she had to get the balance exactly right for Frankie. Convincing, but not too slick. Friendly, but not desperate. All the while fully inhabiting the persona of Ursula

Brown, avoiding any verbal tics, facial expressions or hand gestures that might remind her adversary of another woman she used to know.

The best of all possible outcomes was enough incriminating proof for the police to take over, leaving Ursula far from the eye of the storm. The worst was Frankie smelling a rat and pouncing. She wouldn't do anything in the bar of a hotel, but command her people to snatch Ursula off the street and take her to a remote location, more than likely Dolores's yacht. There she would toy with her victim, like a cruel cat with a mouse. Not for the first time, Ursula considered sourcing some kind of poison she could take if faced with the inescapable prospect of Frankie's sadistic punishments.

She dismissed the idea as impractical and worked on her mind-set. Frankie was only human. A nasty example of the species, to be sure, but she had the same motivations as everyone else. Ursula knew her weak spots and what drove her. Although Berto was insignificant in real terms, she had to treat him with equal deference. Dangling the prospect of maximum dollars for minimum effort would hold them in her thrall. The next steps she would play by ear, careful not to ask leading questions that could look like a set-up. Which led her to the second problem – what to wear to a smart business meeting with enough volume to conceal a wire while looking nothing like her former self. She wasn't sufficiently confident with the sari, fearful it might slip. On top of that, adopting an entirely different style of dress to previous meetings was a red flag even Berto couldn't miss. She had to style designer chic, and wear lots of make-up and jewellery that didn't rattle.

The other thing bothering her was Denzil's advice. *Make a mistake. Lower the bar. Delude these people into thinking you are no threat.* Somehow she had to prove she was not a cop. To do that, she'd need to become a criminal. She ran up the dune to her house, sweaty, tired, out of breath and ideas. Everything looked the same, but she circled the house, performing her checks as she always did.

After a shower, she stood in front of the wardrobe, trying to recall all the advice from her police training. *Keep it clean. No noisy jewellery or rustling neckwear. Nothing distinctive, just a simple shirt with a collar. Enough room in the waist area for a pack strapped to your midriff. Anything excessively baggy is a dead giveaway.*

She studied her Alexander McQueen dress. It was the opposite of bland, a loud print in red, green and black, with a pert collar and cap sleeves. Berto had snapped her wearing it last time they met. To wear the same outfit twice would appear cheap, inexperienced and clumsy. *You've got to fall flat on your face in order to save it.* Problem partially solved. Talking of face, she should get started on her make-up.

By 11.15, she looked polished and well groomed. She considered a little pair of lace gloves to cover her scabby knuckles, but wasn't convinced she could pull it off. In any case, a few imperfections could improve her story. The overall look was 1950s, including Mary Janes and scarlet lipstick, pearl earrings and a black Furla handbag adorned with a honeybee. The final touch was less innocent. She strapped a holster to her left leg, twisted it so that the sheath lay against her inner thigh and slid in her knife. Two twirls in the mirror convinced her it didn't show. She was ready. The outfit, while perfect for an air-conditioned hotel or shopping mall, wouldn't last two minutes on a moped. She called the Da Gama Apartments and asked to be put through to Apartment 16.

"Ursula! Hi! I was just on my way to the lobby. Are you already here?"

"Change of plan. Could you get a cab over to my place? I have a proposition best discussed between just the two of us. Pick up something nice for lunch then come up and see me."

He didn't need asking twice and she regretted her word choice. *Proposition, just the two of us, come up and see me?* As if she was deliberately misleading the poor man. She returned to the bedroom and sprayed on some Guerlain Herba Fresca for no other reason than it smelt like springtime and had a bee on the box.

Noah brought sushi. Of course he did. No local street food for this guy. By the time his taxi arrived she had already eaten a couple of prawn *rissois* and was eyeing a flatbread.

He wore a cream linen suit over a blue T-shirt and Hermès navy loafers, with Cartier sunglasses pushed up onto his head. "You look beautiful! I don't think I've ever seen you in a dress." He leaned forward for a greeting kiss.

She dodged away, took the box from his hands and backed into the kitchen. "Hi, Noah, come in and thanks for being flexible regarding arrangements."

"You didn't specify what you wanted for lunch so I got a luxury sashimi and sushi platter."

"Great, I like fish. Take a seat. Sparkling water or herbal tea?"

"Water, thanks. So my guided tour is off?"

"Postponed. Help yourself." She gestured at the jug.

"Oh, could I get some bottled water? My digestive system is still regaining full gut health."

Ursula brought in the plates, opened the box and picked up her chopsticks. "The water's safe, Noah, I have a filter. Thanks for getting lunch."

"You're welcome. Sorry it took so long. Nobody in Goa is in a hurry, right?"

"One of the reasons I like it so much. Are you going to eat?"

"Sure." Legs crossed at the ankles, one arm looped over the back of the chair, the other lifting a slice of sashimi to his mouth, he was the epitome of chilled confidence. "Those colours are perfect on you. Knowing you dressed up for our date blows me away. I can't take my eyes off you."

"I'm afraid this outfit is not for our 'date'. I'm dressed this way because I have two important meetings this afternoon. That's why there was no guided tour on the bike." Noah Lloyd was getting right up Ursula's nose.

He didn't notice. "Mmm, these are pretty good. Gotta say though, nothing comes close to the original Japanese. I had one of the finest meals of my life in Toyama. So fresh and refined, it's alchemical. You ever been to Japan?"

"Only for work. Can we talk, Noah?"

"Yeah, I'm listening, Little Bear. You said you had a proposition?"

"I did and I want to make clear it's a business proposition. I'm meeting a couple of big shots to seduce them into a business deal. Would you have time for a drink at six o'clock this evening? You'd be a great help." *Seduce?* What was the matter with her vocabulary? "What I mean is that you, Kirkland et al showed me an opportunity. I'd like to take the idea and recruit some associates to make it happen." She stuffed a maki roll into her mouth to shut herself up. This was not the calm, persuasive speech she had rehearsed.

Noah scrutinised her face. "That's pretty vague. What about Denzil? He's totally linked up. I mean, I'd love to have a drink with you and your friends, but how do I add value?"

She placed her chopsticks on the wooden rest. "Denzil landed in hospital due to your event and it wasn't an accident. His mistake and not your fault, so don't get your knickers in a twist. Basically, anyone wanting to make money from hospitality in this region must be authorised by the people who run the show. The meeting tonight is with two senior figures. My pitch is exactly how you and Kirkland sold me your bachelor party. The Reset, remember?"

Colour drained from Noah's face and he shook his head.

"Endorse that as an experience? Jeez, Ursula, you saw what a mess I was! Why would you inflict that on an innocent? Sorry, I can't participate in something I perceive as wrong."

She ate in silence, refusing to meet his eyes.

He poked his chopstick at the wasabi, his expression sullen. "More water?"

"I'm good, thanks."

"Fine."

"Look, I cannot get on board with selling an experience I found horrific. Not even for you, Little Bear. I'm sorry."

"Oh, will you ever get over yourself, you egotistical prick? I don't want your assistance in marketing the idea, organising the logistics or lifting one of your manicured pinkie fingers to make it happen. Your role is simple: you represent the target client. You sit there and nod. When I ask you if there's a market, you say, 'Hell, yeah!' That will suffice, but if you wanna enthuse, be my guest. Then you can take me to dinner and elucidate on the other reasons you came back to Goa."

He did the puppy dog eyes. Again. "I think you know the reason I'm here."

"Feel free to tell me in detail later. Straight answer, will you come to the hotel and represent a client base? If not, I'll find someone else."

He took a few bites of a California roll and a slice of sashimi, his eyes downcast. Ursula called upon all her patience, ate some pickled ginger and considered apologising for calling him an egotistical prick. It took no longer than two seconds for her to change her mind.

"I have to say, you asking me to do this makes me feel kinda cheap. My objective in coming here was to develop a personal relationship between us. Now you want to use me in some sort of unethical deal? I'm not happy, Little Bear. This is not what I expected. Maybe I should go."

Because she'd manoeuvred the table into its present location, Ursula knew how heavy it was and how much effort it would take to tip it over. She drew her knee up, placed her foot on the side and kicked like a mule. The table toppled onto Noah's lap, spilling sushi, water and a whole jug of tea onto his suit. His chair fell backwards and he landed like an upended turtle, pinned to the floor by a slab of marble.

"Maybe you should. This conversation is over."

She stalked into her bedroom and locked the door. Using a trick she had been forced to learn in Brazil, she opened the window, hopped outside and crept along the porch until she could see into a window. Noah waved his limbs like Gregor Samsa and finally wriggled his way out from under the table. When he got to his feet, panting and covered in bits of rice, he stood in a state of shock, staring at her bedroom door.

His next move surprised her. She fully expected him to call a cab and leave. Instead, he went into the utility room, found a dustpan and brush, and began sweeping up all the wasted food. He cleaned the floor, righted the table, washed the crockery and used the filter jug to refill the water bottle. He poured himself a glass and made for the deck overlooking the sea. Ursula scuttled backwards, clambered into her room and calculated how to play this.

Noah Lloyd was used to getting his own way. Just like Kirkland C. Reece and the rest of their entitled pals, who believed, and to some extent had been encouraged in that conviction, that the world revolved around them. Whatever they wanted, they could have it. Nothing was unaffordable. Consume, disrupt, destroy, then pay for the damages. Never would it occur to them to wonder how their behaviour inconvenienced the service providers. After all, weren't staff being paid to indulge their every whim? Ursula adopted a meditative posture and focused on her breathing, trying to stem the eruption of outrage. Her rational side offered calming thoughts. *He's not used to being refused. You need his help. Would it hurt to talk to him and find some common ground?*

Unfortunately, her emotional side was in charge. *You babysat him through his trip, to the extent of washing his soiled mattress. You owe this arrogant pillock nothing. In fact, he's the one who should acknowledge a debt. Who does he think he is?*

She glanced at the bedside clock. Quarter past two. She had to be at the police station by four. Time to take control.

She touched up her make-up and put on sunglasses. When she unlocked the bedroom door, Noah was still sitting on her deck, his feet on the railing, rocking back and forward on the rear legs of the chair.

"I'm afraid I must ask you to leave now. Today is a particularly busy day for me. If you like, we can share a cab downtown and I can drop you at your apartment." She looked over his head rather than suffer his sorry-for-myself shtick.

He kept his gaze on the waves. "I got to thinking out here, watching the ocean. We asked you to do something off the agenda for us. You said no, because you disapproved. When Denzil got knocked out of action, you stepped up. You didn't like it, but you overcame your principles to give us what we paid for. I respect that."

Since she was wearing sunglasses, he couldn't see her roll her eyes. "Thank you."

"Then you went the extra mile, taking care of me through the worst moments of my life. You held me, comforted me, anchored me and saw me come out the other side. The only reason I am still here is because you never let me go."

Ursula said nothing because the words forming in her mind were not helpful.

"Personally, I disapprove of your business plan. That said, I'm gonna support you for two reasons: reciprocity and speculation. If the idea takes off, I want a part of it. For the income stream, sure, and because I think we'd make a pretty cool team."

She came to stand in front of him, leaned her back against the rail and crafted her response with care. "That is honourable and decent behaviour. Thank you. My project is still in the viability stage, so let's not get ahead of ourselves. Your presence at the meeting this afternoon would be most welcome. One thing I must insist upon is that I do the talking and you do not question me. Learn your lines, speak them on cue and shut up if I kick you. If you have objections, you can voice them later. Everything is meticulously planned, even if it might not look that way. Let me take the lead. OK?"

He let the front legs of the chair fall onto the deck. His linen suit bore stains of soy sauce, wasabi and indiscriminate wet patches, his loafers were ruined and when he stood, he winced in pain. "Sure. I've learned not to judge a woman like you. Yes, I will follow your lead, but I could use a shower and a change of clothes before we meet your associates. May I use the bathroom?"

The taxi dropped Noah at his apartment and delivered Ursula to the police station. She was hoping Cruz would be there. She was disappointed. Two junior officers led her to an interview room, applied the wire, tested it at various distances and instructed her in protocol. She paid attention, as earnest and under-confident as any woman on the street. Her focus was not entirely an act. Last time she'd worn a wire rather than using a phone recording was a full three years back. A refresher course never hurt.

"Do not under any circumstances touch the microphone. Act normally and try not to fidget with your clothing. Speak at your usual volume. Try to relax as far as possible. Just never forget you're wearing a wire."

As if she could forget. The pack taped to her abdomen was heavy and uncomfortable, and the fear of what might happen should she be recognised made sweat run down her spine. She was putting Noah at risk and even worse, not warning him of the dangers.

She turned to the efficient female officer who was observing her from every angle to ensure the wire was invisible. "You'll be right outside the hotel, yes?"

"That's correct, madam. My colleagues and I will be listening to every word."

"What if I need assistance? You know, in case they turn nasty?"

The tall man tuning the equipment looked up. "The Superintendent has positioned two officers in the hotel and if required, we can provide back-up. Do you expect them to turn nasty?"

Ursula realised her qualms were affecting the young officers, who were exchanging concerned glances. "I doubt it, but as someone inexperienced in this kind of operation, I guess I was hoping for reassurance. Don't worry, I'll be fine."

She was lying. If Frankie Vargas suspected her of surreptitious recording or twigged her real identity, the police would have no time to act. No matter that she was in a public place surrounded by witnesses, Frankie would kill her.

"You will be fine, madam, yes, indeed." He packed up his equipment. "My colleague and I have to leave now to get into position. Please remain here for twenty minutes, then make your way out to the car park. A taxi driver will be waiting. Good luck."

"Thank you." She plastered on a bright smile and watched as they closed the door.

Twenty minutes. Ursula gazed up at the clock and watched the second hand as it made one revolution around the face. She examined the scabs on her knuckles. Maybe gloves would have been a good idea, after all. In the windowless room, the air was stale, despite the fan. She wasn't confined or locked in so nothing was stopping her from going to the loo or using the water cooler. Still she sat, staring at the clock, like a prisoner awaiting the executioner's call.

"Drama queen," she said aloud. Her words triggered a gecko to run across the ceiling and escape into an air vent.

Lucky you.

Oh, stop with the self-pity, will you? The reason you're in this position is because you chose to be. You engineered the whole thing and now you're closing in. In half an hour, you'll be sitting opposite two prime targets. All you need to do is get them to incriminate themselves and the police will do the rest, taking Dolores down with them. Objective achieved.

She acknowledged her inner voice was correct. Rather than sitting here sweating, quaking and wondering if she needed a pee, she should meditate herself into a state of calm. She was a hunter, a fisher casting a hook, using all she knew about her prey to lure them. Unbidden, Thanh's face floated into her mind, his eyes narrowed in concentration.

When first assigned to him as an undercover partner, she found him impressive and intimidating. Stealthy, fast and decisive in predator mode, he had taught her everything she knew. How to read her environment, where to seek weak spots, when to move slowly and when to strike, the technique of sending awareness far beyond her personal space, and how to scrutinise the inscrutable. Thanh believed in visualisation. Picture the perfect outcome, identify the path to take you there and play each step in your head.

The clock said she had fifteen minutes. She closed her eyes and role-played the upcoming conversation in her mind. Guessing the level of hostility or interest was impossible, so she concentrated on her own legend. What exactly did she want? How much did she care? When would she pull the plug and walk away? Deep breaths cooled her skin and channelled her energy. With every rehearsal, she became more grounded and prepared for battle.

She opened her eyes, slipped her bag onto the crook of her arm and walked outside to find her taxi. She was as ready as she'd ever be.

18

From the outside, Hotel Vermelhas Rosas looked the same as usual. A couple of people carriers waited to collect guests, doormen in clean kurtas hurried to open the door, groups, couples and families sat at outside tables, and waiters carried wooden trays of drinks. The heat of the day had dissipated, leaving mellow warmth behind. Tropical blooms scented the air and strains of classical sitar floated out of hidden speakers.

Ursula walked inside to see Noah already waiting on a bar stool. He placed two fingers to his temple in some kind of salute. It made him look like a Boy Scout. With a casual glance around the room, she went to join him, holding out a hand.

"Hello, Noah, and thank you for joining me." Her voice was overly bright. She could imagine a needle on a dial in the police van jerking into the red. She lowered her tone to a natural pitch. "I don't see our hosts just yet. We'll wait a while. Nice jacket."

"Thanks. Pink isn't for everyone, but I find it uplifting. That dress really suits you, you know."

Ursula interrupted before he could go any further. "Compliments exchanged, let's get to business. The people we're meeting operate an interconnected range of services, from hotels, escorts, entertainments and fun activities. We need to show maximum respect and serious deference. I am pitching a new model based on our previous encounter – that is, your colleague's bachelor party. I will do the talking. All I require from you is enthusiastic confirmation there is a market for such events. Talk at length about the changing habits of recreational drug users, play down your own experience and leave the rest to me. Incidentally, should they ask us to stay for dinner, we have another engagement."

"Got it. Am I posing as a potential client?"

"Only in the vaguest ... ah, here they come. Or at least one of them."

Berto stood in the restaurant doorway, dressed in a black shirt and jeans, one hand in his pocket. He scanned the tables until his gaze settled on Ursula. His eyes narrowed, flicked to Noah and back again. Ursula kept a straight face but the urge to whistle an Ennio Morricone theme was all but overwhelming. With one hand, he beckoned them to follow.

She spoke aloud to keep her team informed. "Oh, it seems he wants us to go somewhere else. That's odd. Come along, then, let's see where he's taking us."

Once out of the bar, Ursula asked a question. "Excuse me, Mr Vargas, I thought we were having a drink in the lobby?"

He didn't turn around and started walking along the corridor. "My family never conducts sensitive conversations in public. We use a meeting room."

She gave Noah a reassuring smile, while scrambling to think of a way out. Hotel signage indicated they were going to the Business Suite.

"Wise move to relocate to the Business Suite. Privacy benefits us all. I'm guessing a hotel called Red Roses has lovely garden views from the ground floor. Goa is such a natural paradise."

He ignored her, stopped at a door and knocked. As far as Ursula could hear, there was no reply, but Berto opened the door regardless. While his head was inside, Ursula dropped her voice.

"The facilities here are state-of-the-art. I wonder how much it costs to rent the Magellan Room per hour. I should check it out for future collaborations. Oh, look at that painting! It reminds me of the sunsets behind my house. The sky turns from the colour of your jacket through orange to blood red. Although my view has no boats or fishermen."

Noah looked completely nonplussed.

"You can come in now," said Berto, subjecting them to detailed scrutiny. Standing inside the door was a musclebound bodyguard, dressed imaginatively in a black suit, black shirt and black tie. He averted his gaze as they entered.

The meeting room was unremarkable: a rectangular table with seats for ten attendees, floor-to-ceiling windows displaying the gardens, and a hospitality sideboard with coffee machine, bottled water and herbal teas. At the opposite end, a half-open door suggested an anteroom.

"Take a seat," said Berto, tapping at his phone. Ursula chose to sit with her back to the window with a view of both doors, and Noah took the chair to her right. They waited in silence for seven long minutes. Finally, the half-open door swung wide and Francesca Vargas stepped into the room.

Ursula's fears leading up to this meeting had revolved around concealing her own identity. Not for a second had she imagine her old adversary would be the unrecognisable one. All that remained of Chica's natural teenage beauty was her height and pale green eyes. The rest was surgically enhanced out of existence. Her face seemed simultaneously puffy and tight, skin stretched over infeasible cheekbones but with swollen fish lips. Those thick brows, once so enviable, were plucked and painted into sharp Vs, giving her a cartoonish expression. As for her colouring, highlights masked the original honey-blonde and any trace of her olive complexion was hidden under expertly blended foundation. The surgery had not stopped at her face. Flat-chested as a girl, Francesca now demonstrated an exaggerated hourglass figure: huge breasts, an impossibly small waist and curvy hips. She looked like Jessica Rabbit.

"Hi. I'm Frankie. I understand you have a business proposition. Roberto gave me an outline, and I agreed to hear more detail. I don't have much time, so if you can keep your pitch to five minutes? Thanks." She slid into a chair at the head of the table and placed her palms on the surface as if she was about to get up again. Berto assumed a similar position at the other end.

In order to address them equally, Ursula would have to act as if she was watching a tennis match. She took a long inhale and pushed back her chair. "It seems there's been a misunderstanding. We have no 'pitch' to deliver, simply a suggestion that worked for us. My understanding was that my client and I would be having a casual drink in the bar to offer some friendly advice. Now we find ourselves in a meeting room where we're expected to spell out our model for nothing? The hostility I've encountered in this region is exactly why I'm relocating my operation. Come, Noah, we're leaving."

Noah got to his feet and couldn't have played the confused outsider better. She had been right to keep him in the dark.

"Sit down, both of you. If a casual drink is that important to you, I'll have some cocktails and snacks delivered." Frankie stared at Berto.

"Good idea. A Mai Tai for me." He caught her expression.

"Oh, I see." He picked up the phone. "Bring a jug of Mai Tais and a Piña Colada to the Magellan Room, with three glasses with a bunch of nuts and stuff. Put it on my bill."

Ursula remained standing. "The refreshments are not the problem. It's the attitude. I came here in good faith to expand on my conversation with Mr Vargas. I'm not trying to sell you anything because I have no need. I'm moving on. The intention was to leave you a tip. If that's unwelcome, I apologise for any offence caused and wish you a nice day." She walked towards the door, sensing Noah at her heels.

The bodyguard took a sideways step to block the door.

"Get out of the way, you idiot!" Frankie snarled. "They are free to leave if they want. Before you go, Ursula, I want to say that I too misunderstood the nature of this meeting. Perhaps Berto consumed too many Mai Tais, Banana Daiquiris and fine wines when you explained your idea at Clube Nacional. If you're not proposing a collaboration, could we start again?"

Ursula eased herself into her chair. "Yes, we can start over, Ms Vargas. But you can cancel the cocktails, thank you. I have another appointment later for which I need a clear head. Please allow me to introduce Noah Lloyd from California. I credit him and his friends with inspiring my business model. I came to Goa in order to prepare a bachelor party for a client. Noah came here for very similar reasons. When Denzil asked me to assist at the last minute, I assumed it would be a classic stag do. My mistake. These gentlemen wanted to try mind-altering drugs but not for a short-term high. What did you call it, Noah? I think you described as 'The Reset'? Forget the usual smoking and snorting and resultant behaviour, this is about self-discovery via psilocybin. It's very popular in other regions of India such as ..."

"Tamil Nadu," said Frankie. "We know. Kodaikanal has become a tourist hot spot."

"Exactly. My point is this: taking magic mushrooms and tripping are one thing. Coke and blow are another. The difference is the psilocybin journey appeals to a particular demographic. Therefore less risky and far more lucrative. Noah, please excuse this crass question, but as a rough estimate, what's the net worth of your bachelor party?"

He took a second to calculate. "Five to six billion, I guess. It varies."

"Thank you. Would you describe in a few sentences, what your expectations were when you travelled to India?"

"Like you said, it was supposed to be a reset. Going inwards, letting go of all you know, changing your mind and I mean that in the realest sense. Altering patterns, switching paths, you know? We wanted to discover our true potential, the other selves we might be without our conditioning. It's a big step. A huge, scary step."

With infuriating timing, there was a knock at the door. Ursula was sure it was a waiter delivering the cocktails, but she glanced up, just to be sure. A barman entered, carrying a tray with glasses, a jug and an ornate creamy concoction.

"Supposed to be, Noah? Did things not go to plan?" Frankie's voice was soft.

"Not for me. The others had a great time."

Ursula could see what Frankie was doing. "Yet despite a negative personal reaction, Noah has returned and will vouch for the fact there is plenty of interest."

Frankie ignored her and reached out a hand in Noah's direction. There was no way she could touch him from that distance and probably didn't want to, but the gesture served its purpose. Her sympathy was as fake as her face. "Some people are resistant to mind-altering substances. Is that what you mean? I hope you didn't have a bad trip?"

Berto took the tray, placed the Piña Colada in front of

Frankie, poured three glasses and shoved the empty tray and the barman out the door.

"Cheers." Frankie peeled her lips apart and raised her ludicrous cocktail in the air. Before she could stop him, Noah repeated the gesture. Berto was already drinking and no one seemed to recall Ursula was in the room.

"Cheers, Frankie." He took a long draught of his cocktail and grinned. "This Mai Tai is out there! You know what, I'm gonna be honest and say I had the worst trip ever. I spiralled down a horrible black hole, despairing and torn apart. I didn't think I would ever get out and if it hadn't been for Ursula, I'd have given up. She stayed with me, nursed me through it and taught me a lesson. Strength takes many forms."

Ursula hadn't even touched the jug of cocktails, but still she wanted to throw up.

"That's overstating the case, but thank you." Before he could elaborate, Ursula pressed on. "Noah makes a good point. The principle is low effort, high gain, but at the same time, you will need support personnel. My team in the Maldives will comprise a doctor, chef, housekeeping and hospitality team, counsellors and an overseer like myself. As I explained to Berto, if you can source quality product, guarantee a safe space and ensure a seamless experience, this is the future."

Berto, downing his Mai Tai as if it was water, gave the thumbs-up. "Low effort suits me."

"Don't I know it," said Frankie, her tone dry. "Ursula, it's generous of you to share your insider knowledge. The Vargas family want to express our gratitude. In the spirit of sisterhood, why not join me in a toast? Cocktails don't float everyone's boat, but no one can refuse a glass of sparkles."

Klaxons rang in Ursula's ears.

Insider knowledge. The Vargas family. The spirit of sisterhood. A glass of sparkles.

Frankie knew.

"As I said, I have another meeting, so I won't, thanks all the same. Good luck and I hope our input helped." She stood and pulled the strap of her handbag across her body. She had an inkling she might need both hands free. "Is there a bathroom I could use?"

The glances between Frankie, Berto and the henchman told her everything she needed to know. She was prey.

"You can use that one," said Frankie, pointing at the rear door.

"OK, be right back." She was torn between leaving the door open to hear what went on in her absence and locking it to address the police and remove the wire. The latter took precedence. If they found recording equipment on her person, she was toast. She spoke quietly and precisely into the microphone.

"I believe these people are suspicious and plan an abduction. I am taking off the wire in case they search me. My life, and Noah's, are in immediate danger. Please do not let them take us from the hotel." She tore off the tape, removed the pack and microphone, stuffed it all into a sanitary bag and stood on the toilet to drop it through the window. She flushed the loo, washed her hands and stepped outside, her skin stinging from the ripped-off tape.

The atmosphere had changed. Berto was on his phone, Frankie had her hand on Noah's shoulder and the security guy was blocking the exit. Noah's head was drooping onto his chest.

"Noah? You feeling all right?"

He blinked up at her, trying to focus. "Sure, Little Bear, let's hit the road."

"Little Bear?" Frankie's voice turned acidic. "Why do you call her that?"

"Ursula, ya know? Little b-brown-bear cub." His mouth went slack and he started drooling.

"Noah, what's wrong? Are you still awake? Noah? Talk to me! Sorry, Frankie, this meeting is over, I need to get him out of here."

The French windows opened outwards, sucking air out of the room and destabilising Ursula. Two men rushed in, bound her hands and feet with cable ties, and to stop her yelling, pressed a sponge over her nose and mouth.

19

Pain returned her to consciousness. Her arms, unnaturally twisted beneath her, screamed in agony with every bump of the vehicle. Plastic restricted her wrists meaning she could not lessen the pressure in her shoulders. She opened her eyes, listening for any indication she had company. As far as she could ascertain, other than a muffled conversation from the cab, no one was in the rear. She rolled onto her side, spasming as blood flowed into her arms, tingling like electricity. From there, she tipped herself onto the floor knees first and put herself in Child's Pose to release the stress on her shoulders. The familiar position and directional breathing helped calm her, easing the pain and allowing her to think. The driver's erratic and jerky progress was less distressing since being sandwiched between two rows of seats meant she could not fall over. She flexed and twisted and relaxed, gradually regaining command of her body.

Her head was not such a simple proposition. She inhaled deeply, focusing on her predicament and ways to get out of it. In the next second, fear gate-crashed her mind, along with its friends, panic, brain-freeze and tension, rendering her wide-eyed and helpless.

Noah's incapability was her dominant concern. The man had no skills or experience to equip him for this kind of situation. All she could hope for was abandonment. Maybe they left him in the meeting room and the police found him fast enough to reverse whatever poison was in his system. Did someone spike the Mai Tais? No, Berto was drinking from the same jug. Noah's glass? Possibly. Frankie would be skilled at slipping something into the mix as she poured. The fact that Ursula would not partake must have frustrated that little bitch. Not that it mattered. Frankie, as always, had got her way and now Ursula was tied and trussed in the back of a van, heading to God knows where.

If she had still been wearing the wire, the police could have tracked her. That second of regret was instantly cancelled by the knowledge of what would have happened if those vicious bastards had found the listening device on her body. She'd made the right decision. She pressed her thighs together and found her knife firmly in place. Relief flooded her like fresh air. The question was whether to try releasing herself now or risk her captors discovering her secret weapon.

The minivan slowed, providing her with an answer. The driver's window descended and she caught snatches of conversation in Konkani, the scent of sea air, rotten fish and diesel fumes. In a few minutes, the vehicle came to a stop. A side door swung open and after a moment's confusion and frantic whispers, a light fell on her back. They lifted her up by the waist, dragging her outside. She contracted like a prawn, curling into herself and keeping her thighs clamped, feigning semi-consciousness. One man scooped her into his arms and strode along a jetty, issuing orders in a low voice. His chest smelt of smoke, cardamom and sweat. Next thing she knew, she heard a splash of water and the thrum of an outboard motor. The arms holding her stretched out to be replaced by others, which laid her onto a wooden seat, slick with sea spray. The launch was small and as the aft area was laden with two dirty great diesel drums, there was only room for six people. Two of whom, she was astounded to see, were smoking.

Another crew member leaned over her torso, not in a threatening way, but more as protection. Two minutes later, Ursula understood why.

The little launch was agile and once it cleared the tiny harbour, sped out to sea at full throttle. It bounced across the waves like a skimming stone, tossing into the air anything aboard which was not lashed down. Ursula sent thanks to the woman pinning her to the seat. The voyage lasted ten minutes, by which time she was soaked to the skin but clear-headed and ready to fight.

The light launch manoeuvred itself alongside a larger boat, and like any other slippery catch, she was rolled into a net and hauled aboard. Her skin was greasy with sweat and seawater, causing her concern for her weapon. As far as she could tell, it remained in place. They lugged her up two decks as if she were a sack of garbage, knocking her head against the handrails and her hips against the steps. Eventually, they threw her into some kind of store room and closed the door. Throughout the entire journey, no one had spoken a word to her, which was a very bad sign. Ursula was not a human being, merely a thing.

She struggled into a sitting position and kicked off the wet, slimy net to examine her surroundings. A porthole admitted a little bluish light from the sunken spots on deck. The room, if one could call it that, was the size of a toilet cubicle with life-jackets and sou'westers hanging along both walls. First priority was to free her hands. She wriggled her hips up and down, clenching her thighs together, trying to tease the knife from its sheath. But she was so wet, her skin simply slid over the holster and handle. All she achieved was to irritate the skin of her right thigh. She needed a towel to gain enough purchase. She swung her legs around and rose up on her knees. From there she was able to shuffle along the line of wet weather garments, feeling in the pockets for some kind of warm and dry fabric. No chance. This type of clothing was designed to repel water, not to absorb it. In one of the larger windproof coats, she came across a lanyard. It identified the bearer as CREW, LA CONQUISTADORA. The thin ribbon designed to go around the wearer's neck was white and waxy, so she almost discarded it, until an idea occurred. Pleading with her shoulders to stay in the most painful position, she teased it out, broke off the plastic sleeve and balled the ribbon in her left hand.

A warm draught blew on her left foot and she spotted a vent at floor level. Not exactly hairdryer strength, but better than a cold damp floor. She shuffled towards it, bent over and allowed air to flow up her skirt. She was still in that position when the door opened.

The second she lifted her head, she recognised the man who had attacked her in the garage. Short hair, scars and a truly unfortunate arrangement of features. Last time they met she'd punched him in the nuts.

"Frankie wants you. Come." He approached her slowly, wary of a surprise attack. She allowed him to heave her up by her underarms but refused to move when he pushed her forwards.

"Untie my legs. I'm not hopping around this boat."

"You come with me." He pressed a fist under her chin, forcing her face upwards.

"NO! Cut those ties!" She clamped her knees together and pulled her ankles apart, as far as they would go.

He seemed to understand the problem, but dithered in his response.

She softened her tone. "Cut the ties so I can walk. Then I will go with you. No problems from me, OK?"

It took a moment, but he took out a fish-gutting knife, crouched and sliced through the ties. Instantly, he leapt away from her feet as if they were attack dogs.

She bowed in gratitude. "Thank you. Let's go."

As far as she remembered from her ignominious arrival, she was on the second deck. Her guard prodded her to move forward, indicating left. They climbed another staircase, Ursula slower than usual as she was unable to use her arms. Music was playing from somewhere above and a balmy breeze fluttered her dress. The danger was obvious: the man two steps below might catch a glimpse of what she had between her legs. She stumbled and collapsed onto her left hip with a cry of pain.

"What's going on down there?" A head appeared over the railing. The voice was unmistakeable. Frankie's faux feminine tones barely masked an aggressive growl. "I told you to bring her up here ten minutes ago. How hard can it be? Does someone else need to do the job?"

The guard grabbed Ursula by the waist and threw her over his shoulder in a fireman's lift. Her head dangled halfway down his back and her feet were dangerously close to his testicles, but all her concentration was on the pain in her upper back and inner thighs. She could see nothing but his coarse shirt as they bumped up the stairs, but sensed much more light as they ascended.

Rough hands lifted her up and set her on her feet. In front of her, two women sat on padded recliners. The first was Frankie, her hostess of a couple of hours ago, the other was a semi-mythical creature few people had ever met. Rumours abounded back in the day whether she actually existed. Maria Dolores Consuela da Vargas had a reputation to rival the bloodiest gangsters on the planet. When she took over from her husband and sons, honour and standards went out of the window. The boys played rough, that much Ursula knew, but Dolores went above and beyond. The woman had no empathy, merely a lust for power. She held on to it with an iron fist. Of all the evil people in the Vargas organisation, Ursula feared Dolores the most.

None of this showed on her face. She stood in front of them, in a damp dress, messy hair and smudged make-up, projecting tearful terror.

Frankie stirred a cocktail stick around her martini. "Why is she still wearing shoes? No one wears shoes on this yacht. Take them off."

Her guard dropped to a crouch and unbuckled her Mary-Janes, throwing them into a basket.

Ursula remained meek and kept her eyes down.

"We know who you are," said Frankie.

Ursula did not raise her gaze from the floor.

"Look at me, Ursula. I said we know who you are."

"I doubt that very much." Ursula lifted her chin and glared at them. "You have no idea who I really am. To be honest, neither do I."

Dolores reached into her voluminous robes, pulled out what looked like a cigarette case and handed it to Frankie. "In that case, let's find out the truth." Her voice, coarse and gravelly, gave the impression she was a heavy smoker. Her gaze bored into Ursula's with a vindictive smile. Frankie opened the cigarette case and withdrew a syringe. She held it up to the light. Then she jerked her head at the ugly henchman, who turned Ursula to face him and drew her into an embrace.

Ursula panicked, trying to raise a knee, but he held her fast. All she could do was stamp on his feet, but since hers were bare, it had little effect.

Frankie came close enough to breathe gin fumes into her face. "So." She caught Ursula's wrist, pulling her shoulders into the same agonising position as when she'd woken up. A sharp pain shot up her left forearm and seemed to ground itself like a lightning strike in her right foot.

Tell them everything, the whole story, starting at the beginning of the alphabet. Put it all on the table but muddle the details. Make them take the cuffs off.

The tension left her and she collapsed into the henchman's arms.

"Put her on that lounge chair."

The guy laid her on the cushions and she cried out in pain. "No! My shoulders, please!"

"She's not going anywhere, Chica," rasped Dolores. "Cut the ties."

"You crazy? I don't trust this bitch. Maybe a little discomfort will sharpen her memory."

"How did I raise such a stupid girl? Pain and discomfort have the opposite effect. We want her to be relaxed. She should be lulled into thinking she's in a safe space. Then we'll get some answers. You, whatever your name is, cut the ties, strap her to the chair and bring a blanket. Leave the rest to me. Then you can go."

"A blanket? Are you going soft in your old age, Mama?"

The sound of a slap and subsequent gasp penetrated the fog enveloping Ursula. "Don't you ever speak to me like that again, Chica. Otherwise I promise you'll regret it."

Hands lifted her upper body, and with one slice through plastic her arms sprang free. She wept with relief, only half of which was faked. Warm, soft cashmere covered her damp dress and cold feet. Someone wound rope around her waist, binding her to the lounger, trapping and wrapping her like a burrito.

"Hello there. I hope you are comfortable. My name is Dolores. What's your name?"

"My name is Ann Sheldon. I am a poet and I live on the beach. It's the hut with the white heron on the roof, right at the edge of the jungle. Do you know it?"

Lapping waves and a distant aeroplane were the only sounds to fill the silence.

"OK, Ann Sheldon. Do you like living in your beach hut?"

"I loved it. Not so much in the rainy season, but for most of the year, it was paradise. Then I had to leave. One smartarse thought he could outwit the drug gangs. It ended up in a massive shoot-out and a fire. People died. After that we flew upriver looking for a missing prostitute deep in the jungle and caught a murderer. That was the most terrifying night of my life."

"Tell me about your sister, Ann."

"I don't have a sister anymore. I used to, but she ... went away."

"Do you mean she died?"

Even if she'd known how to answer, Ursula sensed the question was a lure. "I honestly don't know if she's alive or dead. Do you have siblings, Dolores?"

"Not anymore. Let's talk about Olivia. What did you know about your sister's job?"

Even though her brain was operating at one tenth of its normal speed, a realisation lumbered out of the fug like a turtle. Dolores just used the name Olivia. For whatever reason, she knew the same story Ursula shared with Shripal, Perneet and Xenia. Someone had spilled her 'secret'. Ursula changed tack.

"I was never really interested, to tell the truth. It's not that I'm scared of them; it's just that they're so flappy and unpredictable. Apparently a swan can break your arm."

All she could hear was whispers.

"Let's start again. I don't believe you're called Ann Sheldon. I think your real name is actually Ursula, and you are the sister of Olivia Jones, an ex-undercover police officer in London." Dolores lit a pungent cigarette. "Just tell me yes or no."

"You're right. My name isn't Ann Sheldon. That was an alias I used while living in Brazil. It was a tribute to my dad because he loved Del Shannon. What other song could I use as a runaway?" Ursula started humming the song, tears leaking from her eyes.

"What the hell is she on about?" Frankie stormed away to look over the deck towards shore.

Dolores stroked Ursula's shoulder. "Listen to me, my dear sweet girl. I ran away from an abusive situation and never looked back. Trust me, I understand. Why were you running away? You can tell me what happened and I will never judge your actions. You and I are sisters."

Lying evil bitch. Images of what Dolores and her sons had inflicted on other 'sisters' were sealed in an impenetrable vault at the back of Ursula's mind. Now the drugs released each abomination into full horrifying colour, triggering nausea. She began to heave and the henchman ratcheted the sunbed higher until she was upright. Dolores offered some water but even in a state of half delirium, Ursula knew better than to drink anything offered by a Vargas family member.

She coughed and spat bile on the pristine deck. "I ran away because a police detective was on my tail for a crime I didn't commit. In Macau, I became a hustler called Esther. Damn, I was good. You'd have loved seeing me in action. What a player! Esther walked out of there with more money than she could carry. Attagirl!"

"She's delirious. Someone needs to give her a slap." Frankie's drawl indicated impatience.

"Shut your mouth, Chica. You have never learned to listen. It might sound like verbal diarrhoea to you, but we have to sift through the shit to find a nugget of truth. Pay attention to the detail, OK? Right, I think I understand now. Esther was a gambler. Did she work alone?"

"Yes, apart from a driver and walker who got a pretty good

cut. I gamed the system and got away with three million dollars. You heard that right. Three million dollars. For the first time in my life, I was rolling in it!" She laughed, a pathetic kind of exhalation.

"What did Esther do next?"

"Esther did nothing at all because I left her behind in Hong Kong. Who wants to be named after an egg roll? I had money and freedom and for the first time in my life, a choice. I chose to sever all ties with my old life which meant going home to Britain. Under the name Olivia Jones, I entered the country to visit my father and sister. It was an unhappy experience. The weather was foul and I had to kill a taxi driver."

"Wait a minute. Olivia is dead." Frankie's tone was sharp. "You adopted your dead sister's name to visit your sister? This makes no damn sense and I'm losing patience."

"Yes, Olivia is dead. My name is Ursula and my sister's name is Katie. She's the ornithologist."

Frankie was pacing now. "What the fuck is an ornithologist? Something to do with teeth? How many sisters have you got, you stupid cow?"

"One. I have one sister called Katie who works with injured birds."

Dolores growled. "Twice I asked you to shut up and listen, Chica. If you don't think you can do that, you'd better leave us alone."

"That's fine with me. Berto's due here at midnight. We'll drink martinis and make plans. You can sit there and listen to this bullshit."

She swished through the doors and into the salon.

Dolores lit another cigarette and blew smoke into the air.

"I'm going to ask you again. What's your name?"

"My name is Ursula Brown." A sudden panic overwhelmed her as she thought of Noah. *Little Bear, let's hit the road. Ursula, ya know? Little b-brown-bear cub.*

"Was Olivia older or younger than you? Do you know what became of her?"

"Olivia was older. I don't know for certain, although I have a theory. That's why I came here. I want to know the truth."

"I'm sure you do. Tell me, how long did you stay in the UK?"

"A few days. Then I sailed to Spain under the name of Iris. Clear eyes, you get the reference, I'm sure. As Iris, I started a new life on a country farm. Happy for a while until I decided to commit suicide. At the last minute, I had a change of heart."

"What changed your mind?"

"It was a waste. Even if I had nothing to live for, I could give something to others who did. I volunteered at a women's refuge in Africa. By advocating for women's rights, I made myself unpopular and had to flee by helicopter. From there I made my way to Goa, where I started my own business as an international concierge. What next? No idea."

Dolores whacked her across the face with the back of her hand, her diamond cluster ring cutting Ursula's cheek. "Delusional, immature and a ridiculous fantasist. Making up names starting with different vowels? Ann, Esther, Iris, Olivia and Ursula; do you think I'm stupid? You are a waste of time and I want you off my yacht. Crew!"

Footsteps stomped up the staircase and the ugly guy came into view.

"Tie her up and throw her in the sea. I never want to see her face again."

The salon doors opened and Frankie emerged, laughing and carrying two cocktail glasses. "What did I tell you? She's a waste of time. Berto's running late so why don't you drink his?"

The henchman looked from Dolores to Frankie. "You want me to throw her overboard, madam?"

Frankie handed her mother a martini. "I have a better idea.

Let's gift her to Berto. He deserves a little fun. Then when he's finished, he can let his men do their worst. Cheers, Mama!"

"That's a very clever plan. Keep the troops happy by throwing them some scraps. Cheers, my darling." She pointed at the deckhand. "Take her downstairs to Roberto's suite. Make sure she cannot escape and lock the door. Get rid of the evidence after the event, you understand? I mean completely. By tomorrow morning, there must be no trace of her whatsoever. Chica, call the kitchen and order some canapés for when Berto arrives. Oh, look! Isn't that the most beautiful moon?"

The women drifted into the saloon, ignoring Ursula completely. Her head was still hazy no matter how hard she tried to concentrate, so she tucked herself into a ball as the man carried her down a single flight. He stopped outside a door and punched a code into a keypad. She squinted with one eye. 5707. She searched her mind for a way to remember it then turned it upside down. LOLS. Berto was such an idiot.

The guy placed her on an opulent mattress and roped her wrists to the bedstead, this time a hand's breadth apart. Ursula got the impression this was not the first time he'd bound a woman in this position. When convinced she was secured, he squeezed her breast and pinched her nipple.

She gave no reaction, keeping her eyes averted, praying he wouldn't go for her crotch.

He didn't. He grabbed his own, moving into her sightline, grinding and gurning enough to make her puke. She squeezed her eyes shut. He laughed, whispering in her ear, "See you later," and left the room.

The moment the door closed, she tested the restraints. Rope offered more mobility than the plastic ties, but there was no chance of releasing herself without breaking her wrists. How much time was left before Berto came to enjoy himself was anybody's guess. On the plus side, her legs were no longer bound and the knife was still strapped to her inner thigh. The issue was how to get the weapon into a position where she could use it.

She shimmied herself between the pillows and bounced her legs up, once, twice, three times until she was in Plough Pose, her feet above her head. From there, she writhed her legs against each other, loosening the knife. The manoeuvre required muscles she rarely used and since she was hardly in peak form, soon became exhausted. Only the thought of Berto's arrival drove her onward. Her lower back was protesting when the knife finally slipped from its holster onto her chest.

So far, so good. Now to get the weapon into her hands. Her body offered the answer, arching into Fish Pose so the knife tumbled down her sternum to rest against her sweaty chin. If she moved a whisker to the left or right, it would slip off and her only means of defence would fall into a pile of pillows. Using her heels, she pushed herself up the mattress with as much delicacy as if she was balancing fine china on her nose until her head rested on her hands. The distance between the knife and her fingers was no bigger than her thumb, yet might as well have been a light year away. She could not reach. The rough rope refused to give a single millimetre more. She couldn't even cry for fear of dislodging the weapon.

You can escape. Your hands are tied, but your body is not. Neither is your mind.

She took three deep breaths, ignored the screaming of her shoulder muscles and used the restraints to haul herself into a Crab Pose. When she judged the angle was correct, she moved her head to the left and her chin to the right. The knife tumbled into her right palm.

She clenched her fingers around it with a sob of relief. Then with one flick, she released the blade and sawed at the ropes. A flash of panic overtook her as she considered the fact they might be reinforced with steel cables. Then the rope frayed, loosened and freed her. Everything hurt. She sat upright, rolling her shoulders and rubbing her wrists, and took deep calming inhalations. It was vital her head returned to normal and her body relaxed.

She barked out a sardonic laugh and looked at her left fist, clenched so hard her knuckles were white. Gradually, she let go, opening her palm which still held the white lanyard ribbon.

Time to prepare herself for Berto.

20

The stateroom was luxurious, carpeted, cushioned and decorated in deep blue. Ursula glanced around the room, alert for anything she might use to her advantage. A heavy vase, tie-backs around the curtains, a glass coaster on the nightstand, even the Tiffany lamp itself if push came to shove. She slid off the bed and explored the room, always with an ear for footsteps outside the door. Berto was exactly the kind of man to have a concealed webcam. The question was, which angle would give him the most gratification? She dimmed the room illumination and looked for any tell-tale blinks, indicating concealed cameras in the ceiling. She found nothing. The only other likely recording equipment was the TV, which was easily unplugged and disabled.

Two doors revealed wardrobes; another, an ensuite bathroom. Huge windows opened onto a balcony with a deckchair and side table. She pressed the button and stepped into the night air. To her surprise, a strong wind blew rain into her face. The weather was turning, which did not bode well for her getting off the yacht tonight.

While staring out at the inky-black waves, she heard

snatches of conversation from the deck above. One female was speaking and two male voices burst into laughter. When one of the males spoke, Ursula realised one husky voice possibly belonged to Dolores. The family party was evidently having fun and showed no sign of breaking up. Ursula assessed the risk. It would take her five minutes to shower and steal something from the wardrobe. In the worst-case scenario, that Berto opened the door and saw she was no longer roped to the bed, he was stupid enough to come looking, rather than call the cavalry.

Sweat, saltwater and the stench of fear made the decision a no-brainer. She stripped off, still holding her knife, and stepped under a jet of warm water. Relief at sluicing off the filth was tempered by the stinging of her wrists when the water reached her cuts. She wrapped herself in a robe, listened for the sounds of company, and emerged into the main room. She pressed the button for the automatic balcony doors and was immediately buffeted by more warm water. In this case, tropical rain. No sounds came from above deck. Either the group had retreated inside or were turning in for the night.

Ursula dared not delay any further. Using the hood of her robe to towel her hair dry, she wrapped the lanyard ribbon around her wrists and bedstead to give the impression she was still tied. Gripping her knife, she lay back on the pillows. The yacht tilted with the waves, a lulling motion unless one suffered from seasickness. Ursula was still trying to decide if the motion comforted or nauseated her when the door opened.

Berto stood there, a shit-eating grin on his face and a cut-glass tumbler in his hand. She could smell the booze on his breath even at this distance. She made up her mind: nauseated, definitely.

"Mzz Ursula Brown. What a nice surprise! Such fun we get to spend some quality time together." He closed the door and placed the tumbler on the nightstand. "The tables have turned. We know who you are."

She said nothing, tensing herself for action.

"According to Manoj, you came all the way to Goa to avenge your sister. What a waste of time. Zoë was a good-for-nothing slut and deserved everything she got."

It took several seconds before she could speak. "Zoë? My sister's name was Olivia." Ursula played her role while processing his words. *According to Manoj?*

"Whatever. I don't give a shit about her real name. We all knew her as Zoë. Milo, that poor trusting fool, knew her as Zoë. We let her into the family only to find that two-faced, lying bitch was a cop who put my uncle and three cousins in jail. If I'd ever got my hands on her, she'd have regretted it for the rest of her very short life. Oh, well, I'll have to make do with the next best thing." He loomed over her, loosening his tie. "Now I can see the family resemblance. Zoë was prettier, but you've got better tits. You know what? I'm going to enjoy this."

"Roberto, please."

"Please what?" He ran a hand behind her calf and lifted her toes to his lips.

"Please don't hurt me."

He dropped her foot, sat on the end of the bed and started untying his shoelaces. "Here's how it works, sweetheart. You do exactly what I tell you, when I tell you and if you follow my instructions, you won't get hurt, *capisci?*"

It was the *capisci* that triggered her. In one fluid movement, she ripped her hands apart, rolled forward on her knees, caught him by the jaw and yanked his chin to the right. His neck broke with a crunch and he fell forward onto his head and knees, hands flopping by his sides.

Child's Pose.

Not what she'd planned; the knife was still clasped in her hand and not a drop of blood had been shed, but Berto was out of action – permanently. The winds grew wilder, lashing the windows and causing the floor to change angles. The safest place until the storm subsided was in this cabin. Yes, a couple of crew members might be waiting their turn but none would dream of disturbing Berto. Turbulent weather could also assist her in disposing of a body.

She made sure the door was deadlocked then rummaged around in the wardrobe for something practical to wear. Not much to choose from, so she settled on a pair of black silk pyjamas, which swamped her. After slicing ten centimetres off both legs and arms, she was able to move with ease. The one thing she didn't have was pockets. Somewhere on her person she had to hold her knife. Her filthy clothes in the bathroom still contained the holster. She washed and dried it, then strapped it to her upper left arm. The yacht rocked and bucked, throwing a flower arrangement onto the carpet. Water and blooms scattered across the floor but the vase remained intact.

It wasn't the first time she'd tipped a dead man over a balcony, but it never got any easier. Maybe there was a how-to video on YouTube somewhere. Berto was far heavier and drunker than her assassin in Belém. She sat on the chaise longue, swaying with the waves and working out the logistics. First, check for cameras on the deck, although in these conditions, it barely mattered. In addition to the unpredictable wind, the rain was behaving erratically, torrential one minute, then a fine mist the next. She yanked the duvet off the bed and laid it on the carpet. After a quick check of his pockets – wallet, phone, stack of cash and vaporiser which she left on the nightstand – she bundled Berto's body up like a sausage roll. That way she could drag him outside and figure out a way of throwing him overboard.

Just as she began to lug the deadweight towards the balcony, an industrial-style rumble echoed through the vessel. She froze in a squat, trying to understand what was happening.

Chains, winches, metal grinding against metal. The captain was hauling anchor. It made sense. In the midst of a tropical storm, the safest place was in a harbour, even for a boat this big. As if to confirm her guess, the yacht's engines fired, sending vibrations through every deck.

The cabin phone rang. Ursula let go of her bundle and went to stand over it. Twice, three times, the set emitted an electronic purr then fell silent. She waited another moment, terrified the next thing would be a knock at the door. She was reaching for her knife when Berto's phone flashed into life. The screen displayed a message.

Heading to port until this blows over. Nothing to worry about. We'll be back in position for tomorrow's drop at sunset. Have fun, Fx

She noticed the time. 01.09. How was it possible so little time had passed?

In the confines of a port, Berto's body would surface far sooner than at sea. Somehow or another, she had to dump him in the ocean as soon as possible. She heaved the duvet between the doors, which constantly tried to close, repeatedly jamming her and her burden. Without warning, the yacht bucked, throwing her off balance and bouncing her into the air. She grabbed hold of the table, which kept her rooted as it was fixed to the deck. The chair was not, and flew skywards until a downwards swoop crashed them both onto the deck. The chair fell onto its back reminding Ursula of a wheelbarrow. An idea took shape but it was risky. In this weather, she could easily be knocked overboard along with her victim. She snatched up two curtain tie-backs and only then spotted an electronic switch to keep the doors in the open position. The weather grew worse, pitching and tossing the boat as if it were a toy. She knotted the ropes around her midriff and lashed herself to one of the bollards. Whether the decorative ties had sufficient strength to keep her aboard was a risk she had to take.

The duvet, now soaked, weighed even more heavily. Just

rolling the lump onto the upended chair was a struggle. Not a snowball's chance in hell she'd be able to lift him. Instead, she worked with the motion of the boat. When hitting a wave, everything fell backwards. Once over the crest, there was a dramatic dip and momentum swung in the opposite direction. Twice she waited for the shift and heaved the chair forwards. She couldn't get it past her knees. The third time, she managed to get it to her waist. Instead of allowing it to hit the floor again, she slid beneath it, pressing her feet against the chair back. When the full force of gravity swung the other way, she used both legs and arms to stop it crushing her like a bug. For several excruciating seconds, she bore the load until everything seemed to become weightless for just a moment, before crashing in the other direction.

Ursula was expecting a drop, but this occasion the force was three times stronger than previously. She pushed as hard as possible using her thighs and biceps. As if plucked by an invisible power, the chair, complete with its passenger, flew into the air and over the railing. Ursula slid along the deck, her feet hit the wall and her torso tipped over the gunwale. Thankfully, the curtain ties kept her bottom half on board, at the cost of a stinging rope burn.

She heaved herself upright and stared into the roiling ocean. Nothing. His choice of navy-blue bed linen worked to her advantage. Unfortunately, the pyjamas would never be the same again. She retreated inside, closed the doors, drew the curtains and wrapped herself in the towelling robe. Now she had to finish the job and get the hell off this boat.

21

Strange how the mind works. Ursula had just murdered a man and disposed of his body. Pain from lesions around both wrists and the burn around her waist demanded attention. Her head was yet to return to normality after the sodium thiopental, exacerbated by the constant rolling of the cabin. She was closer than ever to her goal – wiping out the Vargas family for good – or trying to escape her captors and survive.

But her stomach took precedence. She was hungry.

The mini-bar contained champagne, spirits, mixers and a bag of nuts. Beside the phone was a list of numbers, including the kitchen. It took her a full five minutes to evaluate the dangers then she picked up the receiver and dialled.

A woman picked up. "Mr Vargas? You wanting something from the galley?"

"Oh, yes, hello, Mr Vargas is in the bathroom. I'm his guest. He told me to call you and order two burgers with fries."

"Two burgers with fries. No problem. Mr Vargas usually likes a bottle of Bairrada with his meal. You want me to add that?"

"I don't know, he didn't say. I guess so. I mean, yes, please."

"Anything else, lady?"

She hesitated and dropped her voice to a whisper. "Do you have a first aid kit? You see, I'm not used to sailing and lost my balance. It's a minor injury, but ..."

"I got you. Listen, the trolley has two levels. Food gonna be on top but underneath, hidden by a tablecloth, you will find various useful items. Due to this storm, food orders gonna take a while, maybe fifteen minutes. Blame me."

The woman's kindness was unexpected. The realisation of the number of women who had suffered at Berto's hands constricted her throat. "Thank you," she squeaked.

While she waited, she made a thorough search of the entire cabin. The bathroom contained various oils and lubricants, but nothing in the way of antiseptic cream. Her main concern was footwear, since her Mary-Janes had been forcibly removed. A less panicky search of the wardrobes showed life jackets, a few items of clean laundry, and a full black-tie ensemble, complete with shined shoes. None of it would fit Ursula. A huge swell threw her against the doors so hard she feared she'd cracked the mirror. But her own bedraggled image looked back at her; runny make-up, wet hair, a cut on her cheek and traces of blood on her bathrobe. She could have cleaned up, but decided against. The chances of gaining any sympathy from female crew members were far greater when looking vulnerable.

In the main room, the nightstands were both locked. Berto had no keys on his person, so the means of access must be in the room. She lifted the Tiffany lamp to see nothing underneath, but as she set it down, something tinkled. A silver key was hooked onto the base. Proud of herself for such a quick find, she removed it and placed it in the first lock.

Then she stopped.

Ursula trusted her instinct and called upon it often. Rarely did her sixth sense speak first. On this occasion and it not only spoke but shouted, '*NO*'. More than a recommendation, this was a flat-out refusal. *NO*.

Ursula let go of the key and sat on the bed. She relaxed, breathed deeply and expanded her consciousness. Threats abounded; she could sense so many above, below and outside that her breathing grew shallow. The drawers in the locked nightstand, however, remained a black hole.

NO. Some places are best left alone. A gut feeling was one thing but experience was another. This was where Berto brought women, voluntarily or otherwise. Items he kept in his bedside drawers weren't hard to imagine and setting eyes on such equipment was guaranteed to give her nightmares. She removed the key, took it into the bathroom and flushed it down the toilet. While she was there, she switched on the shower.

Something shifted in the yacht's movements; a slowing of the engines and less frequent lurches. The bell rang. Ursula checked the peephole and reached for her knife. The holster was empty. Outside stood a young black woman in branded crew uniform, with a classic hotel trolley.

Ursula opened the door with a fearful smile. "Thank you very much."

"Most welcome, ma'am. Enjoy your meal. You need anything else, you hear, just call and ask for Macy. I'm on duty until dawn."

Their eyes met in a mutual understanding. "You're very kind, Macy." She glanced over her shoulder. "I appreciate it."

Trolley in, shower off. The burger and fries smelt so good she could barely wait. Even so, she checked under the table-cloth for the 'various useful items'. A first aid kit, plus a crew uniform consisting of a polo shirt bearing the *La Conquistadora* logo, trousers, deck shoes, a rain jacket and baseball cap. If she bundled her hair under a hat and wore the staff uniform, she had a damn good shot at getting ashore.

She double-checked the deadlock and fell on the burger

like a wolverine. She swallowed three mouthfuls before opening the wine. Just one glass to aid digestion. She looked at the second plate. "No appetite, Berto? Fair enough. Mind if I help myself?"

The turbulence persisted to the point that Ursula needed to hold on to her wine glass or lose the contents. She rejected the buns and ate two burgers with a significant amount of fries. By the time she finished her meal, something had changed. Engine sounds dwindled to nothing. The deck remained steady. Rain still lashed the windows but with less ferocity than before. She checked the clock: 04.56. It would be light in an hour. The wine and the food made her sleepy, but she couldn't rest on this vessel. Instead, she took a cold shower, slathered herself in scented body cream and applied antiseptic to her wounds. Her left wrist looked awful, so she placed a dressing around it, covered by a support bandage. A plaster masked the wound left by Dolores's ring. Everything else would be covered by her clothes. When she judged herself to be as respectable as possible, she tried on the crew uniform. It fitted, if a little snugly, and she focused her attention on getting safely out of the cabin and off the yacht.

Macy said she was on duty till dawn. So now would be the time to act. She wrapped all her clothes and empty holster into a bundle and dropped them into the sea. In the bathroom, she checked the entertainment system for porn channels and selected a movie. When she was ready, she called the kitchen.

"Mr Vargas? How can I help?"

"Hello, Macy. This is his guest again. Thank you very much for the burgers. Mr Vargas is now ready for his breakfast."

"Of course. Does he want his usual?"

"That's what he said. Order me the usual. Would you mind taking out the other trolley? There's some laundry on the bottom shelf. Thank you so much."

"It's a pleasure, madam. What about you? Whatcha want to eat?"

"I'm not hungry, but thank you."

"You're welcome. I'll be there in five minutes."

"Just come right in and leave the food. Mr Vargas is running a bath."

"I understand."

In the final few minutes of her incarceration, Ursula turned the lights up high and checked the floor, the balcony and the bed for any sign of her knife. Nothing. It was probably resting somewhere on the ocean bed. She improvised, wiping one of the serrated burger knives and tucking it into one of the cargo pants' pockets. Berto's wallet, phone and vape she left on the dressing table, but pocketed the roll of notes. She pressed play on the porn film, set the volume high, closed the bathroom door and unlocked the cabin. Then she crawled underneath the tablecloth to conceal herself on the lower level of the hostess trolley. There wasn't much space.

Rather than curl into a foetal ball or lie on her back, she crouched on her knees, head to the ground, arms alongside so her hands lay by her feet. Rabbit Pose was the most stable and agile position, enabling her to spring up fast or roll sideways if necessary. She took deep breaths, bringing her metabolism to a calm watchfulness, rejecting sleep.

A light rap came at the door. Ursula said nothing, waiting till the stewardess entered. The chinks and tinkles of crockery offered a gentler soundtrack than the grunts and moans from the bathroom. The maid abandoned the breakfast trolley and wheeled what remained of the burgers, along with Ursula, into the corridor. The motion was not always easy to predict, so Ursula spread her knees to maintain her balance. Then the trolley came to a sudden halt.

"What's this?" Ursula recognised the rough voice as the man who had tied her to the bed.

"Last night's dinner. I just delivered their breakfast. Gonna be cold by the time they finish fooling around in the bathroom, but that ain't my problem. Can I go now? My shift ends at six."

"Yeah, go. Wait! Give me those."

"What? The burger buns?"

"Yeah, and the fries."

"Take whatever you want."

The trolley moved along carpeted floors and into an elevator. Once the doors closed, Macy spoke as if talking to herself. "Kitchen waste to the galley, laundry to the washroom and one last trip to drop trash onto the quay and I'm done. You know what? I'mma do the garbage run first, while it's still quiet out there."

The doors opened to a similar space where Ursula had first been held. Except this room was filled with grey plastic sacks. It stank to high heaven. Macy pulled up the tablecloth and beckoned Ursula out, pointing to a wheeled contraption.

"Stack that dolly with trash bags and push it down the gangplank. Throw them into the second dumpster along the quay, then turn right and walk on out of here. Keep your cap low and look like you don't take no shit. No one gonna stop you when you wearing this uniform."

"You are my guardian angel. Please take this with my thanks." She peeled off a wad from Berto's roll of notes.

Macy eyed the money. "I won't say no. You take good care, lady." She backed away into the elevator, with a grin. "Pretty smart."

Ursula heaved sack after sack onto the dolly, dragged the contraption to the gangplank and unclipped the chain. A young watchman dozing on the deck opened one eye and relaxed on seeing the uniform. She manoeuvred the awkward contraption onto the quay and pushed it towards the second dumpster, as instructed. Her levels of exhaustion were becoming critical, but one after another, she threw in all the refuse bags and closed the lid. Few people were around, but the port was clearly beginning to wake. She strode towards the exit with a nod to the gatekeeper and walked past the barrier and into the city.

A taxi rank was fewer than 100 metres away. With a lift of an imperious finger, she indicated she needed a ride. The question was, where to? Home was too risky and all her safe places were under suspicion. The driver wished her a good morning and asked for her destination.

"Da Gama Apartments, please."

She needed to know Noah had not been hurt at the Hotel Vermelhas Rosas. Plus he was the one person who could not have betrayed her. When she told the story about avenging her sister, the only people present were Shripal, Perneet and Xenia. Her mind returned to that lunch at Hotel Renascenca, her face still a mess from fighting off Vargas thugs, the fish thali, the surprise at Xenia's accent and ... her drooping eyes snapped open. There was one other surprise.

The man hiding behind the curtains. Shripal's apology. *Sorry, Ursula, but we couldn't be sure you were trustworthy. That's why I stationed my driver and bodyguard outside.*

Berto's loose lips confirmed it. *According to Manoj, you came all the way to Goa to avenge your sister.*

Manoj? The kindly driver who loaned her his Amitav Ghosh book? But if the driver was a spy, where did that leave his mistress? One thing was certain, Shripal should never set foot on *La Conquistadora* again. Ursula's brain was a mixture of feverish concern and near delirious exhaustion.

"Da Gama Apartments, madam."

She jerked awake, horrified she had fallen asleep in the back of a cab with a strange driver. She thrust too much money at the guy and simply bowed her thanks, for fear she would burst into tears. Inside the building, the receptionist was on the phone, so Ursula waved a hand to indicate she needed no help and pointed to the logo on her shirt. Then she made directly for Apartment 16.

It was before seven in the morning. When he didn't answer after the first press of the buzzer, she willed herself to be patient. She counted to twenty, then rang again. No answer. Despair threatened to overcome her when from along the corridor, she heard a rhythmic slapping sound, like wet feet in flip-flops. Ursula stood with her back to the door and reached into her pocket for the steak knife.

Wet, half-naked and very much alive, Noah Lloyd turned the corner.

"Little Bear!" His jaw dropped and he rushed to catch her, just as her knees gave way.

22

A gentle light filled the room, reminiscent of a late afternoon on the beach. In Portugal, she and Sal used to eat lunch, make love and nap during the midday heat, spooning together under a thin sheet. She could feel the weight of him now, his chest against her back, his thighs tucked behind her and his hand resting on her hip. Her eyes flickered open and she saw the bandage around her wrist. With dizzying speed, she returned to the present. Pain, fear and imminent danger sharpened her senses and she tensed, ready to defend herself.

"Hey, there. How you feeling?" Noah's voice was soft, close to her ear.

Tension eased and she addressed the question. Her wrists throbbed, a stinging sensation surrounded her waist, the cut on her cheek was painful and her face was sticky after drooling on the pillow. All things considered, she'd been better. However, she was still fully clothed.

"I need the bathroom."

"Right over there. You hungry? I can order us some lunch."

"What time is it?"

"Twenty after twelve. I was waiting till you woke up."

She rolled over to face him. "Have you been here all the time?"

His face, underneath the tan and teeth, was filled with concern. "Pretty much. You looked after me when I needed it, so I owed you, Little Bear. This is payback. Are you ready to talk about what happened? Those guys were terrifying. I've never been so scared in my life."

Ursula sat up and looked out of the window. "Give me a minute to freshen up. Order us some fish, I don't care what kind. So long as it doesn't come with fries."

They ate fish and seafood skewers on a bed of rice. Noah made several attempts to start a conversation, but Ursula simply didn't have the energy. When she finished her meal, she drained her glass of water and got up to leave.

"Noah, listen to me. This is a serious situation and I'm not sure who I can trust. I don't want anyone to know I'm here. Anyone at all, you must promise me. I will contact you again as soon as I know what's going on. Sorry, I have to go now."

Noah's eyes were wide. "You're freaking me out, Little Bear."

"Deal with it. I don't have time for your issues. Are you going to be useful, Noah, or make this into a personal drama? I appreciate all you've done but I have more important things to do than pander to your ego. I need a change of clothes, a phone and someone I know is on my side."

He folded his arms and frowned. "After all I've done for you? I'd say I've helped you out to the extent of risking my life. Are people only here to serve you, Ursula?"

"Look in the mirror and ask yourself that question, Mr Lloyd. Being disposable is no fun, is it? I'm out of here. Thanks for lunch."

She patted her pockets to reassure herself she still had cash, and reached for the door handle.

"Ursula?"

"What?"

"Whatever you're fighting, I am on your side. Dunno what side that is and if I'm honest, I'm way out of my depth. I just want to say, I'm here for you. Even if that's likely to get me killed."

Ursula's anger fizzled into nothing. "You know the one thing that worried me most when those assholes snatched me? Not my own safety, because I can handle myself. I was terrified on your behalf. I shouldn't have got you involved and I apologise." She sat on the bed. "What happened? I mean, how did you get away?"

"I couldn't tell you, exactly. I was kinda out of it. A bunch of people were yelling and the security man picked me up in a fireman's lift. Then the police came. He dropped me on my shoulder and ran. I spent half the evening at the police station, but couldn't tell them much. How about you?"

The less Noah knew, the better. "They took me onto their boat, but I managed to give them the slip by stealing a crew uniform. Who did you speak to at the police station?"

Noah frowned in concentration. "I don't recall. But he gave me his card. Wait a sec. Here it is: Superintendent Cruz Biswas. That's one helluva name."

"He's one helluva man. And just the person I need to talk to. Listen, I have to make some enquiries but I can't run the risk of being recognised. I want you to go to the market and buy me a sari. Ask the women to help you get all the elements of the outfit and say it's for your girlfriend back home. Here's some cash. Can you do that for me?"

"Sure. You want me to pick up some make-up too?"

"Good idea." She gave him a sincere smile and he softened. She turned away before he could move in for a hug. "Thank you."

At three o'clock on the dot, Ursula entered the Old Goa Police Headquarters. With an imperious tone, she gave her name as Mumtaz Singh, a name she'd seen on a nearby doorbell, and insisted on seeing Superintendent Biswas. In a confidential tone, she said she had some information on the whereabouts of Ursula Brown. Ten minutes passed before a junior officer escorted her to an interview room, where she spent another twenty minutes studying the walls until the door opened.

Cruz Biswas was impressive enough in the grand surroundings of Denzil's home. In this tiny room, he practically filled the space.

"Good afternoon, Mrs Singh. I understand you have some information for me on the subject of a missing person."

She pushed back her headscarf and looked into his eyes.

"Ursula? My God! Is that really you? Everyone has been so worried. Are you well?"

"A little worse for wear, but I'm OK, more or less."

"I can't apologise enough for what happened at the hotel. The police were supposed to protect you. Instead, they allowed you to get kidnapped by a bunch of gangsters."

"Don't blame your officers. I removed the wire myself. I couldn't take the risk of them finding it. Yes, in addition to what your people heard over the transmitter, I have further information on the Vargas clan. But before we get into that, I need some assurances. One, that you will act on what I tell you. Two, you will not ask too many questions about how I came by such information. Deal?"

He gave her a searching look. "Do I need to be concerned?"

"No, but you need to act fast. We only have a few hours. I ask again. Do we have a deal?"

He held out his hand. "Deal." They shook on it.

"Firstly, we have a mole in our operation. I believe Shripal's driver and bodyguard, Manoj, has been feeding information to the Vargas family."

"You have proof of that?" His brows knitted.

"I took three people into my confidence when I told my story: Perneet, Shripal and Xenia. I trusted them and I still do. What I didn't know was that Manoj was hiding on the balcony outside, on Shripal's orders. The Vargas family apparently knew my story and only one of the four people I just mentioned could have passed that information on. The matriarch and her daughter did not disclose their source, but Roberto Vargas, loose-tongued from whisky, mentioned Manoj. That makes me very worried for Shripal's safety."

In one fluid movement, Cruz got up, gestured to Ursula to wait and left the room. He was gone for over twenty minutes. Apart from the ticking clock, Ursula didn't mind. For the first time in fifteen hours, she had uninterrupted thinking time.

She dealt with her ego first. Manoj played the loyal, humble servant to perfection.

I would swear an oath that my driver is discreet.

His kindly manner and deferential respect encouraged her to confide in him. Only about the book club, yet still, he reinforced their private bond by loaning her his copy. She'd taken him at face value for two reasons: Shripal vouched for him and, far worse, Ursula assumed an employee was no threat. *Learn a lesson from that, lady.*

The second issue was the danger of making an accusation based on the mumblings of one drunken fool. If she was wrong, and she could be wildly off base, the chief of police was about to arrest an innocent man.

Point three: perhaps Manoj was merely the messenger, sent

by Shripal to deliver information. What if the three women she thought were on her side were in cahoots against her? In that case, Cruz Biswas was the last person in whom to confide.

She took three calming breaths, shutting out the irritating twinges from her wrists, midriff and cheek, and pulling herself away from the immediate situation. She imagined sitting in a room very similar to this, beside a fellow detective, second-guessing their targets.

Why would Shripal, Perneet and Xenia draw her into a plot to oust the Vargas family unless they meant it? Her mind spiralled away from the first meeting with Denzil to the dinner on Sunday. Either the family were exceptionally clever at deception or her instincts were correct.

Knuckles tapped on the door and Cruz re-entered. "Sorry to keep you waiting. I spoke to Shripal and warned her to stay at home. My officers will pick up Manoj for questioning. I suspect he's a low-level operator, but he may have information about the gang's operations."

"He's not the only one. Their yacht, *La Conquistadora*, docked in the harbour last night, sheltering from the storm. But she heads out again soon for a very important reason. There's a drugs drop tonight. This is your chance to catch Francesca Vargas red-handed."

"Just Francesca? I thought her mother and cousin were part of the plan." Cruz was watching her with the same level of scrutiny she would have used when interviewing a witness. She respected his professionalism.

"As we explained on Sunday, each family member is responsible for a different area of the family business. Francesca, or Frankie as she likes to be called, handles the drugs. Sure, her mother is the overall boss and Roberto is a key distributor as part of his 'entertainments' role. What you need is to catch someone flagrantly breaking Goan laws by importing large consignments of Class A narcotics. Superintendent, I'm handing you an opportunity on a silver platter – the chance to take out the kingpins and break their stranglehold on this region."

He placed his hands in a steeple grip and rested his chin on his forefingers. "So I should mobilise several armed marine police vessels to follow a luxury yacht on no other intelligence than your say-so?"

"Fair point." She assessed the situation from his perspective. "You have drones, right? Send them after *La Conquistadora* and note where she anchors. Have marine police on standby. Listen in on communications. When other vessels approach from out at sea, release your attack dogs. Police speedboats form a dragnet around the yacht and arrest delivery boats plus the owners of the yacht on suspicion of drug-trafficking. You'll need armed officers because these people won't go quietly. Leave the supply vessel well alone. Without military muscle, that's a suicide mission. Snatch the small fish and let the big one get away. For now. It's going to be quite a haul and likely to make headlines. The drop is scheduled for sunset. More than that, I don't know. Can I go now?"

He stood up, towering over her. "Naturally you can go and thank you for sharing your knowledge. Last thing, how to contact you. Where will you be and may I have a number?"

"I'll be at home. It's been a long day. My phone got lost when I was taken, but you can call my friend, Noah Lloyd." She scribbled Noah's number on the notepaper.

"I'll see if the team found your belongings."

"That's very thoughtful. Thank you for hearing me out, Superintendent. Good luck."

"Same to you, Ursula. You know something? You'd make an excellent cop."

She gave a weary laugh. "Once upon a time, I thought so too."

.   .   .

Noah had done as she asked and waited outside while she spoke to the police. He was lounging on a bench in the shade, relaxed and reassuring. He unfolded with a broad grin when he saw her emerge from the building.

On impulse, she reached a hand to his face and kissed him on the cheek. "Thank you for waiting for me. I'm all done here and ready for home. Do you have plans or would you like to come back to my place? I'd appreciate the company."

His eyes lit up. "Sure! That's be great. You want me to get a cab?"

"Would you? I'm worn out."

He lifted his head and raised an arm. A taxi driver across the street yelled, "Over here, mister!" but before they could even acknowledge him, another cab screeched to a halt at their feet. Noah opened the door like a gentleman. Ursula bundled up her skirts and got in, keeping her face veiled, and gave the driver her address.

When the battered Peugeot rattled up the dusty track to her house, it appeared unchanged. Noah paid the driver, and judging by the cabbie's effusive thanks, added a sizeable tip. At Ursula's request, he accompanied her around the property, examined the garage and followed her inside.

"Noah, could you make sure my bedroom is safe? I'll check the kitchen." It was a ruse to get him out of the way, because much as she hated the idea, she needed to retrieve the gun.

It was exactly where she'd left it, at the bottom of an over-sized golden vase. If she'd been wearing her usual jeans and T-shirt ensemble, there would be nowhere to conceal the piece, but a sari was full of hiding places. She didn't dare open the barrel to see if it was still loaded while Noah was in the house. Instead, she did as she had promised and scoured the kitchen, including the utility room, for any disturbances.

"All clear. Under the bed, inside the closets and outside the window. *Nada.* Guess you can relax now, huh? Want me to fix you a drink?"

"I'd love that. Maybe you could rustle up some snacks from the fridge. Mind if I go and change? Then we can watch the sunset together on the porch."

His grin spilt his face. "Go right ahead. I'll improvise."

In her bedroom, Ursula locked the door, unwound the sari and assessed her injuries. Both cuts on her wrists and the rope burn required attention. Her face itched, a sign it was already healing. Her shower sloughed off everything: make-up, sweat, stress and all the tensions of the last twenty-four hours. It was good to be home. She reapplied cream and bandages to her wounds, slipped into a loose linen dress, ignored the jewellery on her dressing-table, and stared at the firearm. Not since her days in the Metropolitan Police had she worn a gun holster, but times had changed. She had to make a choice – cop, or cop-out. In an act of surrender, she let her muscles go limp, collapsed onto the bed and closed her eyes.

Decision time. Her nemesis – the Osman-Vargas clan – was close to extinction. The Osmans were no longer an issue, having been totally wiped out by the turf war. The majority of the Vargas crew were in jail. This was the final stage, taking down the last three members of the family. In an ideal world, it should be legal and permanent. But the world was not ideal, which was why Berto was now 'sleeping with the fishes'. Francesca's casual cruelty in handing her over to Berto was typical. She expected her enemy to die an ignominious and painful death. Even so, Ursula didn't want to kill Francesca. That was too easy. That vile female deserved lifelong punishment for her horrific crimes. Finally there was Dolores, Queen Bee, Mama Bear and top of the shit pile. Still pulling the strings despite the loss of her sons and husband, still a moral vacuum. Ursula had met her face to face, brazened it out and escaped. Then she'd given all her intelligence to the police to finish the job.

Game over.

A voice in her head disagreed. *But* you *didn't finish the job, did you?*

Ursula was marshalling her arguments to defend her course of action when the doorbell rang. She grabbed her weapon and opened the bedroom door.

"You want me to get ... whoa!" On seeing Ursula's hand-gun, even though it was pointing at the ceiling, Noah raised his hands. She flicked her left hand at him, indicating he should hide in the kitchen. Then she heard voices. Loud, female, bossy voices she recognised.

"What did you expect me to do? Hire a helicopter?"

"Please be careful. Keep that basket level or it will leak."

"Bloody hell, Shripal, how much wine have you brought? We're not catering for a wedding!"

"Ring the bell again, she might be asleep."

The doorbell ding-donged twice. Ursula replaced the gun in the urn and opened the door.

"Hello, ladies. This is a nice surprise."

23

"Ursula! Thank God!"

"We were so worried, Ursula! Are you OK?"

"Mate, I'm so happy to see you! We thought those bastards had done you in!"

Ursula met Perneet's, Shripal's and Xenia's eyes with a grateful smile, but glanced over their shoulders at the people carrier.

Shripal caught the look. "Manoj is in police custody. I borrowed my uncle's staff for the afternoon. This is for you, from Cruz, with his compliments. Mumtaz, bring the food in now."

Ursula opened the paper bag to see her Furla handbag, phone, wallet, honeybee accessory and red lipstick all intact.

Two staff members in uniform carried a large tray loaded with various tiffin tins and paper bags to the porch under Shripal's supervision. "Leave it there, thank you. I'll call you when we are ready to depart."

Ursula stood back to let the three women carry in enough food and wine for a banquet. It was not as if she had a choice.

They talked constantly, asking questions they didn't wait to hear answered. While trying to answer three queries at once, Ursula cleared the table. A scream came from the kitchen.

Xenia ran out, slamming the door behind her. "There's a man hiding in there!" she gasped.

"Yeah, I know. Noah, come on out here and meet my friends."

The door opened and Noah emerged, trying not to look nervous.

"May I introduce you to Perneet, Shripal and Xenia? I'm working with these women to rid Goa of the Vargas family stranglehold. Ladies, this is Noah Lloyd, who I mentioned the other evening. He was supporting my pitch to Francesca and Berto. Unfortunately, they drugged him and snatched me. We were lucky to escape unscathed."

Perneet was gracious, placing her hands together and bowing. "A pleasure to meet you, Noah, and I am glad you are unhurt."

"Hello, Noah. I think you met my father, Denzil Fernandes." Xenia held out a hand for him to shake. "Sounds like your first few experiences of Goa have been disappointing."

"The pleasure is mine. Thank you for the welcome and please pass on my warmest regards to your father. Goa has been eventful, that much is true." He turned to Shripal. "Are you also a daughter of Denzil's? I see a family resemblance."

"I'm his niece. Welcome back and thank you for trying to help us."

Noah glanced at Ursula. She was about to offer a truncated version of their mission, but Shripal's phone rang. Everyone fell silent while she listened and said just one word. "OK."

She ended the call and her eyes shone. "That was Cruz. It's on! The police operation has already begun. We have to hurry. Xenia, plates and cutlery! Noah, find more chairs for the deck.

Do you have any binoculars, Ursula? I brought mine and my uncle's plus Xenia has a great zoom lens on her camera. Noah, see if you can find a corkscrew and open these wines. Glasses, Perneet? Maybe napkins too."

Everyone scurried around obediently without questioning Shripal's orders.

"Wait, what's the rush?" asked Ursula. "We won't hear anything about the police op until tomorrow at the earliest. Or is Cruz going to deliver live updates?"

Shripal frowned in confusion. "Cruz told me you were on the Vargas yacht last night."

"Yes, I was."

"So you know where it anchors."

"Not exactly, no. They took me out there on a smaller boat, but I couldn't see much. Then after that storm hit, we sailed back to port. I couldn't have escaped otherwise."

Shripal took her by the arm and steered her outside. "They usually choose a spot between Ilha Grande and the coast. Cruz and his team have pinpointed their location to about four kilometres west of Cansaulim." She tilted her phone like a compass, narrowed her eyes and pointed to a vessel in the bay. "There she is. *La Conquistadora*. That's where the action is going to happen and we have ringside seats."

"You thought we turned up with food, wine and flowers just because you're not dead?" Xenia asked, bringing a kitchen chair and an armful of cushions onto the deck. "Nah, we just want a bloody good view."

"I didn't see any flowers," Ursula deadpanned.

"Perneet! What did you do with that bouquet?"

The older woman stepped onto the deck with a package wrapped in tissue paper and a vase containing a fabulous display of exotic red blooms. "Here it is. Ursula, you looked so beautiful in that red-gold sari, I want to give it to you as a present. The flowers came from a wholesale merchant who remembers you well. I thought the colours were appropriate. Red, yellow and orange – to represent your fiery energy."

"Perneet, what a lovely gesture! I'm touched."

"Yes, yes, so are we all." Shripal clapped her hands together." Come on, let's fill our plates and glasses then sit down to watch the action. The sun is setting, people! Noah, where's that corkscrew?"

In a flurry of activity, they helped themselves to food and wine, settled into chairs and began to eat. Ursula took her binoculars from the living-room drawer and they lined up like ladies at Ascot. The only one at a disadvantage was Noah.

"We can share," said Ursula. "I don't want you to miss out."

"Use your phone, man!" Xenia gesticulated with her fork. "Don't tell me a tech bro worth millions hasn't got a zoom facility. Do you want some of this naan?"

"Ssh!" hissed Shripal. "Turn the lights out. I can see boats coming inwards. That's clearly the drug delivery so where the hell are the police?"

Noah got up to turn off the indoor lights as the sun sank below the horizon with a display similar to Ursula's flower bouquet. Everyone leant forward, looking through their own devices. *La Conquistadora* was only partially lit, upper decks dim and only navigational illuminations below: the opposite of a party yacht.

"The police are more than likely in four locations," said Ursula. "Somewhere close to this beach, hiding behind a nearby yacht, docked in Ilha Grande and further out at sea. When they are sure the cargo is transferred, two police boats will intercept the delivery boats and two to three others will surround *La Conquistadora*. They will not flag their presence until the target is surrounded. My best guess is they already have drones monitoring movements and are definitely intercepting communications."

Four heads removed their devices from their eyes and turned to her.

She shrugged. "Like I said, my sister used to be a cop." She reached for her glass of wine and froze at the sound of a helicopter. It flew low over her house, blades whipping above their heads, directing its searchlight out to sea. At once, everyone understood this was a major law enforcement operation. No one uttered a word.

In the bay, powerful beams hit the dock of *La Conquistadora*, catching two smaller vessels *in flagrante*. Through the binoculars Ursula watched police boats approaching, two aft and one fore. The helicopter circled, intimidating and inescapable. Further out to sea, three more patrol crafts flashed warning lights. The net was tightening.

For several minutes, nothing happened. Ursula assumed the police were negotiating with the crew. Shripal topped up each person's glass. The sun slipped below the horizon and the sky turned from plum to indigo. Sunset into twilight.

"They're boarding the yacht," said Xenia, her whole body stretching forward, with binoculars to her eyes. "Cops going in for the kill. Check this out!"

The helicopter flew lower, police scrambled onto the aft access deck and swarmed over the yacht. From what Ursula could see, an altercation erupted on the upper level. That was exactly the spot Francesca and Dolores had held her, injected her with a truth serum and consigned her to death. At this distance, figures were indistinguishable, but there was no doubt the combatants meant harm.

Gunshots rang across the water. All activity on the top deck ceased. The helicopter flew out to sea and all the police vessels clustered around *La Conquistadora*.

"What now?" asked Xenia.

No one had an answer. They sat in silence, watching blue flashing lights for a few minutes. This stage of a police operation was painstakingly slow. Evidence must be collected, arrests processed and the scene secured. It would take hours.

Ursula was worn out and yearning for solitude. "Why don't we wind things up for the night and wait for Cruz to give us the lowdown? You lovely people have truly lifted my spirits, but after the last few days, all I need is sleep."

"Of course you do."

"Yes, that's for the best."

"I'll message you all the moment I hear from Cruz."

Her guests leapt into action, clearing plates, emptying wine glasses and replacing everything in trays. Shripal called her staff and within twenty minutes, her house was close enough to normal. She thanked them all on the porch and noted the cows were already settled down for the night, eyeing them with equanimity.

Xenia made a point of offering Noah a lift home.

"That's OK, thanks. I'd like a word with Ursula before I leave. It's no problem to take a cab."

"If you're sure?" Xenia looked to Ursula for confirmation.

"Yeah, I owe Noah an explanation for all this." She waved a hand towards the bay. "I really appreciate your being here tonight, ladies. It means a lot."

"You are welcome. We'll talk tomorrow."

"Get some rest. My advice is a cup of Nilgiri before bed."

"Goodnight, Ursula, goodnight, Noah. Thanks for the entertainment."

They waved them off down the drive and Ursula chose to confront the situation head-on.

"I meant what I said about owing you an explanation. But that's all I owe you. We'll have a cup of tea, put our cards on the table and then you have to leave. Understood?"

He paused for a moment, watching the tail lights of Shripal's vehicle merge into the traffic below. "Understood. But I have a whole lot of questions. This is gonna take a while."

Ursula shook her head. "I doubt that. Let's go inside, we're disturbing the cows."

That made him move.

She went into the kitchen to make tea and he leaned against the door jamb. It made her uncomfortable for two reasons. First, he was blocking her escape route. Second, following her into the kitchen assumed a familiarity they didn't share.

"You can go sit on the deck," she suggested. "I won't be a minute. Who knows, there might have been developments."

"Maybe, but I wouldn't recognise them. You got any milk?" He opened her fridge.

She put down the teapot, walked across the room and closed the fridge door. "It might be common practice in the US to treat other people's kitchens like your own, but not here. Go and sit on the deck, please. I will bring tea and milk in a moment."

He backed away, shaking his head like Kirkland.

Ursula crossed her eyes and did a sotto voce imitation. *I'm not angry, just disappointed.*

When she brought the tea tray, he was sitting with his arms folded, jaw jutting. She ignored the sulk, placed the tray on the table and picked up her binoculars. The scene in the bay seemed the same from a distance, but when she zoomed in she could see officers taking people off the boat, some in handcuffs.

"Good job, Cruz," she muttered. "Alright, Noah, let's cut to the chase and you can leave. How about I give you the short version? It won't take longer than a cup of tea."

He stared at her sideways with a quizzical expression, as if she was vaguely familiar. "I wonder who hurt you."

She groaned and clapped a hand over her face. "Sweet suffering shite, don't start with the psychoanalysis. Spare me that."

"All I want is to understand, Little Bear. I returned to Goa with one aim, to tell you I loved you. You are my soul mate and I laid that on the line from day one. Since them you've rejected me, used me as a stooge, almost got me killed and strung me along when I'm useful. Then you go into your room to change into something comfortable and come out waving a gun. Somebody in your past must have hurt you pretty badly for you to treat others this way."

Ursula took three calming breaths and poured the tea. "Hopefully you've not consumed too much wine tonight because I want you to remember what I have to say. This is NOT all about you, Noah Lloyd. I apologise for taking you to Hotel Rosas Vermelhas. I knew the dangers. You did not. That said, I believe I expressed it as a business proposition and not our engagement party. I certainly did not encourage you to think of me in a romantic sense. When I escaped a dangerous situation, I came to you as a friend and safe space. If that puts me in your debt, I'll buy you dinner, take you kite-surfing or teach you how to make a decent caipirinha as payback. As for your declaration of love, seriously? You don't have the faintest clue who I am and if you did, you wouldn't like it. You're in love with an idea of a woman who never existed. Soul mate? Don't be absurd. As for moving to Goa, I'd advise against. Here's why."

She blew on her tea and took a sip. "That yacht down there belongs to the Vargas family, an international mob which took a major hit a few years back. They came to Goa thinking they had enough money, reputation and lack of morality to infiltrate all criminal activity in the whole state. Turns out they're wrong and we can see that playing out in real time. I'm here because the Vargas family killed my sister. She was an undercover police officer who helped root out that festering sack of vermin. But a couple of those nasty bastards wriggled free of the net. That's why I came to India. To make sure not one single member of that corrupt bunch of profiteers remains at large. Unless they're imprisoned or dead, my work is not yet done. More tea?"

Noah shook his head for a long time. She got bored of his theatrics and went inside to call a cab to take him home. When she came outside, his face was in his hands.

"Your taxi will be here in ten minutes. Sure you don't want more tea?"

He didn't look up. "Nuh-uh. It tastes weird. Who *are* you, Ursula?"

"I'm afraid that's none of your business. No hard feelings, it's just a question of survival."

"How do you mean?" He looked up, his eyes red and mouth pouty. "I don't buy the international woman of mystery shtick. You got attack cows, a bunch of suspect friends, a gun you keep by the door and a whole lotta intelligence on me and my friends. What's the angle?"

Two police boats sped away towards Panajii, presumably taking the prisoners into custody.

"If I may repeat myself, it is not all about you. I came here for my own reasons, you for yours. Our paths crossed and as far as I was concerned, once that was over, we had no need to see each other again. You returned of your own volition and inserted yourself into my world, a world that has nothing to do with you. I'm grateful for your help and have apologised for putting you at risk. There's nothing more to say other than goodbye and good luck." She stood up, willing the taxi to arrive.

He started the head-shaking thing again. "I'm disappointed, I gotta say. I thought you were authentic, you know, the real thing. That's what attracted me to you. Authenticity. To me, it seemed you had principles and stuck to them. Turns out it was all an act. One thing I hate is a fake."

Headlights washed across the ceiling.

Ursula opened the front door. "In that case, best hurry back to Silicon Valley. Your taxi's here. Thanks for everything and have a safe journey home. Bye, Noah, and best of luck."

She opted not to do the long wave goodbye from the porch, but returned inside, locked up, switched off her phone and went to bed.

24

Untroubled by her conscience, Ursula slept long and deeply, waking to bright sunshine and eleven voicemails. Before tackling them, she made coffee and took it onto the deck along with her binoculars. *La Conquistadora* had gone, leaving the bay populated only by fishing boats and local pleasure cruisers. She inhaled, filling her lungs with the scents of the morning then opened her phone and pressed PLAY.

Hello, Ursula, this is Superintendent Cruz Biswas. The reason for my call is to express gratitude for your information. We interviewed Manoj Pai and found him to be an informant. As such, he is a danger to my sister-in-law and has been dismissed. Thanks to your intelligence, we intercepted a delivery of Class A drugs yesterday evening and apprehended both the suppliers and receivers. The operation went smoothly considering the last-minute preparations, all perpetrators were arrested and vessels impounded. Unfortunately there were two casualties. If it is convenient, I would very much to talk to you at some point this afternoon. A few questions are outstanding and I believe you could help. Thank you.

The next three were from Shripal. *Oh my God, are you*

watching the news? They caught the whole lot. The Vargas people, the supply boats and even the ship they sailed from. No way can the Vargas family survive this.

Sorry, Ursula, it's Shripal again. I just spoke to Cruz. They seized cocaine, heroin, ketamine and I think he said meow meow, but maybe I misheard. For Cruz, this is an incredible coup. He'll be making a statement in the morning. Call me as soon as you wake up.

Oh my God! I just got word that Frankie is dead! She opened fire on the police and an armed member of Cruz's team shot her in the neck. That's not all. Berto is missing. I'm trying to find out how but I'm going to need more coffee.

Talking of coffee, Ursula finished hers and went inside for a refill. Francesca caught in the line of fire was very good news. Too good to be true?

Hi, Ursula, it's Xenia. It's stupid o'clock and you're probably asleep like a normal person. Just wanted to say, good job, mate! You nailed it. Also, what's going on with you and Noah?

The next three messages had nothing to do with the drugs bust and everything to do with Xenia's question.

Little Bear, I can't sleep for thinking about you. I hate how we left things. You were so cold and dismissive towards me but I'm guessing that's self-preservation. You're scared of vulnerability. Well, newsflash, I'm not. Not anymore. I poured my heart out and lay my dreams beneath your feet. Sleep well and tread softly.

Sorry, one last thing. I guess I rushed you a little. You said I don't know who you are. True. But I want to. That takes time and I have a well of patience.

"Oh, for crying out loud, Noah, will you ever get the message?" She realised she was shouting at an inanimate device and pressed PLAY while gritting her teeth.

Goodnight, Little Bear. You'll be in my dreams. See you in the morning.

"Not if I see you first," she growled.

Good morning, Ms Brown. Denzil here. I am calling to offer my most sincere and heartfelt congratulations. I suggest arranging a celebratory party for everyone involved on Friday. I will host it at my home and make everything perfect. Top-class catering, staff and champagne are on me. All I need from you is a guest list. Well done, Ursula. I'm so very proud of you.

Ursula started to shake her head until she realised she looked like Noah.

The last message was from the same number as the first. The Superintendent of Police.

Hello, Ursula, this is Superintendent Cruz Biswas. The reason for my call is to request a favour. I am well aware of your connection with a certain family and I must ask you to say nothing to any one of them until you have spoken to me. A car will collect you at ten.

Ursula jumped, splashing hot coffee over her hand. *I am well aware of your connection with a certain family?*

She spoke aloud. "He means the family Fernandes, you idiot."

It was twenty past nine. Ursula abandoned the coffee and got into the shower. By the time the car arrived, she was dressed in palazzo pants and a loose shirt, both the colour of sand.

Cruz presented a very different image to the first time she'd met him. His shirt had sweat stains, his chin was stubbly and the skin around his eyes looked ashen and lined. He offered her coffee but with that morning's track record and the colour of her clothes, she asked for water.

He poured himself a large cup, black. His eyes, when he fixed his gaze on hers, were similar. "I'm going to ask you to swear an oath. This is not a court of law, but I'd like you to treat it as one." He produced a small leather-bound Bible from under his desk and placed a laminated card beside it. "Will you swear?"

"Of course." She placed her left hand on the book, held up the right as if answering roll call and read the words on the card. "I do solemnly swear in the name of God that what I state shall be the truth, the whole truth, and nothing but the truth."

"Thank you." He removed both objects and rested his fore-arms on the table. "What happened to Roberto Vargas?"

"I don't know." It was far from the first time she'd been interrogated by a senior police officer and not the first time she'd lied under oath. The trick was to stay as close to the truth as possible and answer with complete conviction.

"You were the last person to see him, according to the crew. What happened?"

She took a sip of water and looked him in the eye. "Dolores Vargas injected me with sodium thiopental to force me to tell the truth. Turned out the truth wasn't to her taste. Hence this." She pointed to her cheek. "The old lady can deliver quite a backhander. She wanted to have me killed but Francesca, never one to resist a little casual sadism, suggested me as a plaything for Berto. A deckhand took me to his cabin and tied me to the bed to await his arrival. Hence these." She pulled back her cuffs to show her cuts from the plastic ties and bruises from the rope.

"Where was Roberto at that time?"

"Still ashore, I believe. Francesca mentioned he was due shortly, but why he wasn't on the yacht with them, I have no idea."

"And then?"

"And then the weather started to get a little wild. Berto came into the room, drunk as a skunk and told me what he planned to do. When he'd finished, he would kick me out so the crew could have some fun. I pleaded with him to let me go. He laughed and said he knew who I really was. That's when he mentioned Manoj. He found it hilarious that I came to avenge my sister only to receive the punishment she deserved. He sat on the bed and began to undress. I tried to keep him talking, to delay the inevitable, but the movements of the ship seemed to make him nauseous. He puked all over himself and the duvet, then slid onto the floor. The smell was disgusting. After that, there was nothing, so I guessed he'd fallen asleep."

Cruz was making notes. "I'm also interested in your sister but that conversation can wait. What happened to Roberto?"

Ursula looked at her wrists again. "As I said, Dolores injected me with a relaxant. When that guy first tied me up, I fell asleep. Only when the ship started to roll and Berto came in with his pornographic fantasies did I start to sober up. The deckhand had tied my hands but not my legs. I pushed myself up by my heels and used my teeth on the plastic. It was agony to stretch my back and neck for so long, but I gnawed through one tie. Then I could release the other. The storm was ferocious and the stink was foul. I opened the balcony doors and rolled Berto onto the deck, throwing the duvet after him. My only plan was how to get out."

"What time was that?"

"Twelve forty-five. I remember seeing the clock."

Cruz pressed his fingers to his temples. "How come Roberto Vargas ordered two burgers and a bottle of wine at half past one if he was passed out on the balcony?"

"He didn't. That was me. I figured that so long as the crew thought he was still ..."

"Alive?"

"Awake. So long as the crew thought he was still awake, they wouldn't come into the cabin. That's why I ordered two burgers on his behalf." She shrugged. "In any case, I was hungry."

Cruz rasped his nails against his stubble. "You have quite an appetite. Two burgers at quarter to two and then a tomato, cheese and ham omelette at half past five. Did you see any movement on the balcony at all?"

"I closed the curtains." Ursula tried to look shamefaced. "But I didn't lock the door. If he'd woken up, he could have come inside anytime he wanted. The breakfast was a ruse. I played a porn film on the bathroom TV to make the maid think we were still at it. I asked her to take the dinner trolley and told her there was some dirty laundry on the bottom shelf. In fact, that's where I hid. I waited till until she had taken it below decks to sneak out. I stole a uniform, took out the trash and walked out of the harbour. Where Berto is now, I couldn't tell you." She kept her gaze level while massaging her left wrist.

"Did you kill him, Ursula?" Cruz studied her from under heavy brows.

"How could I have killed him? The guy weighs twice as much as me and I had no weapon. What, you think I'm capable of killing a man with my bare hands? Seriously?"

Not exactly a lie.

"I'm not sure what you're capable of, but I do know under-estimating you would be a grave error. Processing this drugs bust is going to take considerable time, especially with press interest, meaning I'm busier than usual for a few days. Can I kindly request you return here on Monday for further ques-tions? Please don't go anywhere."

She bit her lip. "I can't go anywhere? But Denzil is throwing a party at his place tomorrow night, celebrating our victory. Do I have your permission to attend?"

"Am I invited?" He cracked the first smile of their encounter.

"You would be the guest of honour. Yes, of course I'll come back on Monday to answer any questions. Thank you for your faith in me, Superintendent. I hope you can get some rest now."

"Me too. I have to look my best at the press conference. See you tomorrow."

"One last thing before I leave. Dolores Vargas. Is she under arrest?"

"No, she will be released later today. She claims to be elderly and infirm, unaware of what her daughter and nephew were doing."

"And you believe her?"

"Unless I have proof of her involvement, I have no choice but to let her go. My officer will see you out."

The heat on the street hit her like the blast of a hairdryer. She rebuffed all the eager taxi drivers and walked a couple of blocks in the direction of the shopping area, by which time she was sweaty and flushed. Normally a street café with an umbrella would have sufficed. Not today. For some reason, she required another layer of protection. One had to pay three times the price for a cold drink on a hotel terrace, but it was worth it to sit anonymously in a shady garden.

Her calm demeanour as she sipped iced cucumber water gave no hint of her inner turmoil. Get out of Goa, ideally today. Her job was done. The Vargas family, with one exception, were all dead. The matriarch was powerless. No celebratory parties, no lovelorn Californians, no police superintendents, just a quiet departure with no regrets. One last trip to Nostromo to collect the essentials and she could leave that afternoon. She was making a mental list of what to pack when her phone vibrated.

"Ursula, where are you? I'm at your place and there's no one here."

"I'm in Panajii, Xenia, just left the police station. What's up?"

"What's up! We've got a ton of stuff to talk about. You

want to have lunch? Shripal and Perneet are still out for the count and I can't blame them. Which police station? Have you spoken to Cruz? Hold up, there's a Jeep coming up the drive. Maybe it's your boyfriend ... oh shit!"

Ursula could hear nothing but muffled shouting and then everything went silent.

"Xenia! Xenia! Talk to me!"

Nothing. Ursula flung some cash on the table and ran through the lobby into the street.

For the first time since she'd arrived in Goa, there was not a single cab in sight. She sprinted up the street, yelling 'Taxi' at the top of her voice. When she turned the corner, she saw three taxis at the rank while their drivers drank tea and smoked at a roadside stall. She hurtled towards the first vehicle in line.

"Emergency! We have to go now!"

A young man dropped his cigarette and raced into the driver's seat.

"Where do you want to go, lady?"

She gave him the address and exhorted him to hurry. "Any speeding fines, I'll pay. But I have to get there fast. My friend is in trouble."

"No problem, lady, I'll get you there in a jiffy."

As he careered through the streets, blasting on his horn more or less constantly, she tried Xenia's number. An electronic voice repeated the message that number was unavailable.

Just as she spotted her house from the main road, a bus stopped to disgorge its passengers, forcing them to wait. Ursula's frustration built into a barely suppressed scream. Finally the cabbie tore up the track like a rally driver and pulled up in front of her house. She could see no one on the porch.

"Wait a moment, please." She got out of the car and walked to the front door, with a skin-crawling feeling. Halfway to the house she spotted Xenia's phone, crushed as if under a tyre. A blood splatter patterned the sand like a Rorschach test, still liquid in places but drying rapidly in the heat. She ran around the house, cautious as she rounded each corner, until she was sure no one remained outside the property. Then she paid and thanked the taxi driver.

"What about your friend, lady?"

"She's not here. Thanks for all your help. Bye-bye."

Once he'd driven off, she went inside, checking every room including the garage for unwanted visitors. Then she tore off her sweaty clothes, changed into jogging gear and poured a glass of water to make a decision. Call Cruz and report Xenia missing? That would be the most logical step. Or consult Denzil to make an educated guess as to who had taken her? One question buzzed around her brain: why Xenia?

Panic and fear for her friend was not helpful when applying logical thinking. She stared out at the waves and breathed, watching the gulls glide, dive and swoop above the ocean. Like a flash of sunlight on the water, Ursula realised. Whoever it was had not taken Xenia. Those lumpen idiots had come to Ursula's house, found someone who looked similar and snatched the wrong woman.

She went inside, looking for her mobile to call Cruz. Poor man. Yet another drama triggered by Ursula Brown. The phone was already ringing, with the number unknown.

"Hello?"

"There you are." Those rasping tones chilled Ursula's skin. "What kind of woman sets up a stooge to be kidnapped in her stead? You truly have no sense of sisterhood."

The reverse victim and offender tactic was nothing new but to hear such a blatant attack from a notorious bully left Ursula open-mouthed.

"This girl claims to be the daughter of Denzil Fernandes, but dresses and speaks exactly like Ursula Brown. Copycat behaviour is unhealthy. You should watch yourself."

Ursula chose her words carefully, giving nothing to Dolores, not even Xenia's name. "Yes, I should have learned that lesson a long time ago. The girl was in the wrong place at the wrong time. Your people came here for me. Let's switch. I offer myself in exchange for her."

The matriarch let the silence stretch out for a long time. "We can arrange that. One thing, if you involve your little friends, the police or any other person, neither of you will make it to the weekend."

"I understand. This is between you and me. Where do you want to meet?"

"I'll let you know." She rang off, leaving Ursula in limbo.

Obligations and responsibilities clashed in her conscience, exacerbated by terror for Xenia. Her thinking was frantic and muddled, exactly the kind of mind-set where she would make a mistake. She needed to go for a run. Her mental energy always fired after physical exertions. In this heat, running was out of the question, she'd collapse in a matter of minutes. So she swam. Powering up and down along the beach, she sloughed off everything and refocused.

An hour ago, she had seriously considered yet another cut and run. Now she judged that behaviour as despicable. Throughout her life, she had never left a job unfinished. This was her chance to obliterate the Vargas family forever. Xenia was a relatively innocent victim and certainly did not deserve to suffer at the hands of Dolores.

She swam further out to sea, filled her lungs and dived to the cooler depths. Each time her lungs were about to burst, she kicked towards the surface, trusting her body's survival instinct. The third time she floated on the surface, gazing into the infinite blue. A seagull crossed her sightline and squawked its plaintive shriek. She rolled over and used her front crawl to make for the shore. Her decision was clear. She had to face down her nemesis: Mama Bear versus Little Bear. Ursula's sacrifice meant the end of this violent, relentless vendetta.

Informing Cruz, Denzil or Shripal would put not only Xenia's life in danger but each of theirs. It was an insane risk to tackle the situation alone, that much was clear, yet she had to try.

Sopping wet when she emerged from the ocean and practically dry by the time she got back to the house, she had a cold core of certainty. One way or another, this was the endgame.

25

Hi, Denzil, and thanks for the message and your vote of confidence. The party is a great idea. Other than your family, Perneet, Cruz and Noah, maybe invite Sandeep from Palolem? Do you need my or Xenia's help in organising? If not, we plan to have lunch and go shopping. Neither of us has a thing to wear!

Lying to Denzil came harder than being economical with the truth to Cruz. Senhor Fernandes had a right to know his daughter had been kidnapped. Ursula was making exactly the same mistake as all relatives of kidnap victims. She used to warn them in no uncertain terms. *Don't try to fix this yourself. If you do, you put your loved one in worse danger.* She ignored her own advice while digging through her lockable suitcase to find the items she needed.

When she located what she was looking for, she filled the remaining space and the second suitcase with all her belongings. If things went to plan, she could leave tonight. In the worst-case scenario, at least her personal belongings were all neatly organised after her death.

"Hello, can I speak to Perneet, please?"

"Perneet is unavailable at the moment, madam. Can I take a message?"

"That's very kind of you. This is Ursula Brown. Could you please tell her that as we agreed, I am sending two bags to be stored in the garage. Someone will collect them later today."

"Ursula Brown, two bags in garage. I will give her the message."

Once she had put all her essentials in her rucksack, she called a cab to take the cases to The Blue Moon. Everything was ready.

She poured herself some juice and sat on the deck to think. Even though it was one of the most toxic environments imaginable, Ursula had to get into Dolores's head. How did she feel? The woman might lack any resemblance of empathy but right now, she was grieving. Francesca, her jewel, her beloved only daughter was dead. It must hurt. And when Dolores hurt, everyone suffered. She'd played the fragile old lady card with Cruz and got out of police custody, probably with the same request – don't go anywhere. That promise was as binding as wet tissue paper.

Then her first act was to come after Ursula. Why? To get answers about Berto? To avenge Francesca with an eye for an eye? Perhaps she had realised Ursula was actually Olivia, the woman who had deceived and jailed her sons, then brought down her whole family. Nope. None of this sat comfortably. If Dolores even suspected her true identity, she would have sent professionals to catch her unawares, not a bunch of amateurs roaring up in a Jeep to grab the wrong person.

It had to be simpler than that. The matriarch could do nothing about Berto's disappearance, the drugs bust or Francesca's death. The one thing she could ensure was the death sentence she decreed. *Tie her up and throw her in the sea. I never want to see her face again.* Dolores wanted to see her die and this time, she'd do it herself. The woman couldn't fight with her fists or even a knife, so she planned to shoot her enemy.

Ursula interlaced her fingers and stretched her arms above her head. "OK, Mama Bear, let's finish this thing. You against me. May the best woman win or die trying."

La Conquistadora was a floating crime scene and Dolores must be planning to sail into another jurisdiction as soon as possible. Assuming they hadn't already killed Xenia when they realised their mistake, she was a liability they'd want to offload fast. All they needed was to lure Ursula to a secure location and plan an escape route. Every indication pointed to today.

Ursula stood in her bedroom, studying the objects on her bed. One roomy white shirt bought in Hong Kong. One pair of three-quarter trousers and a belly-band holster, both in military green. Her loose duster coat with deep pockets. A fully loaded Beretta 92X thanks to Denzil. A custom-designed white ballistics vest, level NIJ IIIA, made in the Netherlands. One pair of ankle socks. One pair of sunglasses. Under the bed, her usual running shoes. Despite not knowing the battlefield, she intended to be fully armed. Which meant getting hold of a second gun. Perhaps she did need to go shopping after all.

The phone buzzed, ushering in a new level of guilt.

Go shopping with my blessing! Tell Xenia to use my account and get yourselves something lovely. Everything is already arranged and we're having cocktails at seven. Enjoy, girls!

She was about to send him a heart emoji when the phone buzzed again.

Your friend and I will be watching the sunset from 17.30 onwards at Grandmother's Hole. We hope you can join us. This invitation is for you alone.

A snort escaped Ursula's nostrils. Grandmother's Hole? It took a few seconds to locate the beach, an unusual site on a promontory past the airport. The only access was via 250 steps down from the Japanese Gardens. Rarely visited with few amenities and difficult to access, it was a classic example of hiding in plain sight. Dolores had chosen well.

She rode her Honda to the Japanese Gardens, a deliberate choice. It was by far the speediest getaway vehicle and in the unlikely event Xenia escaped without her, she could drive it home to Denzil. En route, she stopped to purchase a Sig Sauer P226 at the hardware store. Since she had no arms licence, it took a sob story about a dangerous ex-boyfriend and paying three times the going rate before he would part with it. Even then he refused to sell her ammunition. She didn't press the issue, because she had more than enough 9mm bullets for two guns. In a bathroom at a nearby café, she loaded the new weapon and placed it in her belly band next to the Beretta. She would have dearly liked to try out the Sig, but couldn't see a way of doing that without attracting attention.

Her penultimate stop was to buy some paan. Normally she avoided the betel leaf mix, mainly used as a mouth freshener and mild stimulant, but it had some other useful properties that might come in handy. She parked on the sandy street close to the entrance, and noted a couple dragging their child away in a hurry. It was not yet sunset so the place should have been popular, yet was strangely empty. It wasn't hard to guess what was going on. Dolores had sent her henchmen to clear the gardens, making certain there were no observers.

She took off her helmet, put on her sunglasses and scanned the area, first with eyes and ears, then pushing her conscious-ness outward. Her radar warned of danger and malevolent observers. She slipped gloved hands into her pockets and sat back as if killing time. When a couple of joggers had passed by, she withdrew her hands, slipped off her gloves and dropped them into her helmet, along with the bike keys and the Sig Sauer. With one last look around, she walked into the gardens, leaving the bike unlocked. She popped the paan into her mouth and followed the signs to the beach steps. The Japanese Gardens were rather a misnomer. More of an unkempt scruffy park, with post-storm detritus still littering the paths and a small children's playground, at least it lived up to expectations regarding the view. Of all the places to end one's life, this was one of the most picturesque. She stopped and recalibrated. This was the reason she had travelled five continents, reinvented herself with five names and ended the lives of at least three individuals. Everything in her life had led up to this moment. Time to finish the job.

The walk down to the beach seemed like a point of no return. Whatever occurred on those sands could never have a positive outcome. Someone had to die. The sun transformed from blistering ball of fire to golden magician, playing tricks with the heavens. Along the steps were various lookout points and photographic opportunities, all curiously empty. Ursula stopped at the first and stared out at the ocean. *La Conquistadora*, anchored out to sea, sat in the centre of her eye line, simultaneously beautiful and menacing.

As she watched, a smaller boat took off from the rear deck, looped away from the yacht and headed towards the coast. Ursula delayed no longer and jogged down the steps, keeping her movements loose and relaxed. Unsurprisingly, the beach was empty. She sat by the cliff, watching the launch draw closer. While trying to discern how many passengers were aboard, she recognised the vessel as the one which took her from the dock. Exactly as she'd hoped.

She got to her feet and walked down to the waterline, raising her hands in the air. The launch stopped just short of the beach, enabling Ursula to see who she was meeting. The ugly guy who tied her up and pinched her nipple was piloting the boat. Dolores sat under the canopy, wearing widow's weeds, one arm around Xenia and not in a comforting way.

The deckhand jumped off the boat, set an anchor and pulled out a walkway to reach the sand. Knee-deep in the surf, he offered a hand to Dolores. She waved him away, walking down the gangplank towards Ursula, her hand clasped around Xenia's wrist. Despite the sunglasses, the sun shone in Ursula's eyes, making it hard to judge Xenia's expression.

She said nothing, kept her hands up and waited for Mama Bear to make her move.

"Throw that away!" barked Dolores.

Ursula showed her open hands. "Throw what away? I have nothing."

"That helmet! Kick that out of here. I don't trust you."

Ursula crouched, one hand still aloft, picked up the helmet and lobbed it gently towards the steps. It landed with a puff around a metre away.

"I obeyed all your orders, Senhora Vargas. We agreed a switch. Let her go and you can do whatever you want with me."

"Let her go? When this is the only person who matters to you? You're so naïve." Dolores pulled Xenia closer, withdrew a gun and pressed it to the girl's temple.

Ursula pushed her sunglasses on top of her head and stared. "You're the naïve one, Dolores. Shoot her, shoot me, sail on out of here and best of luck to you. But then you'll never know the truth of who I really am."

Gulls cackled and squealed, like an ironic audience.

"We know who you are, you stupid cow. A calf to the slaughter. Your sister died in agony at the hands of my family, like the traitorous bitch she was. I have to admire your courage in coming all this way to take revenge. Close, but no cigar." Her voice was strident but her lies let her down.

The sun was setting, a colourful show for a limited audience because no one on Grandmother's Hole was paying attention.

"Don't you remember me, Mama Bear? Sweet little Zoe, the love of Milo's life?"

The matriarch's face sagged and she released Xenia, stumbling backwards. "You're not Zoe. Zoe's dead. She was a filthy spying cop and we had her killed. What the hell are you talking about?"

"Xenia, if you don't mind, this is a private conversation. Please leave us. My bike is outside the garden and my helmet is right over there. Goodbye and have a pleasant evening." Without waiting to see if the girl would go, Ursula continued. "Yes, Maria Dolores Consuela da Vargas, I may look a little different, but I am the same woman you knew as Zoe Jarvis."

The deckhand sat on the prow, slack-jawed as if watching a telenovela, making no move to intervene. A stumble from the steps told her Xenia was on her way to safety, but still within bullet range if Dolores chose to shoot. There was no doubt in Ursula's mind she was capable of such casual cruelty. How else could she overpower two younger, stronger women? Certainly not by relying on a single gormless henchman.

"Didn't Spencer mention he'd seen me? I thought he'd run squealing to you the second I left The Boar's Head. Silly old sod is still loyal to the family and told me jack shit."

"Spencer?" In an instant, Dolores looked her age.

"You remember Spencer, surely? The janitor of the Osman-Vargas operation who had to clean up your messes. Your husband removed one of his testicles."

Dolores stared, but it was clear she wasn't really looking. An internal reel of memory was playing in the woman's head.

Realisation on realisation hit Ursula like ripples from a stone. She kept her voice soft. "Oh, now I understand. Spencer couldn't let slip I'd popped into the pub and bought him a port and lemon, could he? Because he was part of the deception. They told you I was dead and you believed them. Who lied to you, Dolores? It couldn't have been any of your sons, since they were detained at Her Majesty's pleasure. Somebody further down the food chain, desperate for promotion, I reckon. Is that how Berto earned his place in the hierarchy?"

The sky turned from striated yellows and blues to a deeper uniform orange. Warm winds from the ocean lifted Ursula's hair. Dolores remained mute and the deckhand lit a cigarette as if listening to a fireside story.

"No, on second thoughts, Berto's nowhere near smart enough to fool Mama Bear. So the only one left is your darling Francesca. Your daughter convinced you I suffered a horrific death and vengeance had been served. Then she and her brothers spent years trying to make that actually happen. They even sent Uncle Jack. It didn't end well, I'm sorry to say."

"You bitch." The matriarch's tone was cold but concealed a ferocious spite.

"I'm afraid I can't accept that. My methods were sometimes questionable but I was acting out of a desire for justice. You, on the other hand, dropped all moral codes from the organisation, welcoming in prostitution, sex-trafficking and systemic abuse of employees. Is it any wonder your daughter followed in your footsteps, lying, deceiving and betraying other women? That includes her own mother. There's only one bitch on this beach, Mama Bear." She began taking one step at a time in reverse, baiting her to react.

It worked. Dolores drew a gun from her jacket and aimed it at Ursula. "This is for Milo," she called, clasping both hands around her weapon.

"Aim for the heart," Ursula replied. "Presuming you know where that is." She was braced and prepared, but the impact of the bullet knocked her off her feet and left her winded. She fell onto her backside, head forward and mouth open, allowing paan juice to spill onto her shirt.

This was the moment she feared the most. If Dolores chose to finish the job with a slug in her head, she had only one chance. She groaned, rattled her breath and coughed, opening her right eye a slit to watch her enemy. Dolores lifted her long black skirts and trudged up the beach, the barrel of her gun aimed directly at Ursula's neck.

Without warning, a shot punched into the shoreline between them, flicking sand and shells in a spurt upwards. Nobody moved. Then the deckhand yelled something and started the engine.

Delude these people into thinking you are no threat. Then, when they look away, you shoot them in the back.

Ursula collapsed onto her side, paan juice pouring from her slack jaw. Another shot thudded close to Dolores's feet. That was enough to convince the old woman. She holstered her gun, scrambled up the gangplank, huddled under the canopy and shouted at the deckhand to hurry.

The launch sped up, churning water in its wake. Ursula calculated how soon the vessel would be out of reach and counted down from ten. When she got to number three, she sat up, whipped out the Beretta, aimed at the oil drums and pulled the trigger twice.

Two balls of flame exploded, throwing a million tiny pieces into the air. The fire expanded, a sunburst of yellow, then contracted, billowing out banks of black and grey smoke. What remained of the boat was obscured by a blaze on the surface of the sea. As kills went, this one of her least environmentally friendly. But she had no time to sit and watch what she had ignited. She scrambled across the beach in a low run, heading to the steps. Disposing of Dolores was one thing but if her crew were loyal, they would be waiting somewhere on the ascent.

She climbed erratically, taking one pace at a time and then racing up six, hiding under an overhang, before setting off again. Sunset had no patience, allowing darkness to creep over the park. Even the blaze in the bay gave little illumination now the fire had dwindled to a few glowing pockets on the surface of the sea.

She was close to the garden entrance when a voice hissed from behind a boulder, "Get a shift on, will you? I don't plan to hang around until the police arrive. That's not really blood, is it?"

"Paan juice, that's all. Are you OK, Xenia? Did they hurt you?"

"Not in the slightest. Helps that I've got a loud mouth. You gonna drive or shall I?"

"You. Put the helmet on and I'll cling on to your back so as to hide the stains. Where are we going?"

"Dad's house. I heard there was a party going on."

At the Fernandes residence, Xenia spoke to the watchman at the gate and drove the Honda away from the party preparations in the garden. She parked behind an enormous hibiscus plant with yellow flowers.

"We can sneak along the veranda and get into my room this way," she said.

Ursula followed, the sound of a ticking clock in her ears. They crept past several windows until Xenia opened a side door. "In here."

The room was decorated in a similar style to the rest of the house, luxurious fabrics draped over the bed, beautiful rugs on the floor and ornately carved furniture polished to a shine.

"Right, why don't you use the shower first and I'll choose us both something to wear."

"Actually, Xenia, I'd prefer to get changed at home. Could I just borrow a T-shirt to ride home? Promise I won't take long."

"If you're sure." She opened a drawer and pulled out a dark purple top. "Here you go. The paan stains won't show through that."

"Thanks." Ursula unbuttoned her shirt and removed her ballistics vest.

"Ouch," said Xenia, when she saw the large red mark on Ursula's sternum. "You're going to have one hell of a bruise."

Ursula winced as she slipped on the T-shirt. "Yeah and it bloody well hurts." She picked up the shirt and vest. "Right, see you in about an hour."

"You're not coming back, are you?" Xenia sat on the bed, her expression serious and sad.

Ursula stopped, wishing they weren't having this conversation but perversely glad Xenia had twigged. "No, I'm not."

"Are you leaving us?"

"After what happened this afternoon, I have no choice." They both stared at the rug.

"Who are you, Ursula? You told that old witch you were called Zoe."

"Believe me when I say it's better you don't know."

Xenia sighed. "I understand. I don't like it but I understand. What'll I tell Dad?"

"That's up to you. I'm ashamed to admit I lied to him. I told him you and I were going shopping today because I couldn't risk getting anyone else involved. You can stick to that story, tell him the truth, or say something in between. But whatever you decide, please leave it as late as possible to give me time to get away. I'm already packed but I need to get a cab to the airport."

Xenia jumped to her feet and took a key fob from the dressing table. "Take my car. Leave the bike here and take my Hyundai. It's round the back. Park it at the airport and take a photo of where you left it. Lock it and take the key with you. I've got a spare. I can pick it up tomorrow."

"That means a lot to me." Ursula took the key and held out her arms for a hug.

Xenia squeezed her tightly and in a muffled voice, whispered, "I'm going to miss you."

"I'll miss you too. And Denzil and Shripal and Perneet, but you most of all." She broke the embrace and smiled. "Take care of Noah for me."

Xenia's expression brightened. "If you insist. It's a dirty job but someone's got to do it."

Voices came from the corridor and Xenia pointed to the veranda door. "Go out that way, turn left and mine's the red Hyundai. Good luck!"

Ursula grabbed her stuff, blew Xenia a kiss and ran. The car was exactly where she described, beside an SUV that obviously belonged to Denzil. The man was minted. Playing down his wealth, taking taxis and riding mopeds was all part of a calculated look, that much was clear.

Xenia's sunglasses were on the dashboard, so she put them on, loosened her hair and drove past the watchman with a cheery wave. A taxi was turning into the driveway. Ursula twisted away as if to check for traffic. She didn't see who was in the rear.

The ticking in her ears grew louder. It was Friday night and everyone was out to enjoy themselves, so the stop-start journey added one frustrating delay after another. When she finally arrived at The Blue Moon, it was already quarter to seven. Perneet should have already left for Denzil's party, so all she had to do was pick up her bags and adopt her disguise.

The girl at reception gave a sweet smile and showed her into the garage, where her bags were tucked unobtrusively against the wall. Ursula thanked her, wheeled them out and put them in the Hyundai. She'd just slammed the boot shut when Perneet appeared in the garage doorway.

"Hello, Ursula. I wondered when you would turn up."

"Hello, Perneet. You should be at Denzil's party."

"So should you." She beckoned Ursula inside. "I won't ask

where you're going or if you're coming back, but I will say you cannot walk through an airport looking like that. They have security cameras and whatnot. Come into my office. I will dress you in a top-quality sari so that everyone treats you with respect."

"Perneet, I don't have time."

"A woman always has time to look her best. Hurry now."

The church bells were striking seven-thirty when Perneet turned Ursula to the mirror. The transformation was complete. Her blouse was orange, the sari kingfisher blue with an ornate brocade border and light pallu. Perneet gave her an embellished headscarf and a soft peach-coloured pashmina, in case she got cold. Finally, she clasped her face and kissed her between the eyebrows.

"Go now, before they come looking."

Ursula bowed and kissed Perneet's hands. "Please give these to Xenia." She handed over her house keys. "Tell her she may want to redecorate. Goodbye and thank you for everything."

She resisted the urge to run, got into the car, and with a gracious wave left The Blue Moon for the last time.

The sari and headscarf worked their magic. She parked the car, photographed the parking place and sent it to Xenia. She was just getting her suitcases out of the car when an elderly Sikh porter came over to help, lifted her cases onto a baggage trolley. He wasn't wearing a uniform, but a turban, a scrappy grey beard, dusty sandals and dark sunglasses. Even though she must have been twenty years his junior, he addressed her as 'Auntie'. She followed his stooping form across the road towards the terminal, feeling in her purse for a tip. He parked the trolley outside the doors and she reached out to give him 50 rupees.

"Thank you, Ursula, but I can't take your money." He pulled off his glasses and looked at her with warm, familiar eyes.

"Manoj?" She took two paces backwards, assessing if he was accompanied by any other Vargas-employed goons.

"Yes. I couldn't let you leave without apologising. I betrayed you and in doing so, betrayed myself. I am truly and profoundly sorry for my actions."

"Hold up, how did you know where to find me? I'm a little jumpy right now and this is not making me feel any safer."

"You are perfectly safe. The watchman at the Fernandes house keeps me informed of comings and goings. I told him I was worried about you. He called me this evening to say you and Xenia had just arrived on your motorcycle. I came to the property in disguise in case the family recognised me. I am persona non grata in that household and rightly so. You drove away in Xenia's Hyundai and I followed you because it would be my last chance to beg your forgiveness."

She studied his face. "Ratting on me is one thing, but to betray Shripal, your employer who trusted you implicitly, is appalling."

"Had I done such a thing, I could never have asked for absolution. I never breathed a word to the Vargas people about Shripal, or Denzil, or Xenia. They pressured me and forced me to deliver information on the family, but I kept saying I was not privy to their activities. Then you turned up with a secret. To my shame, I saw a way of getting them off my back by telling them there was a stranger out for revenge. Believe me when I say I will regret that till my dying day."

"I trusted you."

"Yes, you did, and I let you down. When I think what might have happened ..."

"Best not. Well, thanks for the apology but the Vargas family are no longer my problem. It's over to the police now."

Manoj placed his hands together as if in prayer. "Thanks to you, the Vargas family are no longer anybody's problem. Goodbye, Ursula, and I wish you luck, happiness and long life." He bowed, replaced his sunglasses and strode away towards the car park.

She watched him go, then hurried to find her departure gate, taking the opportunity to throw her phone into a sanitary bin.

Once she was in a last-minute economy seat on the aircraft to Mumbai, some of the tension left her shoulders. She could not fully relax until she had left Indian soil, because the police might already be searching for the woman who blew up a boat off Grandmother's Hole. But thanks to Perneet's expert disguise, no one looked twice at a wealthy married lady. Gazing out at the coast of Goa as the plane took off, Ursula waved a discreet goodbye to everyone, including the cows.

The longest leg of her journey was a ten-hour flight from Mumbai to Paris. This time, she booked an Air France luxury private suite, the kind which deluded guests into thinking they were staying at the Georges V. Ursula undressed, showered, availed herself of the complimentary silk pyjamas and ordered a two-course Michelin-starred meal with a half bottle of wine. She watched the news while she ate but found nothing about violence in Goa. Then she reluctantly cleaned her teeth, moisturised her face and got into bed, convinced nightmares would haunt her.

What have you done? Where do you think you are going?

She opened her eyes and looked out the window at the stars, glittering like precious stones scattered on velvet.

I finished the job. My name is Olivia Jones and I'm going home.

She closed her eyes and fell into a profound, peaceful sleep.

. . .

The drive from Porto to Viseu took three hours because she stopped several times to stretch her legs. Three flights and the atmosphere of airports made her hungry for greenery and fresh air. Nerves accounted for the rest of her delay. When she finally crested the hill and looked down at the farm, A Quinta Douro looked better than ever, freshly painted and flourishing. She drove up to the gates, which were open, and followed the same sloping track down to the farmhouse. More farmhands than usual seemed to be working the fields and Ursula squinted but failed to recognise them. She parked outside the building which used to be her own. The door opened and two women, one white, one black, emerged.

"Iris! You're home." Lana's smile spread across her face. "Look, Jennifer, I told you she'd be back."

It took a second to connect her previous lives. "Lana! I'm so happy to see you again! Jennifer, is that really you? Here in Portugal? I can't believe this!" She rushed to embrace the older woman, inhaling the smell of hay, baking and comfort, and opened her arms to include Jennifer.

The three women held on to each other as if any one of them could disappear into the ether.

"How is it possible? How come you're here?"

Lana spread an arm out across the fields. "They're all here. At least all those who wanted to come from A Casa da Prata are living and working on your farm. Thanks to Gil Maduro."

"Gil Maduro?"

Lana pointed to the river, where a figure on horseback came cantering closer.

"Gil?" She let out a gasp, released the women and ran to meet him.

The horse slowed to a halt and the rider leapt from the saddle. His face was older, warmer and filled with emotion.

"*Basta?*" he asked.

"*Basta*," she agreed, and wrapped her arms around his neck.

AUTHOR'S NOTE

Thank you for reading BLOOD AND SAND.

Ursula's adventures in Goa have drawn one aspect of her old life to a close. Now she is free to forget about the past and start thinking about the future.

But certain people have long memories. Justice is often slow but once in a blue moon, it strikes like lightning.

VOLCANO BLUE is the final book in the RUN AND HIDE series. To read the first chapter, simply turn the page.

VOLCANO BLUE

Whitemoor Prison is a hellhole to reach even if you've got your own wheels. I been here five times in the seven years since he went down and it don't get any easier. One time he wanted to see me when I'd lost my licence for drink driving. Cadging a lift to a Cat A high-security joint ain't gonna win you any friends, believe me. No choice but to take public transport.

Nightmare. You gotta get a train to Peterborough, another to the village of March and then the nick itself is about two miles away. No buses and I reckon all the taxi drivers take their break when the visitors' train arrives. I had to walk the whole bloody way and ruined a new pair of box-fresh Nikes. Not in the best of moods when I arrived, I can tell you. How losers who don't drive or can't afford a motor manage, I don't know. But that's their problem.

Five out of seven years, how's that for loyalty? Missed two years because he'd got the hump after that cock-up in York-shire. We had solid gold intel, but I was otherwise engaged on a job in Portsmouth. The geezer I sent to do the job got sloppy and wound up in the Calder river. We only went and lost her – again. He wouldn't forgive me for that and I'm not the kind of bloke to grovel. Persona non grata with not so much as a whisper in eighteen months. I heard on the grapevine he hired a freelancer who tracked her to some place in Africa. Dunno what happened exactly, but word is she's still on the run.

Then six months ago, he sends a message. He's got a major job and it's urgent, he says. Can't trust no one else. I thought it was gonna be a hit. Russians and Albanians are crawling all over our patch and causing no end of trouble. Dinis and Alex would have kicked their arses, but that's not so easy when one's banged up in Monster Mansion and the other spends most of his time in an isolation cell. So off I trot to Whitemoor, fully expecting an order to take down a couple of dodgy warlords from Barking. Looking back, I wish it had been. Bish, bosh, job done, home in time for tea and Eastenders.

No such luck.

Everyone knew the old girl was starting a new empire from scratch. Fair enough and good luck to her. But you'd expect it to be on the same bleeding continent, right? Wrong.

I want you to go to India, says Milo.

By India, he's not talking Southall or even Brick Lane, but actual curry country.

Mate, I've never been further than the Costa Brava. Why the hell should I go to India?

He goes silent for ages and I watch the minutes tick away on the wall clock.

Then he speaks, so quiet I have to lean closer to hear. The rumours are true. They're all dead. Mama Bear, Chica and even that sad sack Berto. The only ones left of the Vargas family are three boys, all of whom are permanently residing at Her Majesty's Pleasure.

Milo, man, I'm gutted for you. Seriously, genuine condolences for your loss an' all, but what do you expect me to about it?

He didn't look good, truth be told, his skin all grey and his hair pulled back in a ponytail. The old Vargas light was still in his eyes but you had to look pretty damn hard to find it.

Ask questions, he goes. Poke about a bit and see what you can find. Somebody must know who killed my family.

I was about to argue the toss and state the facts: the old bird's luck finally ran out. Then I saw the set of his jaw. Even now, as defeated as I'd ever seen the boy, he was not gonna take no for an answer. OK, I sigh, leave it with me and I'll see what I can do. Anything else?

Oh yeah, he says, as if he was asking me to pick up a bottle of vodka from Duty Free. Bring *La Conquistadora* home.

You what? How the hell am I gonna get a bloody great superyacht across the ... whatever bloody great sea is between us and India? You're having a laugh, mate.

I've made you my agent. You represent my interests now. *La Conquistadora* belongs to me and I want her in Europe. Hire a crew, sail towards Oman, go through the Gulf of Aden, slip through the Suez Canal and leave her in Malta. Just watch out for Somalian pirates.

He might as well have been talking Japanese for all I understood. Sod that for a game of soldiers. Milo, it ain't happenin', I says. I can't do that.

Oh, I think you can, he says, tapping his fingers to his chin. Because you still haven't finished the last job I gave you.

That's how I ended up spending three months in India and two months at sea – turns out I'm not a good sailor – and only just managed to get home for Christmas. So here I am again at the gates of Whitemoor, ready to earn my Boy Scout's badge. The warder pats me down, takes my phone and the package of goodies I brought then finally lets me into the first of the holding areas. Takes a good ten minutes before me and the rest of those miserable tossers get into the visitors' room.

Milo looks worse if anything. He's not big on small talk, so we shake hands and sit down.

I done what you asked, says I, trying not to smirk. All the documents are in the package I left at reception and *La Conquistadora* is parked in Malta.

Berthed, he says.

You what?

You berth a boat, not park it. What did you find out?

Not much more than you told me. Police raided the yacht one night when the crew were receiving a delivery. Chica pulled a gun and got picked off by a police sniper. Your dear old mum, God rest her soul, was on a little service boat that blew up. Two crew members said it carried fuel and the deckhand was a smoker. An accident waiting to happen, they reckoned. Berto washed up on some godforsaken beach. His body was in such a state, who knows what happened?

Who cares? Anything else?

Yeah, I grin. This is the good bit. Your mum kept a kind of log book. Not a diary, more appointments and stuff. She had a meeting with a woman using the initials U.B. Mean anything to you? Nah, me neither. Thing is, Mama Bear had written something in brackets (*Perhaps the sister of Olivia Jones out for revenge?*). No record of what happened because everything after that went pear shaped.

His eyes are sort of glassy but I think he's still listening.

Anyway, when I got back from Malta, I did a bit of checking on Olivia's sister. She's never been to India, has Facebook photos of herself and kids on that day at some crappy theme park and bears no resemblance to the CCTV pic I found from the hotel. Gotta say, it didn't look much like Olivia either, but you might have more luck. That's in your package too.

Milo nods. Thanks for getting *La Conquistadora*. Forget that woman for the time being. Instead, I need you to locate a certain person.

Not that I expected champagne and a medal, but after what I'd been through in the last six months, I deserved more than just thanks. You're welcome, I say, a bit on the sulky side. Who?

A Brazilian, last seen in Mozambique.

Where the bleeding hell is Mozambique?

East Africa.

Brazil? Mozambique? Do I look like James bloody Bond? Shit, Milo, I just got back from India and let me tell you, that was no picnic.

Just track him down and report back to me. Unless you're not up to the job?

I could just get up and walk out. But I won't. I never do. I sit and wait for my instructions.

That man I want you to find is a police detective. His name is Gil Maduro.

.

ALSO BY JJ MARSH

Other titles in the Run and Hide series

WHITE HERON

BLACK RIVER

GOLD DRAGON

PEARL MOON

My Beatrice Stubbs series, European crime dramas

BEHIND CLOSED DOORS

RAW MATERIAL

TREAD SOFTLY

COLD PRESSED

HUMAN RITES

BAD APPLES

SNOW ANGEL

HONEY TRAP

BLACK WIDOW

WHITE NIGHT

THE WOMAN IN THE FRAME

ALL SOULS' DAY

~

My standalone novels
SALT OF THE EARTH

AN EMPTY VESSEL

ODD NUMBERS

WOLF TONES

And a short-story collection
APPEARANCES GREETING A POINT OF VIEW

~

ACKNOWLEDGMENTS

Thanks to Florian Bielmann, JD Lewis, Gillian Hamer, Jane Dixon Smith and Julia Gibbs.

Printed in Great Britain
by Amazon

47635395R00158